THE
KILL
CIRCLE

A CORDELL LOGAN MYSTERY

THE KILL CIRCLE

DAVID FREED

THE PERMANENT PRESS
Sag Harbor, NY 11963

For information, address:
    The Permanent Press
    4170 Noyac Road
    Sag Harbor, NY 11963
    www.thepermanentpress.com

Library of Congress Cataloging-in-Publication Data
    Freed, David, author.
        The kill circle / David Freed.
        Sag Harbor, NY: The Permanent Press, [2017]
        Series: A Cordell Logan mystery
        ISBN: 978-1-57962-511-5 (hardcover)
            1. Logan, Cordell (Fictitious character)—Fiction. 2. Murder—Investigation—Fiction. 3. Conspiracies—Fiction. 4. Romantic suspense fiction. 5. Mystery fiction.

    PS3606.R4375 K55 2017
    813'.6—dc23   2017037188

Printed in the United States of America

To 2nd Lt. Joe Gold, 96th Bomb Group, killed-in-action, 27 May 1944, whose courage and sacrifice inspired me to fly long after he was gone.

"There is nothing more deceptive than an obvious fact."

—Arthur Conan Doyle

ONE

The blood trail zigzagged through the pines and down a snowy draw, cutting across a stand of aspen trees denuded of their leaves before vanishing at the river's frozen edge.

"You've got to be kidding me. We *had* the bastard."

"Aaron, what have I told you about using that kind of gutter language?"

"Sorry, Dad."

The cold burned their cheeks and stung the walls of their heaving chests. Exhaled breath hung above their heads like cotton candy before evaporating, not unlike their wounded prey, into the thin mountain air. For an exhausting forty-five minutes, the two hunters had tried to get off a kill shot, catching glimpses as he ran for his life.

And now, just like that, he was gone.

Aaron scanned the far bank through the telescopic sites of his .30-06. "He must've crossed over."

"Not likely," said his father, who everybody called Brick because that's how he was built. "See that ice? It ain't all that thick out there in the middle. He would've fallen through. He would've known that. He's still on this side of the river, downstream."

"Why not upstream?"

"Aaron, you're fifteen years old. Start opening your eyes." Brick slung his own rifle, an old lever-action Winchester, and stooped to poke a twig at a glob of blood the size of a nickel, florescent on the snow. "See those bubbles? You shot him in the lung. Big dude like that, sucking wind, no way he'll be running uphill, not if he can help it. He's headed downstream for sure. C'mon."

They paralleled the riverbank, stepping over fallen timber and around boulders the size of Volkswagens, their necks bent like hounds. What little there had been of the sun was kissing the high ridges when they regained his tracks and picked up the trail again. Even in the flat, dimming light, the red globs on the snow were easy to follow—every thirty feet or so, then every twenty.

"He's about bled out," Brick said.

It was a quarter mile before the north fork of the Champ River twisted south and the forest gave way to a narrow canyon. They found him inside the tree line. Aaron let out a whoop and ran the last few yards, sliding through the snow on his knees to grab the elk's antlers with both hands, twisting the animal's lifeless head like he was steering a bus.

"Look at the rack on this bad boy!"

"Not bad for a first kill," Brick said. "Not bad at all."

The buck's buttery eyes were fixed, its tongue pink and lolled to one side. Aaron leaned his rifle against the carcass and snapped a selfie.

"Here," Brick said, "lemme get a couple."

The kid grinned and tossed him the phone. "Make it a good one, Pop."

Brick pried off his gloves and tucked them inside his camouflaged, insulated hunting suit to keep them warm. He raised the phone to capture the moment, then slowly lowered it. He was squinting at something over the kid's shoulder. Aaron turned to look:

Fifty yards upstream, a vintage silver Porsche sports car was sitting upright, slightly nose high, in the middle of the river. They could see the driver slumped back in his seat. He wasn't moving.

"Is he dead?"

"I don't know, son."

How the man came to be there was not hard to reconstruct. Across the river, the snow-covered slope led to a road carved high into the flank of the mountain. An ugly gouge in the snow extended the length of the slope, the kind a car would leave tumbling end-over-end after leaving the road.

Father and son ran toward him, slowed by the thin air and the knee-high drifts, by the weight of their rifles and hunting packs, heavy with ammo and survival gear.

"Hey, mister!" Aaron shouted as they got closer. "Hey, you OK out there?"

There was no response. The driver's hair was white and pulled back in a ponytail that draped across one shoulder, the way a cat curls its tail around its haunches. Rust-colored rivulets of blood had frozen along the side of his face where his head apparently had made contact with the Porsche's steering wheel. Less than thirty feet of ice separated the man from his would-be rescuers. It might as well have been thirty miles for all the help they could render him now.

The two hunters stared in silence at the dead driver. Under the ice, the river currents whispered like ghosts.

"Nice car," Brick said.

"How long you think he's been out there?" his son asked.

"Since last night would be my guess, when that storm rolled through. He probably got going too fast on the ridge up there, missed the turn, and down he come. Driving a car

like that, in the snow, rear-wheel drive, no chains?" Brick
shook his head that anyone could be so reckless.

"I've never seen a dead person before. I mean, on TV,
maybe, but . . ."

Brick put his arm around the boy's shoulder. "We better
call the sheriff's office."

"Phone don't work this low in the canyon."

"Then we best get to higher ground. It'll be pitch dark
down here anyway before you know it."

"What about my elk?"

"We'll dress him out tomorrow. He ain't going nowhere."

The hike back to the trailhead where they'd parked their
truck took nearly an hour. They saved their words for later.
There was no moon. Only the crunch of the snow under their
boot soles and the beams of their flashlights disturbed the sol-
itude of winter in the high country.

A Spruce County sheriff's dispatcher with a tubercular
hack took down the pertinent information. Brick passed along
the location of the wreck as best he could—in the Champ
River below Archibald Pass on federal land, seven miles or so
west of Angel Falls. He could hear the clicking over the phone
of computer keys as she took notes.

"And you're pretty certain the party's expired?" the dispatcher asked between coughing fits.

"Dead certain."

Well, then, there wasn't much to be done, the dispatcher
said. A deputy would be sent out at first light to investigate
further.

The story would rate six column inches inside the next
issue of *The Pinecone*, the county's eight-page, bimonthly
newspaper. The driver was identified as one Rico F. Perris,
an army veteran who'd worked as a statistician for the federal Bureau of Labor Statistics and who lived alone in a small

cabin down a dirt mining road above Angel Falls. Neighbors said he'd mostly kept to himself—but not so much that he fell into the meth-making, AK-47-toting, hermit category, like so many others who'd taken up residence around the small, Gold Rush-era mountain towns west of Denver. He'd served as assistant scoutmaster with the local Boy Scout troop. He'd volunteered with the Spruce County Public Library's "Saturday is Reading Day" program. Workers at the Angel Falls post office and Safeway grocery store remembered him as friendly, if not a little aloof, like maybe he thought he was smarter than everybody else. At the Molly B, Angel Falls's most popular saloon, a barmaid remembered that Perris often ordered red wine, which served to remind other patrons that he was no native of beer-crazy Colorado. After sipping a few glasses, he would talk about having been raised a Puerto Rican Jew in New York's Spanish Harlem, and how it had made him tough.

Who Perris really was and how he had spent his productive life, none of that made it into print. Some preferred it that way, those who realized that if the truth were ever told, the United States would be changed forever.

And not in a good way.

TWO

My toes were itching. I've sustained gunshot wounds that were less annoying. After clawing at my skin for a week and slathering on two whole tubes of extra-strength, over-the-counter hydrocortisone cream, I couldn't stand it anymore. Eight blocks west of my converted garage apartment in sun-soaked, money-drenched Rancho Bonita, California, conveniently located beside an El Pollo Loco fast-food Mexican restaurant, was an urgent care clinic.

I'd never been to an urgent care clinic before, but I presumed that by virtue of the adjective, *urgent*, my toes would receive expedited medical attention. This, I calculated, would leave me plenty of time to grab a quick chicken fajita bowl on my way to the airport, where I had a flight lesson scheduled that morning. My student was a spoiled, pot-smoking, sixteen-year-old ingrate named Zane Gillespie whose software zillionaire father hoped that becoming a pilot would afford the kid some structure in his life, even if during our previous lessons, Zane had demonstrated about as much interest in earning an airman's certificate as I did mastering origami. More than an hour later, however, I was still camped in the waiting room of the urgent care, still clawing at my toes. I'd removed my socks and low-top Merrell hiking shoes, the brand of footwear I

came to favor back when I worked for Uncle Sugar. I phoned
the kid's father and canceled the lesson.

After I was finally ushered into the examining room, where
I waited another twenty minutes poking through drawers and
playing with medical equipment, the doctor made her entrance
to spend all of thirty seconds assessing my tootsies.

"Athlete's foot," she said.

I smiled.

"What's funny?"

"Nothing. It's just I haven't been particularly athletic of late."

"Could've fooled me. You look like you're in terrific shape
for a man your age."

My age? Ouch.

She squeezed my arm, but not necessarily in what I interpreted as a physician's manner. More like a "Let's have dinner
on Saturday" manner. "Yep," she repeated, "in excellent shape."

She had a few miles on her, a lot of mascara, and enough
hair spray to make a climatologist weep, but she was hardly
unattractive. She reminded me a little of an older Her Hot-
ness, the platinum prom queen I lusted after without success
more than thirty years earlier in high school. I wasn't looking
for any new romantic entanglements, though, not even of the
short-term variety.

"Kind of you to say," I said, breaking eye contact to pull
my socks back on.

She watched me for a second or two before respond-
ing with an almost imperceptible murmur, a guttural kind
of "hmm"—incredulity, perhaps, at my disregard for what I
took to be romantic interest on her part. As I bent forward
to tie my shoes, she swiveled away on her padded chrome
stool toward a small desk and crossed her legs, her white lab
coat revealing more thigh than I really needed to see. I waited
while she scribbled out a prescription.

"Keep your socks clean, your feet dry, and apply this cream twice daily. Any problems, you've got our number." She handed me the slip of paper in a physician kind of way, offered me a physician smile, and left. Whatever regret I might've felt at not having taken advantage of her overture came and went. There comes a point in life when you grow tired of playing the game, when you've lost enough and would just as soon be left alone.

Most of the time anyway.

ACROSS THE street was a CVS drug store. The line to drop off prescriptions stretched all the way down the oral hygiene aisle.

Ten minutes came and went before I found myself number three in line. Ahead of me was a gray beard wearing a Korean War Veteran ball cap. Ahead of him was a young Latina with Jesus inked on her left shoulder and a sleeping infant cradled in her arms. Behind us, bouncing impatiently from one foot to the other, was a bad ass who looked like he'd just made parole. Thirties, shaved head, neck tats, absurdly saggy jeans, tight white T-shirt, ham-hock arms from slinging iron on some prison yard somewhere.

"I can help whoever's next," said a pharmacist assistant, opening a second register.

Without hesitation, the bad ass bypassed those of us ahead of him in line and strode to the counter. Nobody protested. They were too intimidated. Somebody should've said something, but they didn't, so I did.

"Excuse me?"

He craned his bullet-shaped head around and glared at me with reptilian eyes.

"That was rather rude, don't you think, cutting ahead of everybody like that?"

"My bitch needs her medicine," he said.

"Your concern for her welfare is admirable. I hope it's nothing serious, but here's the thing: See all these nice people in line, some of whom were first, in front of you? They need their medicine too."

"Mind your own business, asshole."

"This is my business. And yours. In a civilized society, we all want to be treated with respect and consideration. The old Golden Rule. Otherwise, heck, we might as well all run around speaking monosyllabically, eating mastodons, and beating each other to death with clubs, am I right?"

He suggested I perform an anatomical act on myself that I'm fairly certain is impossible.

I suggested that he might benefit greatly, as I had, from the teachings of the Buddha who believed behaving civilly has its karmic rewards.

It was at this point he called me a name implying that I enjoyed engaging in intimate relations with my own mother, a woman who put me up for adoption and whom I never met. He then added that if I cared to discuss things further, we could do so outside in the parking lot.

Once upon a time, I wouldn't have waited to discuss those things. We would have continued the conversation right then and there, and our little talk would have ended with him in intensive care or, quite possibly, the morgue. But with maturity, if you're at all fortunate, comes the dawning awareness that 10 percent of life is what you make it; the other 90 percent is how you take it. You learn when to pick your battles, and the wisdom that most battles ultimately aren't worth fighting to begin with. Discovering Buddhism late in life had helped me understand that lesson, even if I sometimes fell well short in practicing it. The yin and yang. The lover of peace. The purveyor of death. I didn't want to harm anyone, but I would if I had to.

"Let me give you a bit of advice, courtesy of the Buddha," I said. "Holding on to anger is like grasping a hot coal with the intent of throwing it at someone else, only you're the one who gets burned."

"What the hell does that mean?"

"It means have a nice day."

I lowered my eyes and turned the other cheek. Playing the peacemaker. I have to say it actually felt kind of good.

There's hope for you yet, Logan.

The dude was waiting for me when I came out of the drug store twenty minutes later.

"Hey," he said, sucking down a longneck Budweiser.

I ignored him and angled toward my old truck, dodging trouble, a boatload of which I already owned. I was pushing the half-century mark, a chronically underemployed civilian flight instructor who lived largely on a government pension in a detached, converted, garage studio apartment, rooming with earth's most self-absorbed, intellectually challenged cat. Plus, my feet were still itching like a pair of flea-covered dogs. All I could think about was getting home, getting my socks and shoes off, and restoring my toes to their unathletic status.

"Hey," he repeated, more adamantly this time, "don't you walk away from me, motherfu—."

Again there was that word. Only this time, he hurled it without regard to the fact that he was within earshot of an old lady shuffling in from the parking lot, green tennis balls on the feet of her aluminum walker. She bore a faint resemblance to the Quaker Oats guy or maybe former first lady Barbara Bush, and the reaction on her face at his unbridled profanity hovered between revulsion and fear. Something inside me snapped. I stopped and faced him down.

"Are you talking to me?" Fine, so it wasn't the most original line, but it was a classic, and I delivered it with aplomb, if I do say so myself.

"Yeah," he responded, "I'm talking to you, you piece of"—and here he let loose with a long, grammatically incorrect, albeit impressively creative string of profanity. "Nobody tells me what to do. Ever."

"Somebody should," I said. "Somebody, friend, also needs to teach you a few manners."

"And that would be *you?*"

"That would be me."

His lips curled into a threatening smile. He was missing a few teeth. Why is it dudes like that never practice good dental hygiene?

"Your funeral," he said, casually setting his beer down on a newsstand, like he wasn't even going to break a sweat snapping me in two. "OK, old-timer, let's do this."

In my younger days, I would've waited for him to take the first shot. That way, if anyone asked later, I could've said he started it. But, again, with maturity, along with learning when to pick your battles, one also learns that waiting to be fired on before firing back is a real good way to end up taking that long dirt nap.

"One thing first," I said, walking up to him, "but we go any further, we need to establish a few parameters."

"Parameters? What the hell are you talking about?"

"Rules."

"*Rules?* You're about to get your ass beat, old man. Ain't no rules in an ass-whupping."

"You're right. How silly of me."

I drove my left palm up and into his nostrils.

You can easily kill a man that way. The septal cartilage will separate and drive into his brain's prefrontal cortex as readily as a spear point. So I didn't hit him all that hard, only hard enough. He crashed backward into the newspaper rack, spilling his beer as well as his blood, which came cascading down the front of his T-shirt like he was playing an extra in a Quentin Tarantino movie. I waited a sporting moment, long enough for him to regain his balance and to launch a punch at me, a ragged haymaker that I easily ducked, before pirouetting and slamming my right shoe like a piston into his seed factory. Down he went and down he stayed.

Granny was leaning on her walker with her mouth open. "That wasn't necessary, young man," she said.

"With all due respect, ma'am, you're wrong. It was absolutely necessary. He'll think twice the next time before picking a fight."

Might rarely makes right, except when it does. I left before the Rancho Bonita cops showed up. Like I said, I wasn't looking for trouble. My toes already were giving me plenty.

THE FOOT cream afforded some relief, enough that I was able to take Kiddiot, my orange blimp of a tabby, to the vet. He'd been throwing up of late and I was worried, no matter how one-sided the nature of our relationship was.

"I've treated pet rocks that were more cooperative," said the veterinarian, whose name was Dr. Lucero, as he wrapped a bandage around his hand where my cat had bitten him. He was a balding young man with a small diamond stud in his right earlobe and what looked to be a Labrador retriever puppy tattooed on his left wrist.

Kiddiot was holed up under a chair in the examining room like a barricaded murder suspect.

"He's not what you would call sociable," I said.

"He's not what *anyone* would call sociable," Lucero said. He finished dressing his wounded hand with professional expertise before reaching into a cabinet over the sink and extracting a pair of heavily padded gloves not unlike those worn by hockey goalies. "H-T-H" was scrawled in Magic Marker on each glove.

"H-T-H?"

"Hard to handle," Lucero said, handing the gloves to me. "Here, try 'em on."

They fit me, well, like gloves.

"OK," he said, "now haul that little antisocial critter on up here so I can take a good look at him."

I knelt down on the linoleum-tiled floor. Under the chair, Kiddiot pressed himself as closely as he could to the wall, away from me. I knew I couldn't talk him out of there. His ability to understand words was on a par with a house plant. I reached in and dragged him out by the scruff of his neck. He hissed and yowled with his ears back, whipping his skinny little tail around and trying to bite me. The gloves worked great. I got him up on the table and held him steady while Dr. Lucero listened to his heart and lungs with his stethoscope. Kiddiot squirmed and growled.

"This cat is obese," the vet said.

"It's my landlady's fault, Mrs. Schmulowitz. She makes him brisket. Occasionally chopped liver. It's basically the only things he'll eat these days."

"Cats are not designed to eat brisket and chopped liver, Mr. Logan."

"Tell it to Mrs. Schmulowitz."

Twenty minutes and $220 later, Dr. Lucero issued his diagnosis: Kiddiot had been barfing because he was eating too fast. All those delectables from Mrs. Schmulowitz he'd been wolfing down had been irritating his lower esophageal sphincter, causing him to regurgitate. He was otherwise healthy as a horse, the size of which he was rapidly approaching, given his caloric intake. I put the bill on my credit card and left.

"Your problem is you think I'm made of money," I told the cat as we drove home. "Two hundred and twenty bucks to find out you're not chewing your food properly? You should be ashamed of yourself."

Kiddiot seemed anything but ashamed. He purred in his cat carrier on the passenger seat beside me with his front legs tucked underneath him, pleased, apparently, at having taken a piece out of the vet.

I let him out when we got home. He immediately climbed into the oak tree in Mrs. Schmulowitz's tiny backyard. A scrub jay sitting close by didn't even bother getting out of his way. Every bird in the neighborhood seemed to comprehend intuitively that Kiddiot lacked the talent, if not the interest, to catch any of them. I shook my head. Somebody once said that time spent with a cat is never wasted. Obviously they'd never met Kiddiot.

I had just slid my key into the door when the back gate clicked open behind me. I pivoted reflexively and shifted my weight to my back foot with my right fist cocked. The gate, like the privacy fence surrounding Mrs. Schmulowitz's yard, was constructed of six-foot redwood pickets, which meant I couldn't see who was approaching. Friend or foe, regardless, I was ready.

"You must be Logan."

Stunning was the word that first registered, but not in the bleached and plasticized Southern California definition of the word. She was Eurasian. Midforties. Five seven with indigo eyes. Dark shoulder-length hair with subtle red highlights. Zero makeup. She wore a conservatively cut gray pants suit over a black silk blouse, collar flared, modestly buttoned, and stylish but sensible black flats, the kind she could run in if she had to. Slung over her shoulder was a well-worn calfskin bag large enough to conceal a full-frame pistol. I realized I was staring at her.

"Excuse me?"

"You *are* Cordell Logan, right? Because if you're not, holy smokes, you're a dead ringer for his file photo."

Her imperfectly perfect smile was distracting. I had trouble focusing. *File photo? What the heck was she talking about?*

"Sorry," I said. "And you are . . . ?"

Before she could answer, Kiddiot jumped down from the tree, trotted over, and rubbed up against her ankles, making little chirping sounds in that high-pitched voice of his. Cozying up to a stranger? That happened approximately never.

"Is this your cat?" she asked, stooping to scratch him behind his ears.

"A cat doesn't belong to anybody. Dogs have owners. Cats have staff."

"Not to hurt his feelings or anything, but he could stand to drop a few pounds."

"He looks like a feline Hindenburg. He makes sumo wrestlers look svelte. He has smaller cats orbiting around him. Yeah, he gets that a lot."

She smiled again and stood. "Your friend Buzz sends his regards," she said.

I'd made her for a police detective. I was wrong.

Dropping Buzz's name let me know she hailed from the dark recesses of the federal intelligence community. It's where he and I had toiled together for more than seven years after the air force concluded that an old football injury had rendered me no longer physically fit to pilot fighter jets. Along with a handful of other special operators culled from the various service branches following the terrorist attacks of September 11, he and I had been assigned to Alpha, a direct action, highly classified Tier One Ultra unit based on the East Coast. Our mandate was straightforward: Rid the world of evil. No more innocent-until-proven-guilty tribunals. No Guantanamo. We got paid to take out the trash wherever we found it.

That was before the Obama administration quietly disbanded the unit as a potential political liability. Buzz, an opera-loving, former Delta Force operator who'd lost an eye in combat and kept on ticking, would remain in government service afterward, taking command of another, smaller intelligence-gathering operation, this one reporting directly to the White House and headquartered in Cleveland, of all places. He had wanted me to come work for him full-time, but I'd had enough cloak and dagger by then. Too much gore. Too much time glancing over my shoulder. Not that there's anything wrong with Cleveland. I just didn't want to go there. And so I relocated to Rancho Bonita, the most civilized place in the country I could find, and got back into flying. I desired nothing more than some small measure of Zen, a place to calm my mind. It didn't always work out that way.

"You didn't answer my question," I said.

She held out her hand. "I'm Layne Sterling."

Admittedly this might sound like a smitten school boy talking, but her skin felt like rose petals warmed by the sun. I'm not saying she wasn't beautiful—she was—but there was something else about her, a seductive allure, I couldn't quite put my finger on. Most attractive women you meet don't radiate it, mainly because they don't have to. They know how they look and that's usually good enough for them. Maybe I was reading tea leaves, but I got the impression Layne Sterling didn't seem to realize how good she looked. Or maybe she didn't care, which made her all the more attractive. But if you learn anything stalking bad people in hell holes around the globe, as I once did, it's that death can come beautifully gift-wrapped. Skepticism can be a lifesaver. I tried not to look at her breasts.

"You don't work for Buzz, which begs the question: who *do* you work for?"

"Who says I don't work for Buzz?"

"With your looks? He would've given me a heads-up if you were coming, believe me."

"OK, you're right. I don't work for Buzz." Layne Sterling glanced over her shoulder, toward Mrs. Schmulowitz's house, as if to make sure we were alone. "I'm with the CIA."

THREE

I asked to see her company ID. She asked me if I was kidding. I took that as partial confirmation of her bona fides. No real spook carries CIA-issued badging on assignment. Her familiarity with the agency's organizational structure and vernacular convinced me that Layne Sterling was indeed a member of Christians in Action.

She said she was assigned to CAM, the Central Intelligence Agency's Casualty Assessment Matrix. I'd never heard of that section. To hear her tell it, most folks in the agency never had either. Sterling explained that whenever a retired case officer or intelligence analyst passed away from anything other than old age or a fatal disease, it was up to CAM to determine whether that ex-employee's seemingly otherwise ordinary death was instead part of some insidious, counterintelligence action executed by foreign powers hostile to the United States.

The job, she said, was rarely pulse pounding. Most retired spooks died like everybody else. They got cancer. Their hearts blew out. They slipped off ladders cleaning leaves from their rain gutters. All too often, bored by the mundanities of retirement following lives of shadowy intrigue, they destroyed their livers with opioids or alcohol. Very occasionally, however, the true circumstances of their deaths pointed toward something larger and more conspiratorial.

It was nearing lunchtime. Why she was confiding all this as she watched me heat up a can of chili on the two-burner stove in my garage apartment, I had no idea, but I tried not to interrupt. I hadn't felt anything approaching genuine attraction to any woman in what seemed like forever, certainly not since the death of my ex-wife, Savannah. I liked the twinge of nervous excitement this woman produced in my stomach. I liked her obvious intelligence, her self-confidence, her eyes, her hair, the lilt of her voice, the near-hypnotic, hula-like gracefulness with which she moved her hands in illustrating her words. I liked that Kiddiot liked her. Then I came to my senses. I'd known Layne Sterling all of about fifteen minutes, which is to say, I didn't know her at all.

"You sure you don't want any chili?"

She surveyed the contents of the pot I was stirring on the stove. "I'm good, thanks." As if to escape the aroma of greasy red beans and mystery meat, she wandered over to my plywood bookshelf, bending at the waist to peer at the titles. "Buzz tells me you're a Buddhist."

"I wouldn't go that far. The Buddha believed you should never fantasize about wanting to dismember any motorist who tailgates you. Let's just say I'm a work in progress."

Sterling smiled. "I've never known anyone who lived in a converted garage. I like what you've done with the place."

I poured the chili into the only clean bowl I could find and sat down at my folding table on one of my two folding chairs. Sterling pulled out the other chair, crossed her legs placidly, and watched me dig in.

"A man died last month," Sterling said. "He was driving through a blizzard in the mountains outside Denver. The car went off the road and ended up in a river."

"And he worked for the CIA."

Sterling nodded. "Directorate of Operations. Senior analyst. Thirty-two years on the job. Numerous sensitive assignments."

"And this concerns me how?"

"The driver's name was Rico Perris." She waited, gauging my response.

I shoveled a spoonful of chili in my mouth. "Sorry, doesn't ring any bells."

Sterling leaned closer, elbows on the table, her hands folded in front of her. "Back about ten years ago," she said, "Mr. Perris was assigned to Red Lancer."

Red Lancer. Now, *that* rang a bell. The code name for a CIA task force formed in-house in 2007 to investigate long-standing rumors that rogue operatives working for the nation's most powerful intelligence-gathering organization had been complicit in the 1963 assassination of President John F. Kennedy. Perhaps predictably, the Red Lancer task force (so named because "Lancer" was Kennedy's Secret Service call sign and "red" was the color of the blood he shed the day he was killed) eventually would clear the CIA of any involvement in the president's murder. How the task force reached its conclusions, what evidence it considered, was never made public.

"You knew all about Red Lancer when you worked for Alpha," Sterling said.

I shook a liberal amount of Tabasco on my chili and stirred it in. "Doesn't ring any bells," I said.

"Oh, c'mon, Logan. You know exactly what I'm talking about." She reached over, grabbed my spoon, and tasted the chili. "How could you even eat this stuff? It's disgusting."

"Help yourself, why don't you?"

"What about Sergei Bezmenov?" Sterling asked, handing me back the spoon. "That ring any bells?"

"Nope."

"OK, then allow me to refresh your memory: Bezmenov was a double agent working for Soviet intelligence. In the twilight of his long, illustrious espionage career, forty-five years later, Mr. Bezmenov was helping divert Russian oil money to al-Qaeda bomb makers in Pakistan. You, Buzz, and other members of your team lured Bezmenov, a notorious pedophile, to the Hotel Pulitzer in Amsterdam by posing online as a twelve-year-old willing to spend the weekend with him. When he showed up, you then proceeded to inject him with a lethal dose of potassium chloride, then dropped his body from a chartered helicopter into the North Sea, where it was never found."

"And you know this how?"

"Buzz gave me copies of your operational and after-action reports."

My appetite was gone. I got up from the table and rinsed out my bowl in the sink. I didn't like where this was going, my past coming back to haunt me. Rule No. 1 at Alpha was that, as in a street fight, there were no rules. Mission by mission, target by target, we terminated dozens of miscreants like Bezmenov. I was happy to have expedited his exit from the planet, no matter how many international laws may have been broken along the way. Yet I was well aware that others, particularly the press, might not have been so understanding of our efforts. The fact that the CIA or anyone outside of Alpha's food chain knew details of what had happened to Bezmenov, or to any of the many others we disposed of in similar fashion, was worrisome. It spelled criminal liability. It spelled the potential of standing trial at the International Court of Justice in The Hague and going to prison.

Sterling walked over and leaned against the sink, close enough that I could smell the perfume in her hair. "We'd like you to help us determine conclusively what happened to Rico

Perris," she said, "whether in fact he died in an accident, or was murdered."

I wiped my wet hands on a red-and-white-striped dishrag and turned to face her. "I'm not interested."

"The agency is prepared to pay you $500 per day, not including expenses."

"I don't need your money. I own a thriving business."

"*Thriving?*" Sterling tilted her head and smiled condescendingly. "I hate to break this to you, Logan, but you live in a garage."

"I think we're done here," I said.

"We need your help, Logan. So does your country."

"I'm sorry. I already gave at the office."

She held her ground, hands on hips, her eyes defiant. We stood there, waiting for the other to blink. Had she been a man, I might've put her in a come-along hold and shown her the door but Layne Sterling was more woman than I'd seen in a long time. I tried hard not to let that sink in before walking out the door. I really didn't know what else to do.

Kiddiot was back up in his tree, dozing, all four paws sticking up in the air like a poster bed. I picked up a hose and began watering the geraniums.

"Sergei Bezmenov," she said, following me outside, "that Russian you tossed out of that helicopter? We have reason to believe that in November 1963, less than a week before Kennedy was assassinated, he was in Dallas, attending a livestock trade show, working for the KGB under diplomatic cover. We also believe he may have been in direct contact with Lee Harvey Oswald."

"Look, I don't mean to be rude, Ms.—?"

"Sterling. Layne Sterling."

"Ms. Sterling, but you're talking ancient history. This has nothing to do with me."

"What I'm talking about, Mr. Logan, is American history. As a loyal American who has served his country more than honorably, I would think this has everything to do with you. With all of us."

I watered the flowers and tried to ignore her.

"Rico Perris became something of an in-house expert on the Kennedy assassination," she said. "Every time CIA headquarters decided to reopen the investigation, he was assigned to it. Only the deeper each task force dug, the murkier things got. Some findings indicated possible involvement on the agency's part, others not." She paused, then added, "Another Red Lancer analyst who worked with Perris died last month in Phoenix. Joe Zyra. He went out for a walk one night after dinner and got hit by a car. Driver didn't stop. One of my colleagues is handling that investigation."

"People get tagged by cars all the time," I said. "They drive off mountain roads all the time too."

"Your point is what?"

"That it could be coincidence, the deaths of Perris and this guy Zyra. That it probably has nothing to do with their having worked for the agency."

"That's certainly true," Sterling said. "Or it could be somebody silenced two retired intelligence analysts who had particular insight into the murder of an American president. We're hoping you'll help us find the truth, one way or the other."

I didn't like this woman knowing any of my illicit history. And I didn't like her lobbying me to take on the kind of work that was no longer a part of who I was or what I aspired to be. I'd be lying, though, if I said that I wasn't impossibly attracted to her. I wanted to ask her out. I wanted her to leave. Hell, I didn't know what I wanted. Some women can have that effect on a man.

She told me she was staying at a hotel down by the beach and was booked on a flight out of Rancho Bonita the next afternoon, back to the East Coast. She gave me her card and told me to think about it. I said I would, but that I would probably decline the job, and turned away from her.

When I glanced back, she was gone.

Buzz was livid. I could practically feel the wetness of his angry spittle in my ear as he ranted over the phone. He'd not only tossed me a good-paying gig, he said, he'd gone out of his way to hook me up with Langley's "hottest skirt," as he described Sterling.

"And this is the thanks I get? You telling her and her employer to get lost?"

"I didn't exactly tell her to get lost, Buzz. I *sort* of told her to get lost."

"You're a regular laugh riot, Logan, you know that? You think this is a joke? You think this is some kind of yuck fest? Jesus."

"No, I do not think this is some sort of yuck fest."

"I would hope not. Because for your information, Logan, her boss, the deputy DCI? He just called me screaming like he had gerbils in his pants. Do you have any idea the shit storm I'm now dealing with because of you? Everybody's preaching interagency cooperation. No more firewalls. Let's all work together. One big happy intelligence community family. Her section, they've had some turnover, OK? They're short on experienced operators. So I tell them, 'Hey, I know this guy out in Cali. He's the best there is.' Which may or may not be a stretch given your checkered history, Logan. Irregardless, this is what I told them, OK? So they bite. They send this hot chick out to come see you—who, by the way, I have met in person and I would crawl over broken glass just to pick up her undies."

"Thanks for that image, Buzz."

"Irregardless. I was trying to do you a favor. Kill two birds with one stone. Help out Langley and help you out at the same time because, God knows, I'm tired of watching you wallow. You need more purpose in your life, Logan. You need to be more mission-oriented like you once were. I'll tell you what you really need. You need a steady woman. I figured you'd be all over her like a fat kid on a cupcake, and you blow her off? I mean, Jesus."

Next to Jesus, "irregardless" was one of Buzz's favorite words, even if there was no such word. Regardless, you don't offer grammar lessons to a man who's saved your life more than once in combat, as he had mine. I wanted to vent, to express my concern at his having violated operational security by sharing incriminating details of the Bezmenov operation with someone outside our old unit, even if that someone was a CIA case officer, but I knew he didn't want to hear any of that.

"I appreciate your concern, Buzz, but you should have talked to me about the job before you volunteered me for it. You could have at least told me she was coming my way. I wouldn't have been caught so off guard."

"*Off guard?* You must be getting spongy on me, Logan. You were trained never to get caught off guard. Ever."

"I don't work for the government anymore."

"Must be nice to be independently wealthy," he said. The sarcasm in his tone was anything but subtle.

"I didn't know it was going to cause you problems," I said. "Give me some time to think it over. I'll get back to you."

"I'll give you 'til tomorrow, close of business," Buzz said. "I got no shortage of other operators looking for work."

The line went dead.

I turned my face to the sun and tried to live in the moment, allowing myself to think about the positive things in my life: My health. My airplane. My landlady, Mrs. Schmulowitz, as close to a grandmother as I'd ever known. The roof over my head. Kiddiot—OK, maybe not Kiddiot. Truth be told, my feel-good inventory didn't take long.

One thing I realized I was genuinely appreciative of was the weather. Rancho Bonita boasts what may be the world's mildest, most predictable climate. Rarely does it get too hot or too cold, too dry or humid. If it's seventy degrees and sunny one day, chances are it's going to be seventy degrees and sunny the next day. And the day after. In fact, pretty much every day. Weather is a major reason why the rich and famous pay big money to live there, and why those of us who will never be rich or famous struggle financially to do so as well. But as I lay there on the hammock in my landlady's backyard, genuinely living in the moment in a way I rarely do, a chill wind came barreling in from the north, rustling the leaves of the oak tree above me and dappling my arms with goose pimples. Some will tell you such winds are fraught with foreboding, as ominous warnings of danger ahead.

I only wish I had listened to them.

FOUR

The New York Giants were losing badly that night to the Philadelphia Eagles, down by three scores late in the second quarter. Mrs. Schmulowitz, a retired gym teacher from Brooklyn garbed sweatshirt-to-headband-to-yoga pants in officially licensed Giants apparel, insisted she wasn't worried, but it was obvious she was. Unable to sit still, she paced back and forth in front of her ancient, mahogany-encased Magnavox television set, periodically throwing up her hands in frustration at each Giants' miscue and muttering, "*Oy gevalt.*" During commercials, to relieve her anxiety, she knocked out jumping jacks like an army recruit at boot camp. This, in turn, made me anxious. I don't care what the American Heart Association says. Ninety-pound women closing in on ninety years of age should be doing crossword puzzles, not vigorous calisthenics. Her joints sounded like hiking boots on a gravel trail.

"Where's the defense?" she shouted at the TV. "My first husband, he could put pads on right now and wrap up tackle better than these schmos—and, by the way, did I mention he's been dead since 1971, may he rest in peace?"

Mrs. Schmulowitz's tidy little house, with its doilies and tchotchkes, was redolent with the mouthwatering aroma of boiled corned beef and cabbage, our usual fare on Monday nights during football season. We normally ate at halftime, but given the way the game was going, dinner appeared to be the last thing on my landlady's mind.

"You know, Mrs. Schmulowitz, you've never really told me how old you are."

"And I'm not about to now, bubby. Let's just say I'm old enough to remember when there was only one way to skin a cat." She glanced up at Kiddiot, who was perched atop her china hutch, and blew him a kiss. "Nothing personal, doll face."

Kiddiot looked like he couldn't have cared less.

"The vet told me to tell you that you're feeding him too much," I said. "It's not like he just got off the boat from Biafra."

"Vet, schmet. If he knew anything, he'd be a *real* doctor, doing boobs in Beverly Hills. The cat appreciates my cooking, bubby. Reminds me of a cat I had when I was living in Brooklyn. Same appetite, this cat, but not nearly so nice. Hated everybody. 'Adolph Kittler,' my father named him."

I sighed. "Whatever you say, Mrs. Schmulowitz."

She stopped exercising and looked over at me, hands on her hips. "All right, OK, so what's with the frowny face?"

"No frowny face. I'm good."

"And if you expect me to believe that, I got a bridge for sale." She sat down beside me on her mohair couch and patted me on the thigh. "We've known each other too long, Cordell. Let's go. Tell Mrs. Schmulowitz. Out with it."

There was no way I was going to confide the details of Layne Sterling's visit that morning, or the subsequent fallout from my having rejected an offer to accept an assignment with the CIA.

"Seriously, Mrs. Schmulowitz, I'm doing OK."

"This is about John F. Kennedy, isn't it?"

I looked at her hard. "You were listening in on me?"

"Listening in? Me? Psshhh. Fuggedaboutit. I heard a couple things, that's all. This and that. No big whoop. C'mon, let's get you fed. Enough with this *fakakta* football game."

WE ATE in silence at her kitchen table. I picked at the food on my plate. Mrs. Schmulowitz focused on her glass of Manischewitz, sighing melodramatically every few seconds. The tension between us was as palpable as it was unusual.

"I'm so sorry," she said after a few minutes. "I was in the bathroom this morning, touching up my roots because, God knows, they needed it. I heard you talking to somebody in the backyard, so I looked out. I saw this very attractive Asian lady and I got curious, that's all. I'm thinking maybe she's your new squeeze and, if so, va va voom. But I didn't hear hardly anything, bubby, I swear. Believe me, your business is your business."

I asked her what "hardly anything" meant. Something about President Kennedy being killed, she said. Something about my having once worked for the government. That was it.

"Whatever you think you heard," I said sternly, "you didn't."

"Ab-so-positively. Not a single word." Mrs. Schmulowitz motioned like she was buttoning her lip. She hesitated. Then she said, "But if I did *hear* anything, I would tell you this: I voted for that very handsome young president. The world changed the day he died, and a part of all of us died with him. Call me crazy, OK? I don't believe in flying saucers or little green men or the Easter Bunny—but I do believe that what happened in Dallas, they haven't told us everything. We still don't know the whole truth. And that's a crime."

Staring up at the ceiling later that night when sleep wouldn't come, I thought about what she'd said. I thought about Layne Sterling. I remembered what Buzz had said, about how he'd grown tired of watching me wallow. Savannah had been dead for three years and not a day went by, not an hour, when I didn't think of her. Buzz was right. Maybe I did need more purpose in my life. A job would have helped, but not as much as a woman.

THERE'S A difference between death and having sex: Death you can do alone and nobody laughs at you.

My flight instructor during primary jet training, a chain-smoking Alabaman named Bob Chitwood, who'd racked up a couple hundred missions flying F-105 Thunderchiefs over Hanoi, laid that line on me one sweltering morning when I was transitioning to T-38s. Then, with no forewarning, he hauled back on the stick from the back seat, stomped on the right rudder pedal, and stalled the jet into a graveyard spiral.

"Your airplane," he said calmly.

With the altimeter unwinding in fast motion and the lush green landscape of south Texas spinning up through the wind-screen to kill us, I could hear him cackling demonically in my helmet. He suggested that I might want to find a solu-tion to our predicament, and soon, before we both left one humongous, flaming divot in the planet. Had I panicked, I likely would've been washed out of flight school and ended up working somewhere like Sears, selling refrigerators. But I didn't panic. I immediately chopped the throttles as I'd been taught to do, neutralized the ailerons, and held full opposite rudder to break the rotation of the spin. Chitwood slapped me on the back in a congratulatory way after we landed other-wise uneventfully and told me I'd "done real good." I would go on to graduate and ultimately advance to A-10 Warthogs, enjoying many rewarding years blowing up terrorists real good, after which, as a special operator assigned to Alpha, I killed them good from the ground. Now, years later, here I was caught in another death spiral. Only this one, I wasn't so sure I could get out of.

It was the morning after Monday night football with Mrs. Schmulowitz, and the predicament I found myself in was my own fault. I had just lifted off from the Rancho Bonita Municipal Airport with a first-time student in the left seat of my tired, forty-year-old Cessna 172, the *Ruptured Duck*. A Skywest regional jet had launched a minute earlier. In clearing me onto the runway, the tower had issued its standard warning of wake turbulence—invisible whirlwinds that come spinning off the wingtips of larger planes and can wreak havoc on smaller ones. I should've waited another minute or two before departing behind the jetliner, long enough for the dangerous mini tornadoes to play themselves out, but I was anxious to get through the lesson and get back to Buzz with my decision. I had decided to accept the assignment with the CIA, if for no other reason than to get to know Layne Sterling better. And so I rushed the takeoff.

Big mistake.

We were at about 700 feet and climbing out over the coast. My new student, a snappily dressed, forty-something Lexus salesman with slicked-back hair who insisted I call him "Frankie," was taking his introductory lesson. First of all, what kind of grown man calls himself "Frankie"? In any case, I was explaining the various flight instruments to him, letting him get a feel for the controls, showing him how easy it is to fly a plane straight and level, when the yoke suddenly and violently wrenched sideways from his grip. In an instant, the *Duck* rolled over and pitched straight down in what airmen like to refer to in typically understated fashion as an "unusual attitude." The truth of it was, we were out of control and plummeting straight into the Pacific.

"This kind of sucks," I heard Frankie say in my headset.

Kind of? There was nothing "kind of" about it. Time slowed to nothing as the seconds ticked down. To this day, I cannot recount in detail how we ended up not becoming fish food. Much was lost in an adrenal blur. What I do remember is yanking back on the throttle and jamming the wheel forward to break the stall as I cranked the wings hard right to retard the spin, in much the same way I did while avoiding disaster in that T-38. The *Duck's* landing gear was virtually skimming the waves before I was able to fully recover from that nosedive and begin regaining altitude.

The tower controller, who'd been watching us on radar and probably visually, asked if we were OK. I said we were. Looking over at Frankie, I wasn't so sure: He'd wet his very expensive trousers.

"Can we just go back?" he asked. You could have spotted the terror in his eyes with a satellite.

"Sure."

I thought about explaining to him the physics of wingtip wind vortices and how getting caught in them rarely occurred, but I could tell by his trembling hands and ashen hue that I'd be wasting his time and mine. He managed to dig an embossed business card out of his eel-skin wallet after we taxied in and told me to give him a call the next time I was in the market for a new or used Lexus.

"You've got me pegged," I said. "I'm all about luxury."

Frankie took one last look at the *Duck* as if to say, "What the hell was I thinking, leaving mother earth in that thing?" and ambled for the parking lot, crossing paths with airplane mechanic Larry Kropf, who had emerged from his cavernous,

World War II-era hangar where I sublet a windowless storage closet that served as my flight school office.

"Am I wrong," Larry asked me, glancing back at my now-former student, "or did you make that guy piss himself? That's getting to be sort of a habit with you, isn't it? Scaring the pee out of paying clients?"

I jotted notes in my logbook and pretended not to hear him.

Larry tipped the scales at close to 300 pounds. His weight was outsized only by the expanse of his generally cynical world view.

For as long as I'd known him, Larry had been a model of slovenliness, a man-mountain with a forest of facial fur, Scotch-taped, black-frame glasses with impenetrably thick lenses, and forearms carpeted with hair as dense as Brillo pads. His idea of on-the-job fashion consisted of greasy baseball caps and low-riding blue workpants that always revealed a Grand Canyon of a workman's crack. He favored T-shirts that struggled to shelter his medicine ball belly but whose memes always covered Larry's cynical world view with messages like, "I'm not always rude and sarcastic. Sometimes I'm asleep," and, "The police never think it's as funny as you do." But as he stood there, blotting out the sun, I could see that he'd been transformed—sort of. Hair trimmed. Beard trimmed. Gone were the dirty ball cap and T-shirt. In their place were a new, lime green cap and a matching polo shirt, both bearing the logo and name of his company, "Precision Aircraft Maintenance." He was still garbed in his usual blue work pants, but at least they were clean, properly belted, and riding at an appropriate altitude.

"Wow," I said. "Next stop, the cover of *GQ*. What the heck got into you?"

"The wife said if I didn't start cleaning up my act, she was gonna run off with the mailman. You should see this guy.

Always hitting on her. Little Filipino dude. She outweighs him by sixty pounds easy. I thought about taking a torque wrench to his gonads, but I figured this was probably the better route. I score some new styles, the wife remembers what a complete stud I am, falls in love with me all over again, and, best of all, stops riding me like the friggin' teacups at Disneyland.

"Sounds like a win-win to me." I tossed my logbook in the *Duck* and shut the door.

Larry watched me tie down each of the *Duck's* wings with rope cabled to the tarmac. "You could use a steady woman yourself, you know?"

"Not now, Larry."

"I'm just saying. Believe it or not, Logan, a woman can actually improve your life. I mean, look at me." He flexed both biceps and kissed each one. "Have you thought about one of those dating sites?"

"No."

I strode toward my pickup out in the parking lot and got in. As I cranked the ignition, I could see him through the windshield. He was peering into the engine compartment of a yellow Piper Cub, unconsciously using the tail of his clean new polo shirt to wipe off a spark plug. I was glad I wasn't his wife. Or the mailman.

When I got home, I called Buzz to tell him I'd take the assignment. Then I called Layne Sterling.

I let Mrs. Schmulowitz know that I would be gone for a few days, possibly longer. As always, she agreed to take care of Kiddiot while I was away. What she wouldn't agree to was altering his diet.

"Cats need protein. What am I supposed to do—feed him *tofu*? Before I forget, bubby, and I'm getting to that stage in life where, oh boy, do I forget, have I ever told you my tofu recipe?"

"I don't mean to be impolite, Mrs. Schmulowitz, but I really do have to pack and get—"

"—OK, real quick, my tofu recipe. You ready? Here goes: Step one: Throw the tofu in the trash. Step two: Boil yourself a nice brisket."

There was no use arguing with her about feline cuisine. The woman had outlived as many as four husbands, depending on the version of her personal history she was recounting at that moment. I hugged her and told her I'd be back as soon as I could. She knew enough not to ask where I was going, or why.

STERLING HAD booked us on the first scheduled departure to Denver the next morning, with a connection through Los Angeles. She was looking forward to working with me, she said, and was anxious to get to Colorado, to get to the bottom of what had happened to former senior analyst Rico Perris.

Then, as they say, complications ensued.

Somewhere in the cavernous expanse of the United Airlines operations center in Chicago, a mainframe computer hiccupped and hundreds of domestic flights, including ours, were grounded until the glitch could be fixed. Fortunately I owned an airplane. I checked the aviation weather app on my phone—high pressure, no airmen's advisories, and VFR conditions from California to the Midwest. In other words, excellent flying weather. If the federal government was willing to reimburse me for fuel, I told Sterling, I could get us both to Colorado by late that afternoon.

Sterling was skeptical. She also was more exquisite than I remembered from our having met the day before. In skinny jeans, knee-high calfskin boots and a black leather waist coat, she surveyed the *Duck* with obvious trepidation. In the sunlight, her almond eyes shone like polished jade.

"I've never been in a plane this tiny before."

"Then you're in for a real treat."

"These things crash all the time, do they not?"

"You only think they do. Crashes only make the news because they're so infrequent. Most are the result of pilot error. Limit those and small planes are actually pretty safe."

"Ever made any errors?"

"Occasionally."

"Any close calls?"

I wasn't about to fill her in on the one I'd had a day earlier. "A few," I said.

"A *few*?"

"Most were when I was in the air force. I flew A-10 Warthogs."

"Close air support. I read your 201 file." She peered in at the *Duck's* instrument panel. "Which one was the worst?"

"You mean close call?"

She nodded.

There were so many. It took me a second. "I was making a thirty-mill pass one day on a T-72 outside Al Kut. Came in too low. The tank exploded. Some shrapnel lodged in my left engine intake, along with some Iraqi's head."

"Did you crash?"

"Thankfully, no."

Sterling stared at me.

"Look," I said, "I promise we won't crash."

"Care to put that in writing?"

I crossed my heart.

She sighed, opened the passenger door, and climbed in. I admired that kind of moxie.

Four hours later, we were at 7,500 feet over central Arizona when I smelled smoke in the cockpit and began wondering if I'd made a promise I couldn't keep.

FIVE

We were streaking above the ground at more than 150 knots—almost like a real airplane—enjoying a thirty-knot tailwind. Stretched horizon to horizon, ahead of us and behind, was the great expanse of the American Desert Southwest. Minutes passed without either of us speaking. She gazed out at the vista, seemingly mesmerized by the view. The air was as smooth as the skin on the side of her face. I couldn't stop stealing glances at her.

"It's not fair," I said.

"What's not fair?"

"You read my personnel file. You know my story. I know zero about you. You work for the CIA. Beyond that . . ."

There wasn't much to tell, she said. Born and raised in Hawaii. Pre-law at UCLA. Seven years on the Los Angeles Police Department, including two years working counterterrorism, before being recruited by the agency. Married and divorced.

"I was also divorced," I said. "She left me for my boss at the time. We were hoping to get back together, but . . ." The words were lost before they reached my lips.

"She was pregnant with your baby when she was killed."

"That's in my file too?"

"Buzz told me. I can't begin to imagine how difficult that must've been for you."

I nodded and tried to put out of my mind what I knew I never could.

"I'm sorry, Logan."

"Me too."

I dialed in 125.8 on my No. 2 radio to pick up the automated weather and field conditions at Flagstaff, where I intended to land for gas. The airport was still nearly fifty miles ahead of us, according to the GPS, but it's always good to be ahead of the airplane, as we pilots like to say. It was in that moment I smelled something electrical burning. Sterling did too.

"What is that?" she asked.

I didn't have time to speculate or answer her. I was too busy pulling the fuel mixture control, closing air vents, pulling circuit breakers, shutting down everything I could think of to starve what fire there may have been or what fuel might have been lost because of it. I also was too busy keeping one eye on the airspeed indicator, making sure the wings didn't rip off as we rocketed toward earth in a sixty-degree dive to get us on the ground as quickly as possible.

The engine sputtered. The propeller froze. At a maximum controlled descent rate of 2,000 feet per minute and a ground elevation somewhere around 4,000 feet in that area of Arizona, I figured we had to survive about two minutes in the air until we reached terra firma. In other words, an eternity. During World War I, before parachutes were commonly used, combat pilots often leapt to their deaths when their ships caught fire rather than be burned to death on the way down. I might have made the same choice myself. I've seen men incinerated. It's as painful a way to go as there is. In any case, I had no parachutes. Our only hope was to ride the *Duck* down and hope we didn't combust before we got there.

I reached under my seat without looking, unlatched the small fire extinguisher I kept there, and handed it to Sterling. Her eyes were wide with fear. She yelled something, but I'd flipped off the avionics master switch. With my headphones on, I couldn't hear a word she said. I was following the first rule of piloting: Don't become so distracted by a developing crisis that you forget to keep flying the airplane. My passenger, however, wouldn't be ignored. She slammed her fist into my right thigh and adamantly pointed down, out the right window. I banked the *Duck* hard over to see what she was seeing. There, directly below us, was a runway.

We corkscrewed toward earth. I would've radioed my intentions, only I didn't know the name of the airport we were over, let alone the common traffic advisory frequency, and I didn't have time to go looking for either on my GPS. The smell of smoke worsened as we descended. I kept waiting for flames to come licking from behind the instrument panel but none did.

The runways below us were configured in a rough triangle. A florescent orange windsock at the center of the field was whipping around like one of those crazy inflatable air dancers you see on used car lots, the ones with waving arms, trying to get you to stop in. It told me the winds were essentially out of the east, and that we would be touching down to the west. Landing a single-engine airplane without an engine, especially under gusty conditions, can be a tad challenging. Set up your approach too soon and you can land short of the field, too late and you might overshoot. It's more art than science. I'm no Monet, but I'm happy to report that on that day, I painted it on, rolling to a stop with 2,000 feet of runway to spare. You could still smell smoke in the cockpit, so I shut down the engine.

Sterling crossed herself. Her hands were trembling.

"I didn't know you were Catholic," I said.

"I'm not. Just covering my bases."

I smiled and thanked her for having spotted the airport. We would've likely flown past it otherwise, I said. She thanked me for getting us on the ground intact. "You're welcome," seemed like a cheesy response, so I said something to the effect that it was no big deal, that we were never really in that much danger. She knew I was lying.

I opened the right door and instructed her to do the same with the left. We undid our seat belts. I told her I was going to restart the engine so we could taxi in. If the plane exploded in flames, I figured we could quickly bail out. Fortunately we didn't have to.

The airport's lone fixed-base operation was single story and quiet as an art library. Ours was the only aircraft on the ramp. A well-scrubbed, ginger-haired teenager whose name might have been Opie came running from inside, directed me to a parking spot, and chocked the *Duck's* nose wheel after the propeller stopped turning.

"Welcome to Winslow," he said.

Winslow, Arizona. So, *that's* where we were. The old Eagles song came to mind. We may not have been standing on a corner, but I was indisputably in the mood to take it easy after what Sterling and I had just gone through. I explained to Opie what had happened, a possible electrical fire behind the firewall, possibly involving the alternator. He said he'd arrange to have their mechanic on the job within the hour and offered to let us borrow his FBO's crew car so we could go into town to find a bite to eat while we waited for the airplane to get fixed.

"Are you kidding? I'm never getting in this plane again," Sterling said as she climbed out. "It's a death trap."

"You can't talk to the *Duck* that way. Only I can talk to the *Duck* that way. Anyway we made it, didn't we?"

"Yeah. To Winslow." She turned and asked Opie if there were any rental cars available.

"There's a couple places in town. We can get you one out here pronto if you'd like."

"Outstanding. Let's make that happen."

"Yes, ma'am," he said.

Sterling turned to me. "You can come with me to Colorado or you can stay here. Either way, I'm going."

"Yes, ma'am," I said.

We were headed eastbound toward Albuquerque on Interstate 40 in an all-wheel-drive, gunmetal gray Subaru Outback when Opie's mechanic called to report that he'd isolated the problem on the *Duck*. My ancient airplane's antiquated audio panel, the one I'd had to smack with some frequency over the years to get it to work properly, had finally taken enough of my abuse and blown a major circuit. Considering the panel's age and condition, there was little point in repairing it, the mechanic said. It would probably take him a couple of days to find a suitable replacement. I told him there was no rush.

"Electrical issue," I told Sterling after I hung up. "Could've been worse."

She stared straight ahead with her hands at ten and two on the wheel, maintaining the stony silence she'd established since we'd hit the road from Winslow.

"There's a file in my pack on the back seat," Sterling said after a while without taking her eyes off the road. "It'll tell you everything you need to know about yourself. We work for a life insurance company, First Mutual of Lexington. I'm a senior claims adjuster. You're my trainee. You'll want to study your cover."

I turned and reached back for the pack, a fancy leather rig embossed with the First Mutual of Lexington logo—a chisel-jawed Revolutionary War minuteman in a tricorne hat, clutching a Kentucky long rifle. The first thing I observed inside was a semiautomatic, Walther PK380, and two extra magazines of ammunition. I had thought about bringing along my own personal protection, a two-inch, .38-caliber revolver I'd carried as a backup during my days with Alpha, but decided otherwise at the last minute. The Buddha doesn't condone violence, and I was trying hard to follow his example, even if there were moments when, admittedly, I failed miserably.

Under the Walther was a manila folder containing my manufactured work history, along with a dozen or so First Mutual of Lexington business cards bound by a rubber band. My name was embossed on the cards. As my fake résumé indicated, I was extremely organized, adept at multitasking, possessed of excellent customer service skills, and a proud graduate of something called the "prestigious" International Insurance Institute. I had worked as an auto insurance special-ist for several companies before "being honored" to join my current employer. I was happily married to my high school sweetheart. We had two wonderful children. In my spare time, I enjoyed bowling, crossword puzzles, and cheering for the Chicago Cubs.

"For the record," I said, "I don't follow baseball."

"You do now."

"Why the Cubs?"

"Because they're universally loved."

"You printed all this stuff up before I even agreed to take the assignment. Because you knew I would."

"How 'bout those Cubbies?" she said, giving me a quick, sly glance.

Damn, she was beautiful. Sterling still may have been put off by my having persuaded her to come flying in my old airplane, but her testiness at that moment did little to dampen her appeal. Had we known each other better, I might have told her that, but I didn't. I forced myself to look away from her face and studied the file.

"There are some things you should know before we get much further," she said.

"About you?"

"About why we think Perris's death and Joe Zyra's in Phoenix may not have been a coincidence."

Back in 1992, as Sterling explained it, Congress passed something called the "JFK Records Act." It required that the federal government by 2017 make public 40,000 investigative documents relating to Kennedy's killing that had remained classified and buried under seal since shortly after the assassination in November 1963. About 3,600 of those documents, according to Sterling, were produced by the CIA, including at least 332 pages on the activities of iconic spymaster Howard Hunt, whose team of burglars in 1972 broke into Democratic Party headquarters at the Watergate Hotel in Washington, DC, setting in motion the eventual resignation of Richard Nixon. It was Hunt—shortly before his death in 2007—who claimed that in 1963, while under contract to the agency, he had been privy to what he described as "The Big Event," a conspiracy among several CIA-affiliated operatives to kill Kennedy.

There was more. Among other documents that had been withheld from the American public since that day in Dallas, Sterling said, were more than 600 pages detailing the activities of one David Atlee Phillips, who ran the CIA's Latin American section and who played a leading role in the agency's attempts to assassinate Fidel Castro. Before he died, Phillips, like Hunt, also was said to have attributed JFK's death to "rogue" CIA officers.

"You can appreciate the potential implications," Sterling said.

"The implications being that those sealed files are potentially incriminating, that there still may be people out there who don't want their names associated with the most notorious murder in modern American history."

"No statute of limitations on the death of Camelot," Sterling said.

We drove past billboards promoting "genuine" Navajo jewelry—"Artist-Direct Prices! Next Exit Only!"

"How many other CIA analysts were assigned to Red Lancer?" I asked.

"Five that we're aware of," Sterling said. Four had succumbed over the years to disease. The fifth had died in 2009 alongside forty-nine other victims when their commuter airliner crashed during a snowstorm while on approach to Buffalo, New York. The only other former member of the task force, retired CIA Deputy Director Glenn Moore, suffered from late-stage Alzheimer's disease and resided in a Scottsdale, Arizona, nursing home.

"In other words," I said, "Misters Perris and Zyra were it. The last known surviving participants with knowledge of the task force's activities and findings."

"Correct."

"What you're suggesting is that they could have had information so sensitive to the Kennedy assassination that it got them both killed."

"That's the crux of my assignment and, by extension, yours."

"It doesn't make sense."

"What doesn't?"

"Even if Perris and Zyra possessed that kind of information, why would anyone want to kill them, considering the government's obliged by law to release it anyway?"

Sterling looked over at me. "Some of those documents," she said, "have gone missing."

SIX

We stopped for an early dinner at a hole-in-the-wall Mexican food restaurant west of Albuquerque. I ordered a chile verde burrito. It tasted like it had been cooked by somebody who'd once seen a picture of a burrito, but who had no idea how to actually make one. Sterling's cheese enchiladas looked as if they'd been thrown down a flight of stairs before landing on her plate.

Our server was a sweet older woman with gold-veneered front teeth and a ruffled skirt the colors of the Mexican flag. "How's everything tasting?"

Sterling smiled bravely. "Delicious."

"Sir?"

"I'd rather not taco about it."

The waitress gave me a quizzical look for which I instantly felt guilty.

"I'm with her," I said, lying. "Delicious."

She left a check on the table and returned to the kitchen.

"You hurt her feelings, Logan."

"No more than this alleged burrito hurt mine."

I pushed my plate aside and mulled over what Sterling had told me before we'd stopped to eat. The classified Kennedy documents, she said, had remained locked away since the early 1960s in a highly secure, climate-controlled vault at the sprawling National Archives complex in College Park, Maryland. No one was certain when or how, specifically, they had vanished, only that apparently hundreds of pages slated for release in 2017 were now gone. No one had thought to make duplicate copies.

Sterling took a tepid bite of her enchiladas. A thin strand of cheese dangled from her lip.

"You've got something . . ." I pointed.

"Thanks." She brushed at the corner of her mouth.

"Other side," I said.

She brushed again and missed. I reached out and took care of the problem for her.

"Thanks."

"My pleasure."

She hadn't resisted my touch. If anything, she'd leaned forward slightly to accommodate it. A promising sign? I wondered. Layne Sterling was difficult to read. Most women are, but Sterling was one who made such evaluations all but impossible. Much, I suspected, had to do with her government training. She was in all likelihood as schooled in the arts of observation and obfuscation as I had been. This made me doubt the potential of my parlaying our professional interaction into something more personal. I resolved to not force the issue, to wait and see how she might play her cards, if she was willing to play them at all. But that didn't stop me from imagining what she looked like without clothes.

If only to get that image out of my head, I asked her opinion of the pistol in her backpack.

"It's OK, not great," she said. "There's no slide release and no de-cocker. To cock the gun, you have to put the safety on, then pull the trigger to drop the hammer. It has its virtues though. I like the locked-breech design. Easier to rack the slide. Mild recoil, good ergonomics. Eight rounds, one in the chamber."

"More than most conceal-carry .380s," I said.

She nodded and looked away. Then she said, "The gun's not mine. It's yours. It's also, by the way, untraceable."

I studied her face. She wouldn't meet my eyes. "This is a domestic assignment," I said. "Why would I need an untraceable, semiautomatic pistol."

"We can talk about this later."

"I'd like to talk about this now."

"We need to go. I'd like to be in Denver by tonight so we can be up in the mountains by morning. Busy day tomorrow." She scooped up the check and headed to the cashier's stand. I followed her.

"You want to tell me what's going on?"

"Not here," she said.

I tailed her into the parking lot, passing an incoming family whose many members were emerging from the van beside our rental SUV like endless clowns climbing out of one of those teeny circus cars. The temperature was dropping, as was the sun. The dry winter wind of New Mexico cut through my leather flight jacket like I was wearing nothing at all. I couldn't wait for Sterling to unlock the passenger door. Neither of us spoke a word until we were back out on the highway.

"I've never shot anybody before," Sterling said.

"But I have. Is that why I was hired for this assignment? Because I've killed people?"

Her eyes were on the road. "Partly."

"What are the other parts?"

"You're a good investigator. You come highly recommended."

"Who else am I supposed to kill?"

She still wouldn't look at me.

"I'm not going to Denver with you or anywhere else. Not until I get some answers."

No response.

"I'm serious, Sterling. The whole truth. And, I mean, right now. Pull the car over. If you don't, I will."

"You're not in charge of this operation, Logan. I am."

"If that's how you want to play it." We were doing seventy-five in the fast lane. I reached for the steering wheel and twisted it. The car tires screamed as we veered toward oblivion.

"Are you crazy?" Sterling let up on the gas. "Okay, okay!"

Slowly we eased onto the shoulder of the highway. She turned off the ignition and stared straight ahead. Eighteen-wheelers whizzed past, buffeting the rental car. "I didn't mean to scare you," I said. "I apologize."

"Accepted. I probably would have done the same thing."

Her shoulder bag had tipped over in the melee, spilling out a 9-millimeter Glock pistol at my feet. I put the gun back in her bag.

She drew in a breath, exhaled, then asked me how familiar I was with something called the "Petrini family."

"Is that like *The Partridge Family*? A divorced mother and her kids put together a rock band? Quite possibly the dumbest show in the history of television."

Sterling gave me a look. "No, Logan. Not *The Partridge Family*. Carlos Petrini rode herd on a Gulf Coast subset of the Carlos Trafficante crime syndicate based in Florida," she said. "They were active during the fifties and sixties, before Kennedy appointed his younger brother, Bobby, as attorney general."

"Before Bobby started going after the mob, you mean."

She nodded.

That part I already knew. So did anybody who'd spent any time studying the assassination. There was abundant evidence proving that Mafia bosses had used their money and muscle to help win Kennedy the White House, rigging votes especially in crucial Illinois. They believed that the new president would go easy on organized crime considering that Kennedy's own father had been a bootlegger during Prohibition. But when Bobby Kennedy made it his stated priority to aggressively prosecute cases against the mob, the godfathers felt betrayed. No conclusive proof had ever surfaced that any of them had played any part in JFK's murder, yet organized crime links to accused assassin Lee Harvey Oswald were many. Dallas strip club owner Jack Ruby, who shot Oswald to death in the basement of Dallas police headquarters before Oswald could tell his story, also was linked indisputably to the mob. What I didn't know, as Sterling explained it to me, was that shortly before he himself was gunned down in 1967 by killers unknown, Carlos Petrini had gone to the FBI and provided names of conspirators he alleged were involved in the plot to kill Kennedy.

Among them was an ex-marine named Harlan Weber who, after leaving military service, was said to have worked briefly as a bill collector for organized crime in South Florida. Though it was never officially verified, Weber, according to Petrini, had been peripherally involved in the murders of two Mafia associates believed to have possessed incriminating information about the mob's involvement in Kennedy's assassination. Their murders were never solved, nor was Petrini's. Weber escaped prosecution, eventually cleaned up his act, and somehow ended up in law enforcement. For the past two decades, he had served as sheriff of Colorado's Spruce County—the same county where former CIA analyst and Kennedy assassination expert Rico Perris had been killed when his Porsche mysteriously ran off a mountain road during a blizzard.

"How old is this guy Weber?"

"He turns seventy-seven in two weeks," Sterling said.

"So that's why I'm tagging along? To take out an old man with a nontraceable, government-issue .380 auto?"

"You're 'tagging along,' Logan, to back me up should I need backup. And, as far as that 'old man' is concerned, you haven't read his DD-214, most of which remains classified. I have. Weber was a thug, a stone-cold killer, both in the Marine Corps and afterward. You don't just turn off those instincts once you reach your golden years."

"A senior citizen sheriff in rural Colorado whacks another senior citizen, a retired CIA analyst, to help keep the truth of JFK's death covered up? I don't know. Sounds pretty dubious to me."

"You're not listening to me, Logan. I'm saying that we don't know if Perris was murdered or died accidentally. That's what I'm trying to find out. *We're* trying to find out." She exhaled in exasperation and ran her hand through her hair.

"Has anyone ever told you you're very appealing when you're agitated?"

She cocked her head and smirked. "Did you just make a *pass* at me?"

"Me? Never. I'm a total professional. Isn't that what Buzz told you?"

"He told me you were still very much in love with your ex-wife."

There was more than a little truth there. I was going to tell her that, and grief coupled with guilt can be a long, tortured road. I also was going to tell her that I found myself attracted to her in ways I couldn't explain, and that I hadn't felt that way about anybody in a long time. But that was before the New Mexico State Police black-and-white pulled in behind us with his rooftop candy bar lights on.

The cop bore a defensive end's brick wall girth and height. He was about thirty, his hair cut high and tight, military style. It was below freezing, yet he wore no coat. His biceps bulged like coconuts under his shirtsleeves, on which were sewn sergeant chevrons. The chrome nameplate over his right breast identified him as "R. Urlacher."

"Afternoon." His right hand rested lightly on the butt of his holstered pistol as he leaned warily into Sterling's window and surveyed the interior of the vehicle. "License and registration, please."

Careful to keep her Glock concealed, Sterling dug her driver's license out of her bag and handed it up to him while I retrieved the rental car contract from the glove box.

"Is there a problem, officer?"

"There's no stopping along the shoulder of the highway unless it's an emergency."

"Sorry," Sterling said, passing him up the registration. "I didn't know that."

"It *was* an emergency, Sergeant," I said. "My girlfriend and I were having a disagreement that required immediate resolution. Perhaps you can help."

Sterling looked over at me with her mouth slightly open, incredulity sketched on her face. Sergeant R. Urlacher narrowed his eyes, not at all sure what to make of me.

"What kind of disagreement?"

"She insists that New Mexico State has the better football program. I keep telling her it's the University of New Mexico."

"New Mexico *State*?" He grinned broadly. Gone instantly were any suspicions he may have had about us. "C'mon, man, everybody knows those losers in Las Cruces are nothin'. Lobos, baby. All the way."

"That's what I told my girlfriend."

What I told the cop was how my own playing days at Air Force had ended my senior year on a road trip to Albuquerque, when a New Mexico linebacker de-cleated me on a crossing route over the middle. Sergeant Urlacher volunteered how his own playing days on the New Mexico squad had been cut short by a shoulder injury.

"Football's easy if you play nuts," I said.

"You got that right," he said.

He handed Sterling back her driver's license and car registration and let us off without even a warning. We watched him drive away.

"Just so we're both reading off the same page, I'm not your girlfriend, Logan."

"Just to be clear, I'm not looking for one."

I thought I caught a flash of disappointment in her eyes, but it passed in an instant. Like I said, Layne Sterling was a hard woman to read. "I'm just glad he didn't decide to search the car," I said. "We would've had some splaining to do with those guns."

"Agreed."

She fired up the engine and eased us back out onto the interstate. Miles passed before she spoke again.

"How did you know?"

I looked over. ". . . Know what?"

"It's like you knew what that cop played and where."

Clearly Sterling didn't know anything about football. A true fan would have readily made a familial connection between Sergeant R. Urlacher of the New Mexico State Police and Brian Urlacher, the great Chicago Bears linebacker who played his college ball at the University of New Mexico. I could've explained all of that to her, but why? I wanted her to believe I was special and mysterious, even if I was neither.

"Well," I said, "you know how it is. You work in a particular field long enough, you pick up a few skills."

"You mean, like Brian Urlacher. Forty-one career sacks, twenty-two interceptions. First-round Hall of Famer inductee in all probability."

Correction: Clearly Sterling knew a *lot* about football.

Who *was* this woman anyway?

A LIGHT snow was falling on Denver when we arrived. Sterling wasn't feeling well. Her stomach was upset. She blamed the enchiladas she'd eaten for lunch.

We spent the night on the government's dime in separate motel rooms, one of those two-star budget inns as seen on *Cops*, where an apt corporate slogan might've read, "Sure you could stay somewhere nicer, but then you wouldn't have money left over for meth." I pulled off my shoes and socks, rubbed anti-itch cream into my toes, and called Mrs. Schmulowitz to check on Kiddiot. Her machine picked up.

"You've reached the residence of Mrs. Schmulowitz. She does not require the services of a licensed contractor, nor does she need her heating ducts cleaned. She does not wish to donate to your charity because we both know it's a scam. Is this what you aspired to do for a living when you grew up, ripping off little old ladies over the phone? You should be ashamed of yourself. Really, you should. Anybody else, I'm happy to call you back." Beep.

I said I hoped all was well, that I was doing fine, and fell asleep.

The next morning, Sterling and I rendezvoused in the lobby. She'd called ahead, she said, and arranged a meeting with Spruce County Sheriff Harlan Weber at his headquarters

in Angel Falls. I didn't need to ask her how she was feeling to
see that she was sick. Her color was wan and she clutched her
stomach. Still she insisted we press on. After what passed for
free breakfast in the motel's dining nook—the usual assort-
ment of stale pastries and burned coffee that Sterling didn't
touch—we headed into the mountains, west on Interstate 70.
With the snow, the journey would take us close to two hours.
I insisted on driving. Sterling, nauseous and grimacing with
each wave of stomach pain, was more than happy to let me.

"Weber can wait," I said. "Let's get you to a doctor."

"I'll be fine."

"I really think—"

"—I said I'll be fine, Logan. I'm in charge of this op.
You're not."

"Whatever you say."

Angel Falls was a tourist trap, but not without its charm.
Main Street was some three blocks long, built by hard-rock
miners whose fortunes were made and lost more than a hundred years earlier quarrying molybdenum from the surrounding hills. Old wooden saloons and brothels were now mostly
souvenir shops, craft breweries, and overpriced burger joints.
The sheriff's office was located on the west end of town in a
squat, sandstone building with the year, 1889, carved over the
main entrance. We parked in the sheriff's lot next door.

"Let me do the talking," Sterling said.

"What about the Walther? Do you want me to lock and
load?"

"Too risky. They may have a metal detector or want to
pat us down. You never know. Let's just leave it in the car
for now."

"So you just want me to sit there?"

"You know what to do, Logan. Pay attention to Weber's
microexpressions, his nonverbal communication. We're looking

for any tell that might indicate he knows something about Perris's death he's not saying."

Microexpressions. Nonverbal communication. I wish it were that simple. It never is. Those little eye movements we all make unconsciously, the set of our mouths, the placement of our feet—they never tell, they simply suggest. Walking into Sheriff Harlan Weber's office, I had no idea who he was, or of what he was capable. Nor could I have foreseen that I would come as close to death that day as I had ever been.

SEVEN

For an ex-marine and reputed former hitman tied however thinly to the assassination of John F. Kennedy, Harlan Weber couldn't have been more friendly or less threatening. Sausaged into his green sheriff's uniform, he was a stocky, hair-challenged man whose office walls featured framed crayon drawings by his grandchildren and plaques honoring his many years of service to the Boy Scouts of America. He wore an oversized gold wedding band. He sipped his coffee from a "World's Greatest Grandpa" mug. The guy clearly was trying too hard. No man is that overtly domestic without overcompensating for something, especially no lawman. Naturally I had my suspicions about him from the get-go.

"You sure I can't get you two some joe? Made it myself just before you all came in."

Sterling and I were seated on a pair of unpadded wooden chairs opposite Weber's ornate, oversized executive desk.

"We're fine, thanks," she said, but the thin smile masking her stomachache told me she was hardly fine.

"So," Weber said, easing into his big executive chair, "how can we help you today?"

"Well, sir," Sterling said, "as I explained to you when we spoke earlier this morning, Mr. Perris held a fairly sizable term-life policy with our company. Mutual of Lexington routinely follows up whenever a policy owner dies under other-than-normal circumstances such as age-related illness, to ensure that certain provisions of that policy—say, those relating to suicide, for example—do not invalidate any payouts to the policy holder's designated beneficiaries."

Weber blew on his coffee mug and smiled at us both. "And that takes two of you to do it?"

"Mr. Logan is in training with our company," Sterling said. "He's here to observe, aren't you, Mr. Logan?"

"Yes, indeed."

"Well," Weber said, "I'm sorry to say you've come a long way for not much."

His department's investigation of Rico Perris's death, the sheriff said, had proven cut-and-dried. Roads in the area that night were snowy and slick. Perris missed a turn doing an estimated forty-two miles an hour when he should have been doing less than ten. His 1959 Porsche 356 coupe went over an unreinforced embankment, rolled at least three times, and ended up in the Champ River. He'd been dead for at least twelve hours before two elk hunters found him. Dispatched the following morning, members of Weber's search and rescue team extracted the body and roped it to shore.

Nothing in Sheriff Weber's demeanor suggested he was trying to hide anything in his telling of the incident.

"Why was Mr. Perris going so fast?" Sterling asked.

"You'd have to ask him that."

"Mr. Perris is dead, sheriff."

"I'm aware of that, Ms. Sterling. A tragedy. Anytime a life is cut short."

"Any idea where he was going at that hour or why he would've even been out, driving around in the middle of a blizzard?"

"We really didn't get into any of that. There was no need." Weber sat back in his chair and put his boots up on his desk. "All I know is, people do crazy things sometimes. It was an accident, pure and simple. You could say it was his time, I suppose."

"What about Mr. Perris's background. Do you know what he did for a living?"

"He was retired. Worked for the Bureau of Labor Statistics, if I recall correctly." Steam from his coffee fogged the sheriff's glasses. Outside the snow was coming down harder. "I know he was from back east somewhere, but where, I wouldn't begin to hazard a guess."

"We'd heard somewhere he had another government job," Sterling said. "You wouldn't know anything about that, would you?"

Weber gazed serenely out at the snow. "No, ma'am. I surely don't. Beautiful out there, isn't it?"

Breaking eye contact might've indicated he knew more than he was telling, but I couldn't be certain. We waited for him to elaborate, watching his behavior intently, but he said nothing more.

"We'd like to inspect the wreckage," I said.

"The wreckage?" The sheriff grunted. "Why in the world would you want to do that?"

I couldn't think of an answer that didn't sound deceptive, then it hit me:

"Product liability."

Sterling stared at me for a long uncomfortable moment before picking up on my lead and running with it. "Product liability, exactly," she said, turning back to Weber. "If there was some mechanical flaw with the vehicle—say, with the braking system—that has the potential to produce litigation. That, in turn, could influence the assignment of policy benefits."

The sheriff turned from the window. "The poor fool went out into the snow, in a rear-wheel drive vehicle, with no chains, and drove off a mountain when he should've been staying home, sitting by the fire. Period. End of story."

"That aside," Sterling said, "we'd still like to take a look at the car."

Weber shook his head. "You want to inspect the wreckage? Be my guest. It's still sitting out there in the middle of the river. We won't be able to tow it out 'til after the spring runoff."

He gave us the location and wished us luck.

"YOU LOOK like I used to feel when Jim Beam and I were drinking buddies," I said as we left the sheriff's office.

"Thanks," she said. "I feel way better now."

She was holding her stomach. The snow flurries were thick as wool. With the wind blowing, it was well below zero.

"He wasn't what I expected," Sterling said. "I don't know what to make of him."

"Makes two of us."

She stopped abruptly in the middle of the parking lot, leaned against me, and vomited.

"You need to see a doctor, Sterling. You're not getting better."

"You could be right."

Driving into Angel Falls, I'd observed a small medical clinic on the east end of town. I helped Sterling into the Subaru and drove over. Ours was the only car negotiating the main drag. I had hoped that we would find the clinic similarly empty, but it was mobbed. The receptionist was short-haired and broad-hipped. Getting in to see the lone nurse practitioner on duty, she said indifferently, would take an hour at the minimum.

"We'll wait," I said, jotting Sterling's name down on a log-in sheet pinned to a clipboard at the counter.

Every couch and chair was occupied. We sat on the floor.

"I'm not paying you to babysit me," Sterling said, wincing. A thin coat of perspiration glistened on her forehead. "It'll be dark soon. You'll find an evidence collection kit in my pack. Get up there and see what you can find."

"I'd rather not leave you here by yourself."

"I'm not asking you, Logan. I'm telling."

THERE WAS no guardrail where Rico Perris plunged over the edge and into the Champ River. I stood there with the snow whipping and wind howling. Far below, a hundred meters or better, I could make out the remains of his silver Porsche partially buried in the ice. Getting there would prove challenging. Only an idiot would've even tried, considering the weather and my lack of proper winter gear. But, sometimes, taking idiotic chances comes with the turf. "Who dares wins" and all that stuff.

I tossed the keys to the rental car into Sterling's backpack, strapped on the pack, and started slowly traversing the steep slope. Almost instantly, my feet slipped out from under me and I found myself sliding on my assets, quickly picking up speed, unable to stop.

I caromed off jagged rocks, one to the next, at the complete mercy of gravity. And then, just when it appeared as if I was about to be catapulted off a ledge and into eternity, the upper branches of a juniper bush appeared in my path, poking up from the snow. I snagged one and held on for all I was worth.

Some scrapes. A few bruises. To my amazement, I hadn't broken anything. I'd live. Cold and wet, and in pain, I carefully eased my way down on my butt.

What remained of the Porsche had settled deep into the frozen river about thirty feet from the bank. I slid the backpack off my shoulders and surveyed the extent of Sterling's evidence-gathering supplies: ziplock collection bags; three small plastic specimen jars; flashlight; latex gloves; tweezers; a palm-size digital camera; a folding Leatherman multipurpose tool; and what looked to be a fingerprint kit.

Then I assessed the navigability of the ice.

At air force survival school and, later, with Alpha, we were taught that three inches of ice was the minimum thickness needed to support a man's weight. Anything less and you were going swimming. I had no scientific means of knowing whether the ice on the Champ was sufficient to hold me. I did, however, have a large rock. I picked it up with both hands and heaved it as far as I could into the river. It bounced and produced no cracks.

Good.

Tentatively I picked up the pack and stepped out onto the ice. One foot, then two. I jumped up and down in place. The ice under my feet felt solid. It was opaque in color, not clear, suggesting to me sufficient depth.

Very good.

Filling my lungs with cold mountain air I slowly shuffled out onto the ice, toward the remains of Rico Perris's Porsche.

Even from a distance, I could see that the car had undergone a fair amount of restorative work over its long life. A chunk of dried body filler, the kind used to smooth over collision damage, appeared to have been gouged loose along the rear underside of the Porsche's sleek body. This was not necessarily surprising given the car's jarring, violent journey down the mountainside. I snapped a few photos. That's when I noticed the smudge of black paint running roughly parallel to an approximately three-inch dent in the vehicle's chrome rear bumper.

It looked to me like a paint transfer, the kind another vehicle might've left when ramming the sports car from behind.

I snapped more photos, returned the camera to the backpack, and pulled out an evidence jar. My intent was to scrape off some of the paint for lab analysis. There was a good chance chemical assessment could identify the make and model of the vehicle that had left the paint behind. The problem was that most of the bumper and the smudge on it were buried in the ice. The second problem was that I lacked adequate tools to chip out the ice and get at the smudge. The blades of Sterling's Leatherman weren't strong enough to do the job. I needed something bigger:

A tie rod.

One was all but hanging off the left side of the Porsche's front axle. I pried it from the steering arm, got on my knees, and began gouging at the ice. Chips flew. I forgot all about being cold and wet, scraped and bruised. It didn't take long to expose the smudge. I used the Leatherman to scrape several large black paint flakes off of the bumper and into the evidence jar.

I had propped the backpack on the wreckage and was tucking the jar into a side pocket when the ice gave way.

PEOPLE WHO'VE fortunately never experienced it think that immersion in frigid water leads instantly to hypothermia and death. It doesn't. The truth is, dying can take a half hour or more, depending on body mass and how cold the water is, but you might not have more than about five minutes before the body starts to shut down and you cash in the chips. You lose function in your hands and feet. Arms and legs stop working. If you're not wearing a flotation device, you drown before your arteries can fully constrict and your heart stops. Either way, you've got to get out of the water and regain body heat as quickly as you can. Only I couldn't.

As I plunged neck deep into the freezing river, I gasped reflexively and began to hyperventilate—classic "cold shock response," as we learned in training. Waterlogged, swiftly losing feeling in my limbs, my strength waning, I tried repeatedly but simply could not pull myself out of the hole in the ice, while the river's currents tugged at me from below. It was all I could do to hang on and to not be dragged under. For the first time in my life, I felt powerless.

"Help! Somebody! Anybody!"

One would have thought that a man who could feel his life slipping away would have come up with a better plea to save himself, but that wouldn't have mattered. The wind was my only response. I might not have been in the middle of nowhere, but you could see it from there. I knew that no one would be coming to rescue me, not out there, amid a raging blizzard.

So this, I thought, was it. The end of the line. My life didn't flash before my eyes, but I did take clear stock of it. I regretted never having learned to play the trumpet. I regretted never having gotten on a stadium jumbotron by doing something stupid on camera. I didn't regret having killed people who deserved it, though I did having loved women who deserved better than the time I'd given them. I had lived, touched lives, and sometimes took them. I had left my mark on the planet, however fleetingly. Now I was about to go into the fertilizing business. I remembered a line I'd heard once but couldn't remember who'd said it: "I don't fear death, though I'd really prefer not to be there when it comes." That pretty much summed it up. I could feel my brain starting to shut down, my body going numb. There were far worse ways to cash in your chips, I told myself. I was ready. And then I heard:

"Hang on!"

At first I thought I was imagining things—a cowboy on horseback galloping toward the river through the snow on the opposite bank. He was cloaked under a white Stetson and a shearling coat. A woolen muffler was wrapped around his face, leaving only his eyes exposed. I watched him quickly dismount at the river's edge and heard him shout at me in an oddly high-pitched voice. I couldn't register the words.

"Help me." I found that I lacked the strength to say the words any louder.

Again he shouted something. I watched him grab a coil of rope and begin crawling on all fours toward me.

How long I was in that icy water I can't say. What I do know is that it was long enough to convince myself I was already dead.

THE QUILT that covered me on the leather sofa was eiderdown and smelled freshly laundered. I could hear the fire in the river-rock fireplace, the crackling of embers, before I felt the heat from the logs on my face. Warmth. Is there any better sensation to wake up to? I also realized that under that quilt, I was in my birthday suit.

I yawned and stretched. Everything ached. As my eyes came into focus, I could see that I was in a small cabin. Ninety pounds of German shepherd were snoozing in front of the fireplace. Propped in a corner near the door was a bolt-action hunting rifle with a black synthetic stock. Hanging nearby on an antique oak hall tree was the Stetson and shearling coat belonging to the cowboy who apparently had rescued me. A solid six footer, he was sitting across the room at a desk wearing green insulated cargo pants, hiking boots, and a red-checkered flannel shirt, pecking away at an old IBM Selectric typewriter.

Only the cowboy was no cowboy.

"Good," she said, turning in her chair, "you're awake. I was starting to get worried."

Hazel eyes. No makeup. Midforties. Sandy-colored hair tied back in a French braid. Pretty in a hard, sharply angled kind of way. I watched her disappear into the kitchen. She emerged a minute later with a chipped cup of steaming tea.

"Welcome to Rocky Ridge Ranch," she said.

I sat up and took the cup, shivering. "At what point in the party did my clothes go bye-bye?"

"You were hypothermic. I had to strip you down, then bundled you up, snug as a bug. You don't remember any of that, do you?"

I shook my throbbing head. The dog padded over and licked my hand.

"How long have I been out?"

"Well, let's see. Frou-Frou and I got you back to the cabin last night after six. It's after nine in the morning now."

"Frou-Frou?"

"My horse. She's out in the barn."

"Wasn't Frou-Frou the horse in *Anna Karenina*?"

My rescuer folded her arms across her chest and eyed me with something between curiosity and suspicion. "You know Tolstoy?"

"And Laura Ingalls Wilder. She named her homestead Rocky Ridge, if I'm not mistaken."

"How do you know all that?"

"I studied literature in college."

"You don't exactly look like the literature type."

"So I've been told."

Her name, she said, was Samantha McBride. Friends called her Sam. She stuck a digital thermometer in my ear and volunteered that she was a cardiologist practicing at a hospital down in Denver while pursuing ambitions of becoming a full-time writer. She'd published two books, she said, historical nonfiction. Both had been largely panned by critics—or "vermin," as she branded them.

"In North Dakota, on the cattle ranch I grew up on, we would have de-balled them."

"North Dakota," I said, trying to keep things light, "all the weather of Canada without the health care."

Sam McBride didn't smile. Brusque, I would come to discover, was her default state.

"Still a little hypothermic," she said, checking the thermometer. "Keep those blankets on."

"Thanks for saving my life."

"You can thank Cuddles," she said, nodding toward the dog. "He went chasing after a 'coon, which he tends to do from time to time. Frou-Frou and I went out looking for him before he got mauled or froze to death and, have mercy, there you were. I looped a rope around the saddle, crawled out on the ice, tied the other end around both of us, and told Frou-Frou to start hauling."

"Smart horse," I said.

"Extremely smart."

"I don't remember any of that."

"Not surprising," McBride said. "People tend not to remember trauma. All that adrenaline you had going stimulated your vagus nerve. The vagus promotes an excessive flood of non-adrenaline production in the brain. Non-adrenaline destroys the brain's ability to store memories."

Cuddles was resting his big square head on my right thigh, thumping his bushy tail on the floor and giving me love eyes. I scratched his ears. "He doesn't exactly look like a Cuddles."

"So he's been told," Sam said.

She asked how I ended up in the river. I gave her my cover story, how my partner and I were routinely following up on the death of the Porsche driver, Rico Perris, for life insurance purposes. We needed to check out the car, I said, to make sure there was no issue of product liability.

"Mutual of Lexington, huh? Sounds like a giant load of crap to me." She reached into her pants pocket, unlimbered the .380 pistol Layne Sterling had loaned me, and held it at what some might've interpreted as a threatening angle.

"I found this in your pack," she said. "What I want to know is, what the hell you were *really* doing out there?"

EIGHT

Sam McBride was certain I was an undercover cop. She professed to dislike cops—most of them anyway. Her parents' lives were destroyed, she said, after her father was falsely convicted on assault charges and spent six months in county jail, the victim of circumstantial evidence manufactured by two morally bereft detectives. She'd also treated enough police officers to know that many exaggerated minor, on-the-job injuries to cheat the system, drawing paid leave or early pensions, and that they sometimes lied to cover their tracks after shooting innocent individuals. I pointed out that as far as I knew, members of civilian law enforcement rarely discharged their weapons in the line of duty, and that too many sustained real injuries on the job protecting the likes of us.

"Anyway," I said, "I'm sorry about what happened to your father, but I can assure you, I'm no cop. I'm an insurance investigator."

"Then what the hell is this?" She reached into the pack with the Walther still in her hand and pulled out the evidence jar with the paint scraping I'd collected.

"Paint transfer. We're trying to determine if the Porsche driver went off the road by himself or had assistance. It could affect the assignment of benefits."

"People don't get murdered in Spruce County. They might get high, they might overdose, but they don't murder each other, Mr. *Logan*, or whatever your real name is."

"I'm not saying he was murdered. The likelihood is that he was the victim of a garden variety car accident. But my company needs to be certain."

I was hoping she wouldn't grill me on my résumé, little of which I remembered. Fortunately she didn't. I also was hoping she'd put down the gun. Unfortunately she didn't do that either.

"Why does an insurance investigator need a pistol?"

"Because some people, including present company, apparently, are flat crazy," I said, "and also because I can't throw a rock at a thousand feet per second."

She thought about what I'd said, then, with some reluctance, returned the pistol to Sterling's pack. "I'm not crazy," she said, "just careful. I'll drive you back to your car after breakfast."

WE ATE scrambled eggs and slab bacon, maple-cured, at a crude log table and washed it down with cowboy coffee—the grounds boiled in a can on her ancient, woodburning stove. The bad news was that my shoes and clothes were still wet from the day before. The good news was that Sam McBride had a box of clothes under her bed left behind by her ex. The jeans were a little loose in the waist and the shirt and ski coat a little tight in the chest, but they'd do. She even scrounged up an old pair of his gloves. The bad news was that he'd left behind no shoes. I'd have to wear mine damp. My toes, meanwhile, had stopped itching—the upside of nearly freezing to death.

Her Volvo station wagon was dented, its red paint rusting and mud-splattered. I finished dressing while she pulled it out of a large hay barn next to the cabin, then watched as she got out of the idling car and hurriedly swung the barn's double doors shut. The structure was so old, it leaned slightly to one side.

"You coming?" she hollered.

I nodded through the window and headed outside.

The Volvo's heater was blasting. Cuddles jumped between us and kept trying to lick my face. He smelled like wet gym socks.

"Cuddles!"

He retreated at her admonition to the back seat, smiling impishly and wagging his tail.

Sam McBride drove with skilled abandon, smashing through snowdrifts along the unplowed road leading away from her cabin like she'd done it all her life.

I asked her if she'd ever met Rico Perris.

"Yeah, I met him. Ran into him down in town a couple times at the post office, as I recall, getting his mail. I didn't really know who he was until I saw his picture in *The Pinecone*. Always seemed a little full of himself. Easterner, if you know what I'm saying."

"Would you happen to know if he had any friends in town, anyone we could talk to?"

"I wouldn't know."

"What about any enemies?"

She looked over at me and smirked. "People don't move up to the mountains without having enemies. The *world* is our enemy. It's why all of us live up here. To get away from all the jerks. But if you're asking, do I know if Mr. Perris pissed off somebody so badly that they ran him off the road? That I couldn't tell you."

We came around a corner. McBride slammed on the brakes. Eight mule deer were standing in the road. They surveyed us without alarm, nonchalantly flicking their tails and ears. Cuddles woofed. McBride told him to be quiet. We waited patiently for the deer to move out of the way.

"I don't understand how anyone could shoot these creatures," she said. "I hate guns."

I said nothing. I may have had issues with hunting—why take the life of some beautiful wild creature when you can go to the grocery store and buy a frozen pizza?—but I had nothing personal against guns, only the people who misused them. A gun is nothing more than a tool, same as a hammer or saw. The only difference is that a gun's purpose is to kill. Sometimes that's not a bad thing.

A PLOW had come along at some point in the night, burying the Subaru up to its roof in a frozen slush. Sam McBride offered to help me dig out, but I declined. She'd already done enough, I said.

"Well, if you won't let me help you, at least let me loan you this." She reached into the back seat and handed me a snow brush. "You can return it and get your clothes back when I fix you dinner tonight. They should be dry by then."

I'm not sure whether I had a "type" when it came to the opposite sex, but the woman who'd rescued me from the ice was not it. I thanked her diplomatically for the offer, told her that I wasn't sure of my schedule, and that I'd be in touch. She asked for my phone number. With some reluctance, I gave it to her.

"Try not to go falling into any more rivers," she said.

"I'll do my best."

I watched her drive away, then set to work freeing the Subaru from its frozen tomb, digging and scraping.

Even with my borrowed coat and gloves, I was shivering. I tried to think about some of the ops I'd been on, the ones in warmer climes, where the mercury can hit 120 degrees in the shade, and where I would have willingly surrendered a year's pay just to be cold for five minutes. I thought about the Taliban commander and his two sons we'd shot in that little village outside Jalalabad, how their corpses roasted in the July sun while we waited for extract, debating the best flavors of Popsicles. Buzz went with root beer. *Root beer?* Everybody thought he was nuts.

Unburying the Subaru turned out to be a minor inconvenience compared to the doors being frozen shut. I lacked any deicer or warm water to unfreeze them. What I did not lack, standing there along the roadside, were rocks. I dug one the size of my fist out of the snow and smashed the rear window. Why anyone would ever buy a rental car is one of life's great mysteries. It's like going to a brothel and looking for your soul mate. I cleaned out the broken glass, tossed the backpack into the back seat, and climbed in after it.

My cell phone was sitting on the passenger seat where I'd left it. It, too, was frozen. No juice. I feared the car's battery would be in similar shape, but when I slid the key into the ignition, the Subaru started up no problem. I let the engine warm for a few minutes, rubbing and blowing on my hands, luxuriating in the heater, then drove into Angel Falls. I was not at all sure where to find Layne Sterling.

I was waiting at a red light, the only traffic signal in town, looking over my shoulder for Sheriff Weber and heading to the clinic where I'd last seen her, when Sterling came bounding out of a French bakery, yelling and waving her hands.

I couldn't roll down my window. It was still frozen. I pointed toward an angled parking space a few feet away and pulled in. The driver's door still wouldn't open. I climbed over the back seat and out the broken rear window.

"Where the hell have you been?" she demanded.

"I went swimming."

"Why didn't you call?"

"Phone's inoperable. How's your health?"

"Food poisoning. I'll get over it. What do you mean, *swimming?*"

"Long story."

"And that window? I suppose that's a long story too."

"Rock got it. I'm just hoping you didn't waive the deductible on the rental agreement."

After leaving the urgent care clinic, she said she'd spent the night in a bed-and-breakfast down the street, waiting to hear from me. I told her about the apparent paint transfer I'd scraped off the Porsche's rear bumper. I told her about falling through the ice, and how Sam McBride, MD, had literally ridden to my rescue.

"That's fantastic."

"What, me falling through the ice and miraculously being saved by a physician?"

"No, you miraculously recovering a paint transfer—not that I don't care about your general welfare."

"Thanks for your concern."

She said she wanted to get the sample off to the lab for analysis as soon as possible. The post office was a block away. The sun was out in full. The snow in town already was starting to melt. Maybe by the time we got back, the doors would be unfrozen. I grabbed my pack from the back. We began walking.

"I'm just glad you're OK, Logan," she said. "You had me scared half to death."

"Hey, thanks for caring."

The post office was about the size of a convenience store and stood out like a leisure suit at an Old West costume party—a bland, utilitarian building of earth-tone stucco that practically screamed 1970s. The lone clerk on duty appeared to have hailed from the same era.

"How can I help you?" he asked, ogling Sterling up and down as we entered.

Mid-to-late sixties. Gaunt and sallow. Wispy moustache. Sad, watery eyes. A bulge of tobacco chaw between his cheek and lower lip. He sported baggy, blue-gray postal uniform trousers and a diarrhea brown, moth-eaten cardigan sweater over his uniform shirt. Greasy strands of graying hair were stretched like guitar strings across his pink pate. Pinned to his shirt was a silver nametag: Bart Tolks, Senior Clerk.

"We'd like to mail something overnight," Sterling said.

"Sure, no problem, we can do that."

He handed her a flat-rate, Priority Express box. She filled out the delivery information and jotted a note to her people while Bart Tolks went about his official postal duties, filing this and rearranging that. I slipped her the evidence collection jar from the pack while his back was turned. She inserted it along with the note and sealed the box shut.

"OK, all set," Sterling said.

"Very good. The clerk cocked an eyebrow as he peered at the mailing address and pretended not to look at Sterling's breasts. "Langley, Virginia. Home of the world-famous Central Intelligence Agency, is it not?"

"Home of many things," she snapped, "including the insurance company we work for. Not that that's any business of yours."

"Relax, doll, I meant no offense."

"I'm sorry. What did you just call me?"

"None taken," I said as pleasantly as I could, cutting off Sterling before she could rip him to pieces. The last thing we needed was some nosy postal clerk opening up the box after we'd left. "We have to get our travel expenses in by tomorrow or we don't get reimbursed."

"Well, we can't have that, can we?" Tolks said. "That'll be $22.95. Cash, check, money order, or credit card?"

Sterling paid him out of two twenty-dollar bills. He made change and asked her if she needed any stamps. She said no.

"Again, no offense. I didn't mean to pry," Tolks said. "It's just that, when you've worked at the post office as long as I have, you pretty much get to know everybody's business in town. It can be kind of a bad habit to break, I guess, asking questions. Most folks around here, they don't think nothing of it though."

"I'm not from around here," Sterling said.

"Obviously," he said, his smile a collection of mismatched, tobacco-stained teeth. "Anyway, you both have yourself a great day."

"You as well," I said.

Sterling said nothing.

We left.

"Can you believe that guy called me *doll*?" Sterling said after we walked out. "That dude gave me the creeps. Something about him just didn't sit right."

"Must've been that Chester the Molester moustache and cardigan."

"I wasn't aware molesters wore cardigans."

"Are you kidding? The guy could have a career in Hollywood if he wanted one. 'Hello, Central Casting? Get me a molester.'"

She smiled despite herself. "You're a pretty funny guy, especially for somebody with so many sanctioned kills."

"The old me," I said.

We reached the car. The air was biting. I could still see my breath.

"We're going to need to get that window fixed, unless we want to get snowed on when the next storm rolls through."

"It'll have to wait," Sterling said. "We have places to go."

"Like?"

"Like Rico Perris's cabin. I'd like to get inside if we can, go through his papers, see what we can turn up."

"Last time I checked, that was called residential burglary."

"Only if we get caught."

"And here I always thought Christians in Action regarded risk as a four-letter word. I like your style, Ms. Sterling."

She smiled and slid the key into the ignition, then paused and turned toward me. "Do you mind me asking you a personal question?"

"Probably."

"Your wife, how did she die? I hope you don't mind me asking. I read in your file that she'd been kidnapped."

The memory of that day rose, foul and acidic, from somewhere near my center. My impulse was to say nothing, to paper over my grief as I had every day since Savannah's death, but the empathy in Sterling's eyes seemed genuine. I suppose I owed her an answer, however incapable I was emotionally of articulating it.

"She died because I got involved in something I shouldn't have. Anything beyond that is window dressing."

Sterling nodded. She knew enough to let it go. That kind of understanding doesn't grow on trees.

Rico Perris had lived the last days of his life five miles outside Angel Falls, just below timberline. Snow had drifted four feet deep in places, making the unplowed, quarter-mile dirt road leading into his place all but impassable. We parked below in a turnout along two-lane Colorado Highway 103, ignored the "Private Property, Trespassers Will be Shot" sign and metal guard gate, which was open, and walked in.

Almost instantly, our jeans and footwear were soaked through.

"Are we having fun yet?"

"Tons," Sterling said, struggling with each exhausting step to extract her legs from the drifts.

I took her hand. "I'm guessing you didn't have this problem growing up in Hawaii."

"You're nothing if not astute, Logan."

Perris's tired, tin-roof cabin was little bigger than a shed and sat perched in an aspen grove. Next to it was a one-car garage, one of those modern, pre-fab aluminum numbers that look out of place wherever they are. I smelled wood smoke long before I saw it curling up from the cabin's chimney.

"Still want to break in?"

"Probably not," Sterling said, frowning.

"I thought he lived alone."

"That was my understanding."

"You sure we got the right address?"

"Pretty sure."

We were about twenty feet from the cabin's front porch, still trudging through virginal drifts, when the door flung open and a woman emerged. She was holding a pistol to her right temple.

NINE

Tears streaked her noticeably high cheekbones. She was a tall, angular brunette in her late fifties with stylishly short hair, designer jeans, and a gold brocade sweater that suggested she was no stranger to money. Even with a gun to her head, she conveyed a certain regality. The pistol was small—.25 caliber, or possibly .32. I couldn't tell from where I was standing.

"Please don't take another step closer," she said in a Boston accent that was decidedly upper crust, "or I swear I'll kill myself."

Her right index finger was resting on the weapon's trigger. I took her at her word.

"It's OK, relax," I said, showing her my palms. "We just want to talk to you, that's all."

She slammed the door and disappeared inside.

"Go around back," Sterling said, drawing her Glock. "Pound on the walls, whatever. Soon as I hear you, I'll boot the door."

Back in the day, I would have been the first guy to boot that door. "Dynamic entry," as we used to call it. But you kick in enough doors, leave enough blood of other people's blood on the floor, and after a while, something shifts at your core. Maybe you get softer. Or wiser. Maybe you just get tired of playing god. Whatever the reason, I didn't want to see this woman hurt, whoever she was.

"This isn't a SWAT action, Sterling," I said. "This is a distraught, middle-aged woman. We have no idea why she's upset. We have no idea who she is. We have no idea what she's doing here. Now holster your weapon."

"I'm not going to stand out here, Logan, and wait her out. It's too damn cold. If you have a better plan, I'm all ears."

I walked up to the cabin's front door, positioned myself beside it in the event the woman inside decided to start squeezing off rounds, and gently knocked.

"I said go away. I'm warning you."

"Ma'am, we're from Mutual of Lexington," I said. "It's an insurance company. Maybe you've heard of us. The gentleman who used to live here, Mr. Rico Perris, held a fairly substantial life policy with us. We're reaching out to his beneficiaries so that they can receive what is legally due them."

Silence from behind the door. Then the woman said, "You're not with the sheriff's office?"

"No, ma'am. We're not with the sheriff."

"I just don't want to be evicted, that's all. I've got nowhere else to go."

"No one's here to evict you."

"What company did you say you were with again?"

"Mutual of Lexington," Sterling said. "We're wondering if you might be a named beneficiary."

The door cracked open seconds later. The woman peered out. "How big is the policy?"

✈ ✈ ✈

WHEREVER YOU looked, Rico Perris's cabin was jammed with books. Stacks of them, shelves sagging under their weight. A

Bach sonata was playing softly on the stereo. The woman said her name was Alessandra Munoz, Perris's live-in fiancée.

"I wasn't really planning to shoot myself," she said, handing me the pistol. "I know they're going to sell the cabin, the county is. I'm just very frightened. I'd prefer not to be kicked out. I've got nowhere else to go."

"You're safe with us, Alessandra."

I unloaded the gun, setting it and the cartridges on the coffee table.

"So," she said, sitting down on a burgundy recliner and primly smoothing her jeans, "am I on the policy?"

"Yes, you are," Sterling said. "To the tune of $25,000."

"Oh, my god." Alessandra covered her face with both of her hands and sobbed, then gazed up toward heaven. "Thank you, dear lord."

I cringed, knowing how cruelly she was being misled, but also knowing that we had a job to do. Sterling gave me a sad little smile as if to say, "We have no choice."

The furniture was mountain-cabin stylish, made from rough-cut logs and upholstered in a nubby burgundy fabric that featured images of bears and moose. I sat on the sofa while Sterling casually perused stacks of papers and snapped photos around the cabin—"Standard procedure," she told Alessandra Munoz, "to document and establish residency for probate purposes."

Whatever the hell that meant, it sounded good. Alessandra didn't question the explanation and spent the next fifteen minutes happily sharing with me her life's story. She was, by her own account, a failed parent, the survivor of three failed, abusive marriages—to a musician, a radio disc jockey, and a jewelry designer—who'd been living in her car when she'd met Perris on a Tuesday all-you-can-eat spaghetti night at the

Molly B saloon in Angel Falls. Both, she said, were lost, lonely souls. Within two weeks, she'd moved in with him.

"A whirlwind courtship," I said.

"Very whirlwind," she said, starting to cry again. "It was kismet. Now he's gone and I don't know what to do."

Alessandra professed to know little, if anything, of what former CIA analyst Rico Perris had done for a living. All she knew of his employment history, she said, was he'd spent the bulk of his adult life working in some capacity with statistics and that he had retired from some obscure federal agency she'd never heard of.

"Anyway, we rarely discussed our past professional pursuits," she said. "Usually, we were too busy making love. Rico was the most sensual man I ever knew. I'm not ashamed to say that."

"How wonderful for you both," Sterling said, trying a little too hard to sound sincere.

Stacked on the floor beside me were two books on the JFK assassination, including, *On the Trail of the Assassins, One Man's Quest to Solve the Murder of President Kennedy.* I'd read the book years earlier. The author, Jim Garrison, had been district attorney in New Orleans and had brought charges against Clay Shaw, a prominent Louisiana businessman whom Garrison accused of conspiring with organized crime figures to kill JFK. A jury later acquitted Shaw, the only person ever charged in Kennedy's death.

The other book on the cabin floor was entitled, *Lancer's Last Day: The CIA and the Murder of John F. Kennedy.* I picked it up and thumbed through it briefly while Alessandra elaborated on how much joy Rico Perris had brought to her life.

"I've never heard of this one," I said, casually handing it to Sterling. "Is it any good?"

Alessandra sniffed. "I wouldn't know. I didn't read it."

"Do you know why Rico was reading it? Or this one?" I held up Garrison's book.

"Not really, no, other than perhaps he was interested in what happened to Mr. Kennedy."

"You never asked him?"

"You make it sound like a crime. No, I never asked him. Was I supposed to? Rico read a lot of books." She got up and put another log in a pot-belly stove. "He always had his nose in some book. He was interested in a lot of things. He was a very well-rounded individual. One of the many qualities I found so attractive about him."

Rico, she said, had been in a book club that met once a month, usually online. He'd served as assistant master of a local Boy Scout troop. Perhaps more than anything, though, her late fiancé had been interested in his vintage Porsche.

"His pride and joy," she said, her eyes misting over yet again. "Always tinkering with it. He so adored that car. He wouldn't even take it out in the rain."

"Then why," I asked her, "did he take it out in the snow that night?"

Alessandra got up and poured herself a glass of cabernet. "I can't be certain, but I think he'd started seeing someone. On the side. You learn to put up with a lot when you have a lover like Rico."

"Do you know who that might've been?" I asked.

She gulped some wine and shook her head no. "The only thing I know is that someone had been threatening him. Her boyfriend or husband perhaps? He never told me. It's why he'd started carrying that gun."

"Do you remember when it was, the last time he got one of those calls?" Sterling asked.

"The night he died. He said he had to go see someone. I told him he was crazy, going out in the snow like that. Kissed me good-bye, grabbed his phone, and away he went. I never saw him alive again."

"If he was being threatened," I said, "why didn't he take his gun with him?"

"He was more concerned about my safety than his own. That's the kind of wonderful man he was. My sweet Rico. I can't believe he left me 25,000."

Again, she wept.

After Rico left that night, Alessandra said, she watched some TV, had a couple of nightcaps, and turned in early, expecting him to return home after a few hours. She awoke the next morning in a panic and claimed to have spent the entire day calling around town hoping someone had seen him. It was not until the following day that a Spruce County sheriff's deputy arrived, bearing the bad news. She was so shocked, she said, she never thought to let the deputy know about the threatening calls. She hadn't called the sheriff's department since, she said, for fear she would be removed from the cabin.

"As I said, I know this isn't my place. I know they'll make me leave at some point, but right now, I've got nobody. My children won't talk to me. I have no other friends. I'd be on the streets. So this money, praise Jesus, it has to have come from heaven."

"What about Rico's friends? Maybe one of them can help you out until you get on your feet," I said.

Alessandra blotted her eyes with a tissue. "The only real friend I'm aware of—other than his girlfriends whom I never had the pleasure of meeting—lives down in Denver. Another Vietnam vet. I've never met him either. Rico would go see him every so often. They were in the book club together but, really, I think it was just an excuse to drink beer together."

Perris had driven to Denver the day before he died to see his friend, who Alessandra identified as one Cyril Tomasello.

Perris told her Tomasello had been a marine and driven a race car at some point in civilian life. He lived near Denver's Mile High Stadium. She didn't know the address.

Sterling handed Alessandra a business card and told her to call if she remembered anything else.

"Do you know when I'll get the money? I desperately need it."

"Soon," Sterling said.

"I HATE all the deception," Sterling said, shivering, as we fought our way back to the rental car through the snow, "but it's part of the job."

"You don't owe me any explanations. I've done my share of deceiving on the job too."

The wind gusted, kicking up snow that blew in our faces. My toes were so frozen, I couldn't feel them.

"She indicated Perris had served in Vietnam," Sterling said. "I'm surprised. It doesn't show up in his file."

That Perris was prior military came as no surprise to me. Many individuals with military experience who transition to the clandestine alphabet agencies purposely have the time they spent in uniform erased from their personnel records. Having it known that you served in the armed forces of the United States, regardless of your assignment, can get you killed in some of the nastier corners of the world if you fall into the wrong hands. There's greater plausible deniability, the theory holds, playing the part of the civilian operating under diplomatic or NGO cover. Personally it never bothered me whether anyone knew about my time in the air force. I figured if I was ever captured while on an overseas assignment with Alpha, any revelations of my having previously flown combat missions would be the least of my problems.

Sterling agreed that we needed to reach out to Cyril Tomasello. Few bonds of friendship are stronger than those forged between men and women who've served together in the military. If Rico Perris had confided to anyone about the threats he'd purportedly been receiving before his death, Tomasello was potentially that guy.

Finding contact information on him took Sterling all of ten minutes. A call to a secure number at Langley, linking her to the sprawling Intelligence Community Comprehensive National Cybersecurity Initiative Data Center in the boonies of Utah, quickly produced Tomasello's current address and telephone number. She could've extracted his shoe size if she'd wanted—so meticulous has the government's cataloguing of personal information on its citizens become. First, though, she wanted to change into dry clothes. She also said she wanted to review Perris's autopsy report before the Spruce County Coroner's Office closed for the day.

I was freezing, too, though I tried not to let my teeth chatter, playing the manly man and so forth. We stopped at McDonald's and changed in the restrooms before grabbing a quick bite to eat. Sterling's stomach was still a little upset from the bad enchilada she'd eaten outside Albuquerque. She ordered a salad.

"Ordering a salad at McDonald's," I observed, "is like paying a hooker to play cards."

"I gather you're speaking from personal experience?"

I ignored the slight and ordered a Big Mac with fries.

"Gotta die of something," Sterling observed dryly. "Why wait, right?"

I pretended not to hear her.

✈ ✈ ✈

JED JONES served as Spruce County's medical examiner, a well-dressed fellow with a perpetual frown and a slightly misaligned glass eye, who sounded a little like Rhett Butler, the kind of guy who garnished the conversation with needless fancy words to let everyone know how smart he was. We found him vacuuming out a hearse in the carport at his day job, running Angel Falls's only funeral home and crematorium.

"The presumption," he said, yelling over the vacuum cleaner, "that I would willingly entertain the release of any autopsy report before first consulting with county counsel is both preposterous and, not to be offensive, somewhat imbecilic."

"Autopsy results, sir, are rarely *not* a matter of public record when the investigation of the decedent's death has been closed," Sterling shouted. "The sheriff's department ruled out foul play in Mr. Perris's case. We're entitled to see that report."

Jones turned off the vacuum. "What establishment did you say you were associated with?"

"Mutual of Lexington."

"We're a highly rated life insurance company," I said.

Sterling shot me a look.

"That may be so," Jones said, "but much as I wish I could render assistance, in this instance, I'm afraid the discharge of my official duties precludes me from doing so, as I've indicated, until such time as I've obtained further direction from legal minds superior to my own. Unfortunately that may take a few days."

I sniffed the air in an exaggerated fashion. "Smell that?"

"Smell what?"

"Embalming fluid and burned human bodies. I can only imagine what a field day the EPA will have up here when they find out the fine good people of Angel Falls are being illegally exposed to the toxic remains of their fellow citizens. They'll be up here in a flash in their little hazmat suits, stringing up 'do not cross' tape. You'll shell out a small fortune in fines and having to upgrade your venting systems, just to keep your doors open."

Jones narrowed his glass eye. "Am I mistaken, or are you threatening me?"

"We're simply asking for what we are entitled to by law," Sterling said.

The mortician glared, clutching the vacuum's wand like a raised sword, before slowly lowering it and letting out a breath. "Give me a couple of minutes," he said.

The odor of death wafted through the open door as he went inside.

"EPA?" Sterling gave me a wink. "Not bad, Logan. I knew there was a reason I brought you along."

"And here I thought I was just eye candy."

As we waited, the sun began to break through the clouds. Muddy, snow-covered cars and trucks rolled past. Sterling's hair glowed reddish gold in the warming light that danced on her porcelain face. Her lips couldn't have been more alluring, her curves more dangerous. I tried not to stare, but I couldn't help it.

"Why do you keep looking at me like that?"

"You have something in your teeth. Broccoli, maybe."

"I hate broccoli."

She started digging at her teeth with a fingernail before realizing by my bemused expression that I was only kidding.

"Very funny, Logan. I remember when I was in third grade too."

"Are you seeing anybody?"

She hesitated, studying me intently. "Are you asking if I have a boyfriend?"

"Or girlfriend—not that there's anything wrong with that."

"No, Logan, I am not seeing anyone currently. I don't have time."

"That's unfortunate. As the Buddha said, all you need is love."

"The Buddha didn't say that. The Beatles did."

"Be that as it may, maybe we can grab dinner sometime, I mean, if you can find room in your busy schedule."

She unconsciously smoothed her hair. "I'll think about it."

We were still waiting for Jones, the coroner, to reemerge from his mortuary with a copy of Rico Perris's autopsy report when a white Chevy Suburban bearing Spruce County sheriff's markings came barreling around the corner and skidded to a stop on the icy street in front of us. The uniformed deputy who was driving looked like a poster boy for steroidal rage.

From the passenger side, out stepped the sheriff himself, Harlan Weber. "You're stirring up trouble in my county," he said. "We don't need any outside agitators here. You got two minutes to get out of town and if I find either of you back here again I will arrest you both."

TEN

If you're a local law enforcement official and you're threatening innocent individuals with arrest on trumped-up charges, let alone those working clandestinely for a federal intelligence agency, the least you could do is come up with something that sounds remotely legit. Sheriff Weber couldn't even do that.

"Obstruction," he said when Sterling pressed him on the issue.

"Obstruction of what?"

"This is my town. It is whatever I say it is. Just so we're all reading off the same page, there was no foul play. Rico Perris died in a car accident. Period. End of story."

Only then did the coroner emerge from the relative safety of his funeral parlor. He stood timidly on the steps, cell phone in hand, and watched.

"I'm gathering," I said, "that this means we won't be getting a copy of the autopsy report?"

"Get back in your vehicle and get on the highway," Weber said as his sneering driver pulled on a pair of leather fighting gloves, black, with hard pads over the knuckles. "If I see you back anywhere in Spruce County anytime soon, I guarantee you *will* regret it."

The cool play would have been to tell him who we really worked for and that he was the one who would end up in jail if he didn't start complying with our demands. That, however, would have violated every spy protocol on the books, along with federal laws which prohibit the CIA from conducting intelligence-gathering operations within the United States.

We got back in the Subaru. I could see Weber and his deputy in the side-view mirror, watching us.

"He's hiding something," Sterling said.

"Jeepers, whatever gave you that idea?"

"*Jeepers?*" She looked over at me. "Why in heaven's name, Logan, would I ever go out with a smart aleck like you?"

"Because I make you smile, and because my cat seriously likes you?"

"Well, I suppose there is that—your cat, I mean."

"Outstanding. I'll take that as a yes."

The smile in her eyes was an encouraging affirmation. She turned the engine over and put the car in gear. A minute later, we were on the onramp to eastbound Interstate 70 and Denver, where Sterling hoped to track down Perris's Vietnam buddy, Cyril Tomasello.

Five minutes after that, it appeared that we were being followed—an SUV, dark gray in color, with a tinted front windshield.

Sterling saw it, too, in her rearview mirror. She asked if I could make out a plate number.

"Negative," I said, reluctant to turn around and let the driver know he'd been made.

Whoever he was, he seemed to know what he was doing, more or less, when it came to the rules of rolling surveillances. When Sterling let off on the gas, he did. When she accelerated and changed lanes, he did as well, erratically and gradually, always careful to keep at least three vehicles between his and ours. I deduced he was working alone; other surveillance vehicles would have rotated in and out of the tail to diminish any suspicions that we were being followed. We watched him in our mirrors.

"Sheriff's personnel," Sterling speculated. "Making sure we left town."

"That would be my guess." The next exit was a quarter mile ahead of us, on the right. "Let's get off."

"Read my mind."

Sterling stepped on the gas and zoomed past a tractor-trailer hauling a load of Budweiser in the right lane, then sliced across the truck's bow, prompting the angered driver to lay on his air horn. Boxed in by the truck and other cars, the SUV couldn't make the exit. Our pursuer overshot and sped on as we pulled off the highway.

"Where'd you learn that, the school house?"

"Tactical driving course," Sterling said.

"Impressive."

We both agreed that whoever it was in the SUV would likely be waiting for us down the road at the next exit if we had, in fact, been followed. We traveled back roads to Denver via the Subaru's GPS, a normally one-hour drive on the highway that became nearly three over hill and dale. The Colorado sky was crystalline, the snow-dusted peaks and pines glorious.

"How does an air force pilot end up in some secret squirrel, Tier One Ultra outfit that nobody's ever heard of, kicking in doors?" she wanted to know.

"We didn't do a lot of door kicking."

"You just killed people."

I said nothing.

"What's it like?" she asked.

"What's what like?"

"Killing somebody."

I looked out the window. "It's like any job. You get used to it after a while."

"How many?"

"How many did I kill? Why are you asking me these questions?"

"I don't know. Curiosity."

I forced myself to respond. "It's not like I kept score."

"Ever think about them, the men you killed?"

"Only when I'm asked."

We drove on. By the time we reached the Mile High City, what remained of the sun was dangling over the Front Range, hovering there like some brilliant gilded crown, before dipping over the edge of the earth. Wispy high clouds hung pink and magenta over the Denver skyline as the last rays of daylight faded. Dusk crept across the sky. I was mesmerized. Sunsets have always been for me a time of reflection, an opportunity to collect my bearings, to assess and reassess my ultimate purpose in the cosmos. There I was, essentially a hired gun, riding right seat in a rented Subaru with a stunningly attractive intelligence officer whom I was having difficulty not imagining nude. I was revisiting the murder of a young president, about which I was once obsessed, behind which the truth remained cloaked in secrecy decades after the fact. All in all, not a bad place to be, I thought—certainly more intriguing and potentially more rewarding than giving flying lessons to ungrateful, sixteen-year-old potheads.

RICO PERRIS's Vietnam buddy, Cyril Tomasello, lived in the front half of a red brick, yet-to-be-yuppified duplex on the hardscrabble northern fringes of downtown Denver. A drunk was curled asleep on the garbage-strewn patch of snow that passed for a front yard, an empty bottle of Night Train wine clutched in his gnarled, ungloved hands. Behind the iron bars of Tomasello's security screen door, affixed to the windowless entry door, was a bumper sticker: "US Marine Corps. Proudly Served." Sterling knocked. There was no answer.

"I'll check around back," I said.

I strode to the east side of the building, unlatched a wobbly chain-link gate, and peered in through the kitchen window. The mini blinds were closed, but I could see that the lights were off. I could also see an older African American man sitting on the stoop of the adjacent unit wearing loosely laced, military-style hiking boots and a blue terrycloth robe over thermal underwear. He was lighting a fat cigar with a match.

"Wife won't let you fire up that bad boy inside?"

He seemed not at all surprised by my presence. "Man, you got that right."

"I'm looking for your neighbor, Cyril. You seen him around?"

The man shook his match dead and puffed. Embers glowed red in the gathering darkness. "You the police?" he asked, squinting through the smoke as Sterling joined me.

"*Us?*" I chuckled. "No, sir, we're from Publishers Clearing House."

"You serious? Publishers Clearing House?"

"Straight up. Your neighbor just won a boatload of money. We're the advance team. We just want to make sure we know when he's home so we don't spoil the surprise when the camera crews show up to give him the big check. You won't tell him, will you?"

"Don't even hardly know the dude, man. I know he hangs at the VFW down on Santa Fe, cuz I seen him down there when I've been—I'm prior military myself—but, no, man, we cool. I won't tell him nothing."

"Thanks for your service."

We bumped fists.

"Damn. Publishers Clearing House." The man shook his head and puffed on his cigar. "Wish it was me."

"Don't we all," Sterling said.

DENVER'S VETERANS of Foreign War Post Number One could be found on Santa Fe Drive, in a modest business district south of downtown. The dilapidated, two-story stucco building was sandwiched between an art gallery and a Crossfit gym. Three men were lingering out front, smoking cigarettes. One of them was leaning on an older Jeep Cherokee, black in color, its right front fender crumpled and bent. The back of the Jeep was plastered with a dozen or more pro-military stickers.

Walking into the VFW, I heard Tomasello long before I saw him.

A loud, overweight man with dark, greased-back hair and a Hawaiian shirt, whose laughter ended in coughing fits to the point of gagging, was holding court at the bar. He was gulping rum and Coke, sloshing the contents of his glass. I gathered by the unsteady manner in which he dismounted his stool and weaved toward the men's room that it wasn't his first drink of the evening.

"I'm looking for Cyril Tomasello," Sterling said, ignoring every ex-military guy in the place, all of whom were staring at her.

"We're friends of his," I added.

The bartender was a redhead whose extensive collection of facial hardware left the impression she'd fallen into a tackle box. "That would be him," she said, nodding disparagingly toward the heavyset man as he walked into the men's room.

"Have a drink," I told Sterling, "while I go visit the oval office."

I followed Tomasello inside the bathroom. We stood side by side at individual urinals, conducting our respective business, staring straight ahead, as men are wont to do. He was breathing hard, labored, one hand tending to business, the other bracing himself on the tiled wall in front of him.

"Looks like we're done with the snow for a while," I said.

"Man, I sure hope so," he said. "I'm sick of the cold and it ain't even December yet."

"You're Cyril Tomasello, right?"

"That all depends on what you're selling."

"I hear you were friends with Rico Perris."

His head pivoted unsteadily toward me, his eyes bleary from the booze. "You knew Rico?"

"Let's just say we traveled in the same circles."

"Do I know you?"

"No."

Tomasello zipped up. "Well, all I can is say is it was a shame. Rico was a real smart guy, but a real piece of work. A lot of those people are. What can I say? *Hebrews*, you know what I'm saying?"

"No, actually, I don't."

The bathroom had two sinks. Tomasello turned to wash his hands. I did likewise.

"If Rico was so smart," I said, "why'd he go out into the snow that night?"

"You'd have to ask him that."

"I'm asking you. You were with him that day, were you not?"

He narrowed his eyes and looked over at me, trying to focus. "What do you wanna know all this for?"

"Did Rico tell you about the threats he'd been getting?"

In an instant, Tomasello seemed to sober up. "Who are you?"

"I work for the government."

"That don't tell me jack."

"We're trying to find out what happened to Rico. The truth."

He stared at me hard, drying his hands on a paper towel. "What happened? What happened is, he drove off a damn mountain."

"We're aware of that. The question is whether he had assistance driving off the mountain."

Tomasello wadded up the paper towel and tossed it, missing the trash can by a foot. "Listen, I don't know who the hell you are or what this is about, but I got nothing to say to you. Leave me alone."

He pushed past me and out the bathroom door. As I followed him out, I could see him brush past Sterling and exit the building in a big hurry.

She was sitting at the bar, nursing what looked to be a club soda and politely fending off the advances of a bearded lug with bushy eyebrows who was leaning in a little too close for comfort. I wedged myself onto the stool between them.

"Hey, I'm trying to talk to the lady here."

"She's busy. If you'll excuse us."

He put his drink down, huffing a grunt meant to intimidate. "Who the hell do you think you are, man?"

All I did was meet his eyes. I didn't have to say anything.

His Adam's apple bobbed. "Wait," he said, "you two are together?"

"Something like that," Sterling said.

"Oh, OK. I didn't know. Cool. Sorry, man."

I nodded.

He retreated to the other end of the bar.

"That really wasn't necessary, Logan," Sterling said. "I had the situation under control."

"Never a doubt in my mind."

"How'd it go in the little boys' room?" she asked.

I told her about Tomasello's sudden sobriety, his disparaging reference to Perris, and his abrupt, agitated refusal to answer any further questions.

"Sounds like he and Rico had issues," Sterling said.

The bartender asked me if I wanted a drink. I passed. She didn't go away.

"Listen, I don't mean to be a busybody," she said, "but I couldn't help overhearing what you were saying about Cyril. You guys cops?"

"Why?" I said, "do we look like cops?"

"Yeah. TV cops."

I smiled noncommittally.

Sterling asked if there was something she wanted to tell us. The bartender grabbed a pack of Marlboro Reds from near the cash register, then announced to all in attendance, "Smoke break. I'll be back in five minutes."

We followed her outside to where no one else could hear us. Sans coat, she fired up a cigarette, sucking the smoke deep into her lungs.

"I'm Kate."

"Logan. This is Sterling."

"Always nice to meet some of Denver's finest." She turned her head and blew smoke into the cold. "Look, for what it's worth, Rico Perris was a super nice guy. Quiet. Polite. Good tipper. Cyril? He's just a dick."

"That doesn't help us much, Kate," Sterling said.

"Yeah? Well, maybe this will."

A couple of days before Perris's death, Kate said, Tomasello had stormed into the VFW and accused Perris of making a pass at Maureen, his on-again, off-again girlfriend who worked part-time as a cocktail waitress at the post. Perris denied the accusation and tried to ignore him. When Tomasello hurled a few anti-Semitic slurs, Perris lunged. Punches flew. Other patrons had to separate the two men. Bloodied, Tomasello vowed payback and left. Nobody at the VFW saw hide nor tail of him for the better part of two weeks after Perris died.

"Cyril's a hothead," Kate said, "especially when he's drunk, which is, like, all the time, OK? He's always talking about what a badass marine he was in Vietnam, lurking around, killing everybody. Pump a couple drinks into him and you'd think he'd won the war all by himself."

"You got a telephone number for Maureen?" I asked.

Kate held the cigarette in her lips, dug her phone out of the back pocket of her jeans, and, squinting through tobacco smoke, read us the number.

"We heard Cyril used to drive race cars," Sterling said.

"Race cars. Yeah, right." She made a snorting sound and exhaled smoke through her nose. "He used to drive at some crappy little track up in Brighton and also in demolition derbies. To hear him tell it, he won *every* race like he was Dale Earnhardt or something."

"Demolition derby?" Sterling had apparently never heard the term before.

"A bunch of beater cars drive around a figure-eight track and try to ram into each other, or avoid being rammed," I said. "The last beater running wins."

"So he has experience crashing into cars." Sterling cocked an eyebrow at me. "Interesting."

Interesting also was the fact that the Jeep I'd noticed earlier parked out in front of the VFW, the one with the crumpled front fender, like it had rammed into another car, was gone.

"You wouldn't happen to know what kind of car Mr. Tomasello drives?" I asked.

"A Jeep," Kate said. "Black Cherokee. Tons of bumper stickers."

"Interesting," Sterling said to me.

I nodded. Interesting, indeed.

ELEVEN

Layne Sterling was no amateur when it came to conducting surveillances. What she'd learned as a police officer in Los Angeles's inner city, she'd refined as a federal intelligence officer: park two or three blocks away, maintain a clear line-of-sight with the location in question, know where the nearest bathroom is, and have plenty of snacks handy because it can turn into a very long wait. Ninety minutes into staking out Tomasello's north Denver duplex, I'd already plowed through a Taco Bell cheesy double beef burrito and two quesadillas.

"Just to be clear," I said, wiping hot sauce off my chin, "I don't consider this a first date."

"Thanks for the clarification," Sterling said.

She'd barely touched her Fiesta Taco Salad. I was tempted to ask her if she intended to finish it, but I didn't want to come off as my usual gluttonous self when it came to fast food.

We'd already confirmed that Tomasello held title to a black, 2002 Jeep Cherokee, thanks to a call via CIA datalink to the cybersecurity center in Utah. There was no record of Tomasello ever having filed any insurance claims on the vehicle, which left unanswered the cause of the damage I'd observed to the Jeep's right front fender—the kind of damage that might've occurred when, say, ramming the rear of a vintage Porsche and sending it flying into a frozen river.

Files showed that Tomasello had served two tours with the marines in Southeast Asia, from 1967 to 1969. He'd been divorced twice. In 1998 police in suburban Aurora, Colorado, had picked him up on suspicion of domestic battery. Twelve years later, while apparently vacationing in Las Vegas, he'd been accused of aggravated assault. Both cases were pleaded down to misdemeanors. The records offered no further details on either arrest or whether he'd done time because of them. There was, meanwhile, another telling bit of information in his file that affirmed Tomasello's apparent proclivity toward violence: He'd once claimed membership in the Posse Comitatus, a loosely assembled organization of far-right, gun-toting, racist, anti-government nut jobs who believed, among other conspiracy theories, that a secret cabal of communist-led Jewish bankers had helped finance the murder of John F. Kennedy. That Rico Perris was a Puerto Rican Jew hardly confirmed any suspicion that Cyril Tomasello was responsible for his death, but it did leave us wondering a little more about him.

"You can have my taco salad if you want," Sterling said. "I'm not all that hungry."

"Waste not, want not."

She handed over her plastic plate. I was just about to inhale my first forkful of oh-so-nutritious iceberg lettuce slathered in sour cream and cheese product when my phone buzzed. The caller ID indicated, "Samantha McBride, MD."

"You were going to check your schedule and get back to me about dinner, remember," she said, "or did you fall into another river?"

I assured her that I had managed to avoid all other bodies of water since being rescued, and that I'd simply gotten busy with work.

"I'm free tomorrow night," McBride said. "I make one mean vegetarian lasagna."

"Sounds great. Unfortunately I'm not certain where I'm going to be tomorrow night."

She knew a rejection when she heard one.

"I saved your life," she said. "The least you could do is be honest with me. Do you want to have dinner or not?"

"I can't. I'm sorry."

The line went dead. I let out a long, slow breath, apparently a little too loudly.

Sterling looked over. "You doing OK?"

"Never better."

Tomasello's Jeep drove past us.

"We're in business," she said.

My line of sight from our vantage point was unobstructed. I observed Tomasello park under a street light in the carport behind his duplex and half fall from the Jeep in a besotted, almost comical fashion, holding a can of beer. Somehow he managed to find his way up the back steps and inside.

Our game plan was to approach on foot—quieter that way. Sterling would cover the duplex, distracting Tomasello should he reemerge while I inspected his Jeep for any telltale evidence of a collision with Rico Perris's Porsche, collecting paint scrapings and snapping photos as necessary. Should we be confronted by anyone, we would explain that we were looking for our dog who'd escaped our backyard a few blocks away. Operators are trained to nail down the details of their lies and rehearse them ahead of time rather than having to concoct a cover story on the spot. Accordingly I proposed that our fictitious wayward pooch be a Saint Bernard named "Tiny." Sterling balked. A Saint Bernard, she said, was too easy to track down. Better to go with a smaller breed.

"I'd suggest a Welsh Corgi," I said.

"What's wrong with a Chihuahua?"

"I like Chihuahuas, but they're not really dogs. I'd never have one personally."

"Fine," Sterling said. "We'll go with a Welsh Corgi."

"His name should be Mr. Clark."

"Mr. Clark? What kind of name is that for a dog?"

"Exactly. Who'd make it up?"

She sighed. Like I said, you learn to pick your battles the older you get.

I grabbed Sterling's pack. We got out and began walking. Ice-crusted slush crunched under our footfalls. The wind was up and out of the north. Another front moving in. The skin on my face tingled from the cold.

The lights were on in the unit next door to Tomasello's. Someone was home there: a shadow crossed behind the curtains, obscuring the two narrow windows flanking the windowless front door. On Tomasello's side of the duplex, meanwhile, all was dark. Sterling and I exchanged a nod and proceeded to our respective assignments. I quickly lost sight of her as she moved into position around the corner where she could observe both front and back doors.

I'd be the first to admit I'm not exactly on the cutting edge of digital technology. I'm old-school. But I did possess enough smarts to have installed a flashlight app on my cell phone. I used it to illuminate the Jeep's crumpled front fender. A quick inspection uncovered no tell-tale paint transfers matching the silver finish of Perris's Porsche, though I did notice something curious: Embedded in a pronounced crease along the fender's front edge was what appeared to be a small, dime-size piece of gray body filler, the same kind I'd also seen on the Porsche.

"Boo-yah."

I got out a knife with the intent of prying the chunk loose when I heard a woman behind me shout, "Drop the weapon!"

I turned slightly to see who was doing the shouting, which admittedly probably wasn't the brightest decision. There, standing a few meters behind me, was a beefy female police officer in early middle age, her peroxide perm poofing out from either side of her peaked hat. She was wearing a blue uniform and aiming her pistol at me with her right hand, holding her flashlight like an ice pick in her left, up high and away from her body.

"They used to teach that kind of flashlight technique at the FBI," I said. "The theory being that you disorient your attacker by holding the light away from you. That way, if he shoots at you, he hits the light and not you. Personally I prefer the Rogers technique. You hold the light between your middle and index fingers, with the flashlight up along the side of your gun. That way, you maintain a nice, two-handed grip on the weapon, with the flashlight still trained on your target."

"Shut up and drop the knife!"

"Yes, ma'am." I let the blade fall.

"Now kiss the ground. Do it!"

"Anything you say, officer. Let's all take it nice and slow. We'll all be fine."

I got down on my knees, and then my stomach, as two more cops showed up in a patrol cruiser. They jumped out with their flashlights and pistols trained on me in the procedural manner I had suggested to Officer Silly Hair.

"Now, *those* guys know what they're doing."

"I said shut up." She advanced cautiously, pistol leveled, tucking the flashlight into her gun belt, and knelt with her knee hard in the small of my back. "You so much as twitch and I'll blow your head off."

I could feel the muzzle's cold hardness pressed into the back of my neck. That's a sensation, believe me, you never get used to. She holstered her weapon and handcuffed my wrists behind me—but not before Sterling came bounding around the corner demanding to know what the hell was going on.

"Freeze!" one of the other cops shouted at her.

Sterling ignored his command and kept coming. "I'm already freezing. This man's with me. He's a licensed insurance investigator and we're conducting official business here. We've broken no laws. Let him go."

I was on my belly, so I couldn't see all that happened next, but I heard it: Sterling being wrestled forcibly to the ground; the cops yelling, "Stop resisting!"; then one of them shouting, "She's got a gun!", followed immediately by the sharp crack of a pistol shot.

THE ROOKIE officer who fired the round would later claim that his Sig Sauer had accidentally discharged as he and his partner struggled to subdue Sterling. Fortunately the only thing his bullet killed was a mailbox down the street. Unfortunately both of us were booked into custody on suspicion of vehicular burglary and, in Sterling's case, resisting arrest. Tossed into separate cells, I wouldn't see her again until morning, which was just as well. I needed some sack time. Again, unfortunately, I would get none.

Nobody who spends the night in a communal holding tank sleeps for more than a few minutes at a time. Too much angst, too much noise. Steel bars clanging, public address speakers blaring with announcements for this or that. All around you are distraught people. Some are quietly sobbing. Some are screaming and swearing. Others are laughing and barking demonically to themselves. You hunker on an unpadded steel bench at DEFCON 1, prepared to repel boarders, dozing for no more than a few seconds at a time. Trust me, I speak from experience. Since leaving government employment and dabbling in freelance investigative work, I'd been introduced to more than my share of municipal lockups. Folks who visit new cities usually find time to take in the sites. I visit new cities and *serve* time. Go figure.

"Man, does this place suck or what?"

I looked over: The tanned preppy on the bench beside me looked more out of place than a bacon sandwich on Ramadan. Tasseled oxblood loafers. No socks. Pressed khakis. White polo shirt with collar popped under a cable-knit crewneck sweater the color of sunflowers. An eighty-dollar haircut. A bleached, toothy smile. He had country club gigolo written all over him.

"I've cooled my heels in worse," I said.

"This is my first time."

"Lucky you."

He asked me what I was in for. It's not an uncommon question behind bars, I've found, but it's not like it is on TV cop shows. People won't automatically fear and respect you if you tell them you're a crazy mad dog killer. Nor will they try to make you their love slave if you admit to having been arrested for jaywalking. As long as you're not in on some sex-related beef, in which case they *will* try to shank you, you should have no problem telling them whatever you want.

"I got popped for practicing podiatry without a license," I said.

"You're kidding me."

"A podiatrist never kids. Feet are serious business. Take care of them, they'll take care of you."

"Yeah, but you're not really a podiatrist. Isn't that what you just said?"

"What, just because I don't have some piece of paper, I'm not fit to be a foot doctor?"

"That's not what I meant."

"Well, what *did* you mean?"

He swallowed nervously and looked away, not sure whether he'd offended me.

"I'm just messing with you," I said. "What're you in for?"

"They're saying I ran over somebody."

"To which, you say?"

He picked at his fingernails. "I say stuff happens."

We didn't do much talking after that. A few minutes later I was called out of the holding tank and into interrogation.

The detective said his name was Steve Weiss. He was dressed in jeans, wore designer-frame glasses, and had a serious case of zits. A holstered pistol peeked out from under a gray, Colorado Rockies hoodie. He was probably thirty but looked about sixteen. Many of the other plain-clothed officers working at their desks in Steve's bullpen appeared to be in their teens as well. That's the problem with getting older. Everybody starts to look like they're in high school.

"Coffee?"

"Sure."

North Denver of late had seen an epidemic of car break-ins, Weiss explained as he poured me a Styrofoam cup from the office pot. Which is why, he said as I followed him into a small, windowless interview room, patrol officers had responded as aggressively as they had after a resident called 911 to report a suspicious white male—namely me—up to no apparent good near a parked car.

"Have a seat."

A metal table. Two unpadded metal chairs. A tripod-mounted video camera in the corner. Acoustic tiles covering the ceilings and walls. Metal shackle rings bolted to the concrete floor. The room was interchangeable with others I'd found myself in, both as interrogator and interrogatee.

I sat on one side of the table. Weiss sat on the other.

"So," he said, "I ran your name and your partner's name through the NCIC computer. All I got back was, 'Contact the Director of National Intelligence.'"

"Weird. You sure you spelled our names correctly?"

His look suggested that he knew I was full of it. "I called the DNI's office," he said. "All I got was the runaround. I also called Mutual of Lexington. You'll never guess what happened there."

"Well, I certainly hope not more of the runaround." I calmly sipped my coffee. "Our company prides itself on our excellent customer service."

"Some cheap-sounding answering machine picked up," Weiss said. "A major insurance company—an *answering* machine? You wanna explain that one to me?"

I shrugged. "Cheaper than a switchboard operator. We pass the savings directly on to our clients."

The kid detective offered me a knowing smile. "Right."

He told me he was convinced I worked for the CIA or maybe one of the alphabet agencies. I chuckled like it was the goofiest thing I'd heard all week.

"So what's the deal with the Jeep?" he asked. "What the hell were you doing out there anyway?"

I said we were routinely confirming the details of a recent vehicular fatality in Spruce County for purposes of life insurance benefits.

Weiss didn't buy it. He was about to get tough with me— to the extent any cop who looks like the before picture in an anti-acne commercial can get tough—when the door opened and another detective motioned him outside. Two minutes later, Weiss was back. He didn't look pleased.

"Well," he said, "you're free to go."

I stood and stretched my legs. "You can do me a favor. I'm looking for a guy. His name's Cyril Tomasello." I spelled Tomasello's first and last. "I'd appreciate any information you might have on him."

"What'd you want with him?"

"Insurance purposes. I'd lay it all out for you, but I wouldn't want to put you to sleep."

The detective knew a bunch of bull when he smelled it.

"I'll see what I can do for you," he said grudgingly.

WEISS'S CALL to the Director of National Intelligence's office had caused the earth to move. Somebody there had called the twenty-four-hour command duty desk at Langley who'd called somebody far up the food chain of the Denver Police Department. That somebody, according to Layne Sterling, had ordered the two of us released.

"Must be nice having friends in high places," I said as we rode back to the rental car in the back seat of a taxi.

"If I had friends in high places, I would not have been thrown in jail to begin with."

She'd never been locked up before, she said. She didn't like it one bit.

"You get used to it," I said.

I started humming Johnny Cash's "Folsom Prison Blues," being the old hand at incarceration that I was, but my attempt at humor clearly didn't sit well with her, so I stopped. Then she started singing the same tune and we both laughed.

"At least they gave you your gun back," I said.

I told her about the chunk of auto body filler I'd seen embedded in the fender of Tomasello's Jeep, how it resembled

the filler I'd seen on Rico Perris's Porsche, and how I had been
unsuccessful recovering a sample.

"Then we'll just have to find the Jeep," she said like it was
no big deal.

The snow was coming down thick as a vanilla milkshake.
The only other vehicles on the flocked streets were plows and
sand trucks, their flashing lights reflecting red and saffron off
the glass and chrome canyons of downtown Denver. It was
0430 hours before we got back to our rental car. Cyril Tomasello's apartment was dark. We went around back. His Jeep
was gone.

"I'm going in," I said, my voice low so as not to wake up
the guy next door. "You maintain security out here. Fire off a
flare if the police show up, or Cyril Tomasello."

"Just make it quick," she said, glancing around anxiously.

The back door lacked a deadbolt, which was most appreciated. From my wallet, I removed my pilot's certificate, which
was slightly larger and more flexible than your average credit
card, forced it into the vertical crack between the door and
the frame at a perpendicular angle to the door. I could feel
the spring on the lock give a little. When the card was in as
far as it would go, I tilted it and pushed on the door.

Open sesame.

Cyril Tomasello would not win any awards from *Good
Housekeeping*. His place defined the word, "mess." Piles of
dirty clothes, wet towels heaped on the carpeted floor, trash
cans overflowing. The air was overheated and reeked of
burned toast and cat urine. I gave him credit for one thing,
though: the man was a reader. Books were piled everywhere.
His kitchen cabinets overflowed with them. There were even
some stacked in the refrigerator for lack of space elsewhere,
heaped among a six-pack of suds, a near-empty bottle of cheap
tequila, a package of moldy sliced ham, a jar of mayonnaise,

something on a dish resembling a tomato or a science experiment gone terribly wrong, half a package of flour tortillas as hard as a Mexican dictator's heart, individual plastic-packaged servings of store-bought tapioca, some dill pickles, and what looked to be part of somebody's wedding cake.

Tomasello's reading tastes were no less eclectic than his diet: Jeep repair manuals, romantic bodice-rippers, a biography of Alexander Hamilton, the sinking of the *Lusitania,* and an entire shelf devoted to the collected works of horror mogul Dean Koontz. On the walls were various framed photos of Tomasello in Vietnam-era combat fatigues. Him standing in front of a Huey helicopter on some tropical flight line, palm trees in the background. Him in the jungle, clutching an M-16 rifle and standing over a pile of dead Viet Cong soldiers. Him grinning at an outdoor table with two Vietnamese bar girls on his lap.

I opened drawers and closet doors, snapping photos of anything and everything because you never know in an investigation what might ultimately prove relevant. There was the pump-action, sixteen-gauge Remington shotgun propped behind the bathroom door, a handmade necklace of five mummified human ears in the shoe box under the bed, the set of handcuffs dangling from the headboard. But what really got my attention was the title of the ruffled paperback book sitting on Cyril Tomasello's nightstand:

Lancer's Last Day: The CIA and the Murder of John F. Kennedy.

TWELVE

You can't go wrong at Denny's. It's always open. Plus, it's next to impossible to screw up a plate of bacon and eggs, even at Denny's.

"You're a regular eating machine," Sterling observed.

I was too busy loading forkfuls of cholesterol into my yapper to respond.

She was intrigued with the fact that Cyril Tomasello and Rico Perris both owned copies of the same book on the Kennedy assassination. So was I.

"I can understand why Perris would own a copy," I said. "The guy worked on the Kennedy case. It makes sense he'd be interested in reading up on the subject. But why Tomasello? We're not talking *Harry Potter* here or the *The Da Vinci Code*. This is a relatively obscure book."

"And a badly written one," Sterling said. She'd downloaded a copy to her phone after we were seated and was now skimming through it while working halfheartedly on an order of french toast.

The book was 230 pages of unsubstantiated bunk with one massive whacko conspiracy theory thrown in for leavening. The theory held that a Mafia hitman hired by the CIA had been hiding inside the trunk of JFK's limousine and fired up through the seat cushions, hitting Kennedy in the back of the neck. This, according to the book, explained why Kennedy was seen clutching the front of his neck moments before a second shot from another rifleman positioned on the grassy knoll at Dealey Plaza blew the president's skull apart. The second gunman in the trunk also explained why First Lady Jackie Kennedy was seen crawling out onto the trunk's lid and pounding on it—to alert Secret Service agents to the gunman's presence.

"Pretty kooky stuff," Sterling said.

I sopped up some fake maple syrup and swallowed down a hunk of buttermilk pancake. "Any mention of Rico Perris or that guy, the analyst who got run over in Phoenix? I can't remember his name at the moment. I'm on too much of a sugar high."

Sterling looked down at her phone. "No appendix, no footnotes. I'm not kidding, this thing reads like it was written by an eighth grader. Listen to this," she said, reading aloud from the book.

"The sun was shining like a big orange balloon that morning in Big D, which stood for Dallas, which stood for trouble. The air was heavy with the methane perfume of the city's many cattle feedlots, but the residents were used to it. For them, it was going to be a special, beautiful day. Why? Because none other than the president of the United States was coming to visit with his beautiful wife who was wearing a strawberry pink outfit from Chanel to mark the occasion! Yet little could the world have known that the game was already afoot! With Secret Service agents who were supposed to be guarding the presidential limousine against sabotage taking a smoke break or relieving themselves of all the beer they had consumed the night before in the bathroom (some were said to be playing poker at the time), the lone gunman, rumored by some sources to be the ruthless Florida Mafia hitman, Jimmy 'The Beak' Viviano, managed to slither like a snake inside the limo's trunk when nobody noticed. He was armed with a deadly 6.5-millimeter Carcano Model 91/38 rifle exactly identical to the one Oswald bought through the mail. It was November 23, 1963, the day Camelot died."

"Kennedy was killed on November 22," I said.

Sterling shook her head. "Like I said, terribly written."

"Who wrote this epic masterpiece?"

"Somebody named P.S. Plaissance, though that's apparently a pseudonym. Says here, 'The author wishes to remain anonymous, out of understandable concern for their own personal safety, given this book's explosive, highly sensitive contents.'"

The book's primary assertion, beyond its second gunman-in-the-trunk theory, was that then-Vice President Lyndon B. Johnson despised JFK to such an extent and hungered so greatly to gain the White House that he conspired with Cuban operatives who hired Viviano and were paid by the CIA on express orders to kill Kennedy. Quoting unnamed sources, the book further alleged that the CIA on Johnson's orders had purposely falsified and destroyed records of FBI wiretaps that could have implicated LBJ in the assassination plot. Of course, none of that made it into the Red Lancer task force's final report, which was supposedly rewritten per Johnson's specifications to avoid any culpability.

Of all the books in Cyril Tomasello's dump of a duplex, why was *that* one on his nightstand? Did it have anything to do with Rico Perris's work investigating the CIA's suspected involvement in JFK's assassination, or the pending release of long-classified documents that could finally shed light on those rumors? I didn't know.

"The bartender described Tomasello as a badass marine," Sterling said. "Harlan Weber, the sheriff up in Spruce County, he was a badass marine, too."

"Most marines are badasses," I said, "or think they are."

"I'm just saying," Sterling said.

"Saying what?"

"What if Weber and Tomasello are somehow connected?"

"What if they are? What does that get you?"

"I don't know yet."

I mentioned the ears I'd found under Tomasello's bed, about how some troops in Vietnam were known to slice body parts off dead enemy soldiers and keep them as macabre souvenirs.

She made a face. "That's seriously disgusting."

Not enough to stop me from finishing my breakfast. "By the way," I said, "this does not constitute a first date either."

"I would certainly hope not." Sterling rubbed her eyes. She was tired. We both could've used some sleep. But first we needed to find Tomasello before he went to ground.

THE SUN was still an hour from its daily debut when we swung by his duplex again. Still no lights on inside. No sign of the Jeep in the carport or on the street out front. No fresh tire tracks in the snow. Tomasello hadn't been home all night. Our next move would be to locate Maureen, his sometimes girlfriend.

She wasn't hard to find, thanks to the phone number the bartender at the VFW provided. A quick call to Sterling's people back at Langley produced the address of a modest, whitewashed bungalow with a black slate roof on South Gaylord Street, four miles south of downtown in Denver's

Washington Park neighborhood. Maureen was Maureen Spencer, sixty-two, a thin-faced redhead with overplucked brows, and a smoker's rasp. She opened the front door, in fuzzy slippers and a pink terry cloth robe, a lighted Salem dangling from her lips.

"Jesus, what time is it?"

"Sorry to bother you this early, ma'am," Sterling said. "We're looking for Cyril Tomasello."

"He's not here," she said, rubbing her eyes with her palms. "And what the hell makes you think he'd come back here after last night anyway?"

"What happened last night?"

She sucked on her cigarette and looked at Sterling through the smoke like it was the dumbest question she'd ever been asked. "I told the other cops all this last night. And now I gotta repeat myself? Jesus Christ, did they not file a report? Did you not read it? What the hell kind of police department are you people running anyway?"

I nodded toward the technicolor contusion under her left eye. "He gave you that?"

"Hell, yes, he gave me that. What is it with these questions? I told all this to the blue-suiters last night."

"It's freezing out here," I said. "Do you mind if we come in for a minute? We just want to ask you a few questions. It won't take long, promise."

Maureen hesitated, then sighed, unlocked the storm door, and stepped aside. Being mistaken for the police had its advantages. Neither Sterling nor I was about to disabuse her of her assumption.

"Nice crib," I said.

"It's a dump," Maureen said.

The living room was a shrine to bad taste. Walls painted the color of bubblegum. Naugahyde lounge chairs covered in plastic slipcovers. A battered wooden coffee table held together with duct tape. An armless orange sofa that looked about as inviting as a church pew.

"Mind if I take a quick look around?" Sterling asked.

"I just told you, he ain't here," Maureen said, folding her arms. "It's two-bedroom. If he'd have come back, I think I'd know it, OK?"

"I'd just like to double-check."

Maureen rolled her eyes and sighed. "Knock yourself out."

I took a seat on the sofa while Sterling ventured down a hallway, her hand resting at the ready on the butt of her holstered pistol.

"How often do you see Cyril?" I asked.

"He lives here on and off—did, anyway. And I have no idea where he's at. But I will tell you this: wherever he's at, he can stay there and rot for all I care. I've had it with him. No more."

As she described it, Tomasello had shown up drunk at her house late the night before. He seemed even more agitated than he usually was. She didn't know the reason. They argued over his drinking, as they usually did. He told her to mind her own damn business and fetched a can of Coors from the refrigerator. When she tried to grab it from him, he punched her.

Sterling returned and caught my eye, subtly shaking her head. All clear.

"We found a book on Cyril's nightstand," I said to Maureen, "about the assassination of President Kennedy."

"So?"

"So, we're just curious if he ever discussed it with you."

"Discussed? Are you serious? Do you know how long it's been since me and him discussed *anything*? We never did much talking. *He* does the talking. I'm just supposed to sit there and listen, nice and sweet. He thinks he's so smart with all his books. My dog is smarter than him, and I don't even have a dog."

"Did he ever mention anybody named Rico Perris?"

"Who?"

"Rico Perris," Sterling said, sitting down beside me. "He and Cyril were friends. Down at the VFW."

"Never heard of him."

She glanced away when she said this. Her reaction gave me pause. I asked her if Tomasello had any family in town, anyone with whom he might be staying. Maureen scoffed. The man who'd punched her in the face, she said, had essentially alienated everyone in his life, including his own children.

"We noticed some body damage on his Jeep," I said. "You wouldn't happen to know when or where that might've occurred, would you?"

Maureen folded her arms across her chest. "What's that got to do with him punching me in the face?"

"If you could just answer the question, please."

"Three, four weeks ago. Hell, how am I supposed to know?" She reached for a pack of Salems on the coffee table, fished out a cigarette, and lit it with a purple Bic. "He went fly fishing somewhere and said he hit a deer. What's this got to do with anything?"

"Did he say where he was going fishing?"

"Up in the mountains somewhere." She exhaled smoke through her nose. "Are you gonna find him and throw his ass in jail where it belongs, or are you gonna sit here all morning asking me stupid questions?"

I stood and apologized for having awakened her. Sterling thanked her for taking the time. Maureen followed us out.

"Do me a favor," Maureen said as she stood in the doorway, pulling the robe tight around her. "If you find that crazy mother, tell him I'm filing a restraining order. Tell him if he comes back here ever again and lays another hand on me, I'll kill him."

We got back in the car. Sterling cranked the engine and quickly fired up the heater, blowing on and rubbing her hands together.

"Gotta get that window fixed," she said.

"Nobody goes up to the mountains in the middle of winter to go fly fishing," I said. "The rivers are iced over."

"Maybe not to go fishing, but Tomasello did go to the mountains. He met with Perris's girlfriend at a bar up there the day Rico Perris died."

"How do you know that?"

Sterling unzipped the side pocket of her shoulder bag and unfolded a small slip of paper, torn from a spiral notepad. "I did a bit of exploring while you were chatting up Maureen. Found this in a pair of men's khakis wadded up in the back of a closet."

In a hurried male scrawl, the note read:

Alessandra Munoz
Molly B Angel Falls
2 P.M.

It was dated the same day Rico Perris's Porsche tumbled into the Champ River.

WE KNEW that Alessandra Munoz had been less than truthful when she said she'd never met Cyril Tomasello. What we didn't know was why. What did she know of her boyfriend's death that she wasn't telling? What was she hiding? We needed to talk to her again. This time, hopefully, she would be more forthcoming.

Traffic was down to one lane on westbound I-70. The Rockies were a pastiche of Santa Claus's zip code. Everything was white. Even with the defroster on high, ice had begun crusting the windshield and wipers. With the back window broken, I could see my breath inside the car.

"Must be nice, living in sunny California," Sterling said after a while.

"I grew up in Colorado. I'm used to this. Mind you, that was before global warming. Back then, I remember, it was so cold, Pamela Anderson was downgraded from officially hot to more or less lukewarm."

Sterling shook her head and smiled, if only a little.

EVEN ON foot, we could forget reaching Rico Perris's cabin. Gale winds had piled the snow chest-high in some places along the road leading in. There were no footprints or tire tracks leading out. Either Alessandra Munoz was still home or she'd gotten out before the latest storm arrived. The bottom line was, we'd come a long way for apparently nothing.

Sterling wanted to drive back to Denver, find a motel, regroup, and take another shot at finding Cyril Tomasello. I didn't disagree with her ambitions. But as we started back down the mountain, karma intervened in the form of an elk herd. The big animals came loping out of the trees ahead of us and across the road. Sterling swerved to miss them and hit a patch of ice. Even with all-wheel drive, the Subaru fishtailed and sideswiped a low rock outcropping.

"That was close," Sterling said.

Too close, as it turned out. Almost immediately, the right rear tire went flat.

We braked to a stop. I got the spare out and the jack, but with the wind howling and the temperature well below zero, my hands wouldn't work. The lug nuts were frozen in place. I couldn't get even one to turn. There was no cell service and nobody was coming to our rescue, not in the middle of a blizzard. Neither of us was keen on the idea of running into Sheriff Harlan Weber, who'd threatened to arrest us if he saw us again, but winter had served us little alternative. We limped down the five miles to Angel Falls, tire thumping, hoping to find someone who could fix a flat.

The Buddha must've been smiling down at us that day because that's exactly what happened. There was a Conoco filling and repair station open for business on the east end of town. Both mechanics bays were empty. Inside, the station's manager, a good-natured, gap-tooth native of Nepal who introduced himself as Ram Bhattarai, was dressed like Nanook of the North, replete with furred collar. He was watching *The Jerry Springer Show* on an old, five-inch, black-and-white television. Two large women were duking it out, throwing angry haymakers at each other, while the audience cheered.

"America," Ram said in an accent still thick with his native tongue, "what a concept."

He assured us he could fix the flat right away. With the blizzard raging, he had nothing much else to occupy his time.

I didn't want to risk Sheriff Weber driving past and seeing the car. "You're going to pull it inside, right?"

Ram looked at me quizzically. "Tell me, who in their right mind would change a flat outside on a day like today if they didn't have to?"

He suggested we take a walk over to the Molly B saloon, a block away, and get something warm to drink while we waited. We didn't so much as walk there as run. Anything to escape the cold.

✈ ✈ ✈

INSIDE, PINON pine burned invitingly in a brick fireplace. The ceiling was covered over in antique tin tiles. The walls were thick with rusting ore buckets and pickaxes, lanterns and hardhats—the accoutrements of nineteenth-century, hard rock molybdenum mining that was once the area's lifeblood.

"Anywhere you'd like," the bartender said. He was a grizzled fellow with a shaved head, sinewy arms, and a big-league handlebar moustache who looked like he would've been right at home, going down one of those mine shafts.

I stomped the snow off my shoes and followed Sterling to a table nearest the fireplace, taking note of a woman's ski parka draped over the back of a barstool. An empty shot glass rested on the bar in front of the stool. Beyond that, we appeared to be the only customers in the place. We peeled off our coats and sat, reveling in the heat and aroma of the wood.

"Our cook's snowed-in up in the hills. Can't get out of his house. So, unfortunately, we're not serving off our regular menu at present," the bartender said. "We do have some popcorn. I could also rustle up a couple of hotdogs, if you're interested."

Sterling warmed her hands. "I'd just like some coffee, please."

"Make it two."

"You got it."

We watched him return to the bar.

"I may only have a few more days," Sterling said. "They're probably going to pull me and assign me another case."

"But we still don't know whether Perris died accidentally or with prejudice."

"Even if we find out that Tomasello ran him off the road," Sterling said, "it doesn't elevate the crime to the level of national security, and that's what my job's all about, making sure the country isn't threatened."

"You've got the pending release of documents potentially sensitive to the Kennedy assassination," I said. "You've got two intelligence analysts dead who worked on that assassination. Seems to me you have an obligation to see this through and get to the bottom of things."

"I don't necessarily disagree with you, but it's ultimately not up to me. I go where they send me. You know how that is, Logan."

"Yeah. I know."

Whether Rico Perris was murdered didn't matter that much to me. Nor did the possibility, however intriguing, that his death was somehow tied to the killing of the thirty-fifth president of the United States. Nor did I particularly care about the decent money I was making riding Layne Sterling's right seat. What *did* matter to me was the chance to get to know her, to maximize my time with her. I didn't want her to leave, not until she realized my many virtues—OK, fine, scratch *many*—and to discover that she was as attracted to me as I was to her.

The bartender dropped off two steaming mugs of coffee. I waited until he left.

"What would you say if I asked you to dinner tonight?"

"You're asking me out? Officially?"

"It could be unofficial if you want."

Sterling cupped her mug in both hands. "I'm sorry, Logan, I don't fish off the company pier."

"Didn't you just tell me you'll be leaving soon?"

"I did."

"OK, so that means we won't be working together, which means no company pier, which means I can take you to dinner. Boom, problem solved."

She stifled a coy smile. "I'll give it some thought."

I was feeling pretty good about my chances when a woman exited the women's john in the back of the Molly B and weaved past us without looking over. I recognized her immediately.

Alessandra Munoz.

She strode unsteadily to the bar, climbed onto the stool where the ski parka was draped over the seatback, and ordered a shot of tequila. Sterling followed my sight line and recognized her too.

"How do you want to play this?" she asked quietly.

"Watch and learn."

Alessandra gulped down the tequila with her right hand, then ordered another. I got up, walked over, and occupied the stool on her right. The stool to her left was vacant. I could've sat there, but I am, if nothing else, a creature of habit, thanks to my days in the field: always confront a right-handed, potentially hostile individual from their right side. That way, if they decide to take a swing at you, they'd have to pivot first, or jab with their weaker, less-dominant hand.

"Hey, Alessandra."

"Hey." She looked over at me in a heavy-lidded haze. It took her a second to connect the dots. "The guy from the insurance company, right?"

"That's me," I said. "We need to talk again. Where have you been?"

"I uh . . ." She stared down at her empty shot glass and bit her lower lip. "I spent the night at a friend's house."

You could've set a match to her boozy breath.

"You lied to us, Alessandra. You *do* know Cyril Tomasello. You met with him here the day Rico died, remember?"

She didn't look over at me. Her hands were shaking.

"Soon as they plow the highway, I'm out of here for good."

"Where you going, if you don't mind me asking?"

"I dunno. Anywhere but here." In an instant, Alessandra Munoz seemed to sober up. Her eyes flashed fear. "Rico, he . . ." She began to cry. "I can't take this anymore."

"Take what?"

She slid off her stool and grabbed her parka.

"Talk to me, Alessandra."

"I can't. I'm sorry."

I watched her hurry out the door and into the snow.

Sterling walked over to me. "Well," she said, "that certainly seemed to go exceptionally well."

Her sarcasm was not lost on me.

The barkeep was polishing beer glasses, pretending not to have overheard every word.

"How often does she come in here?" I asked him.

"Alessandra? Two, maybe three times a week."

"What's she so afraid of?"

He shook his head enigmatically. "You don't know this town, man."

He was right. I didn't know Angel Falls at all. But I knew someone who did.

THIRTEEN

The Angel Falls post office was a two-minute walk from the Molly B and devoid at that hour of customers. The front counter was unmanned. I could smell marijuana as we walked in. From somewhere in the back, the town's self-proclaimed resident busybody, mail clerk Bart Tolks, shouted, "Be out in a minute, folks."

Sterling sniffed the air, looked over, and gave me a confident wink. "Leverage," she said. "Watch and learn."

Tolks emerged seconds later wearing his moth-eaten cardigan and a loopy smile. He was finger-combing his hair with one hand and fanning away the last vestiges of marijuana smoke with the other.

"Hey, I remember you guys. Langley, Virginia, two-oh-five-oh-five, right?" He seemed pleased to see us, though obviously more Sterling than me, his eyes drifting toward her breasts.

She strode to the end of the counter, ignoring an "Official Use Only, No Entry" sign, and pushed through a pair of low swinging doors, the kind you'd find in a courtroom, into the mail sorting room.

"Hey, wait a sec, what do you?—you can't go in there!"

He shagged after her. I followed them both. Sterling sniffed the air once more. The scent trail took her to the top drawer of a gray metal filing cabinet. She opened it, pulled out a green glass bong, and set it on the mail sorting table.

"What the—you can't do that!" Tolks said.

"I just did."

"Yeah? Well, FYI, recreational weed's legal in Colorado, OK?"

"Yeah, well, FYI, this is a federal facility, OK?" Sterling said. "And, also FYI, the federal government still considers pot a Schedule One narcotic substance. Smoking weed in a federal facility? You're looking at some serious prison time here."

"You could lose your pension," I said.

A V-shaped vein rose in the middle of Tolks's forehead. The pulse throbbed in his right temple. "Jesus Christ, who *are* you people?"

"Who are we? We're the people who can make this all go away," Sterling said, nodding toward the bong, "or call your supervisors at the postal service and rat you out right now."

He sat down in an antique wooden swivel chair and ran his hand through what was left of his stringy hair. I asked him if he knew Alessandra Munoz.

"Do I know Alessandra? Yeah, I know Alessandra. Everybody around town knows Alessandra. I can't believe this. I'm minding my own business, doing my work, and you people come barging in here. I mean, Jesus, what the hell."

"There's no need to go postal, Bart," I said.

"No need? Easy for you to say! This is ridiculous! I gotta calm my ass down."

"You do that, Bart," Sterling said. "Take it easy and we'll all get through this fine."

He reached for a pouch of Red Man-brand chewing tobacco and stuffed a healthy wad of chaw into his mouth.

"Something spooked Alessandra," Sterling said. "She says she's leaving town. We want to know why."

"What do you care?"

"That doesn't matter right now. What matters is Alessandra. Tell us what you know, what you've heard, and I promise, we're out of here."

"I don't know anything," he said, turning to spit into a Styrofoam coffee cup.

"Suit yourself, Bart." I got out my phone and snapped some pictures of his water pipe. "Here," I said, tossing it in his lap, "hold this."

"What are you doing?"

"Gathering evidence." I took more pictures of him holding the bong.

"You can't do this!"

"I just did."

He tried to get to his feet. I shoved him back down in the chair.

"My next call is to the postal inspector general's office," I said. "Trust me, they're gonna want to make an example of you."

Sterling rested her hand comfortingly on his shoulder. "Listen carefully to me, Bart. Federal prison isn't like state prison. There's no time off for good behavior. Five years is five years, and that's what you're looking at. Plus, a soft little white boy like you? You'll be somebody's play thing in no time, guaranteed. Now you have a choice here. I advise you to choose wisely."

Tough but smooth. Persuasive but not overbearing. A total pro. Layne Sterling was the complete package. I was beginning to wonder where she'd been all my life.

The mail clerk's upper lip was glistening with nervous sweat. He rocked back and forth in the chair like his stomach was killing him, which it probably was, while his eyes darted left and right, like some feral animal caught in a snare.

We gave him time to sweat, letting silence work to our benefit. A good intelligence collector knows that most people find lapses in conversation uncomfortable. Their impulse is to fill in the gaps. Sometimes they say things they shouldn't.

"OK," he said after a few seconds, "but you didn't hear it from me. I don't want to die."

I crossed my heart. Sterling made like she was buttoning her lip. Thusly assured of anonymity, Bart Tolks talked. In fact, the guy who purported to know everybody's business in town wouldn't stop talking.

What he spilled was a game changer.

WITH OUR flat tire fixed, Sterling and I dined that night at The Basilica, a dark, cozy Italian restaurant in Idaho Springs, twenty miles down the road from Angel Falls. It was far enough away from Spruce County that we didn't have to worry about Sheriff Harlan Weber making good on his threat to arrest us if he found us inside his jurisdiction again. The restaurant offered what was billed as the best pasta along the Front Range, but with the winter weather, there was no shortage of empty tables. I had wanted to put business aside for a few hours, eat a decent meal, and get to know each other better. Unfortunately, no thanks to that gossiping mail clerk, our evening together turned out to be less of a date than a debriefing.

As Tolks told it, Sheriff Weber was as crooked as a crowbar. Everyone in town feared him. While on patrol one summer night two years earlier, Weber was believed to have come across the body of a Mexican cocaine courier killed in a drug deal gone bad. Inside the courier's vehicle was a fat satchel of $100 bills—upward of $200,000. Rumor had it that Weber hastily dumped the body in an old, boarded-up mine shaft and used the cash for the down payment on a swanky condo in Santa Fe, New Mexico. More recently, Weber had found himself the subject of a Spruce County grand jury investigation for allegedly stealing several thousand dollars in charitable contributions intended for the local Boy Scout troop. Weber had volunteered for years as the scoutmaster. Rico Perris, who'd served with Weber as assistant scoutmaster, had purportedly provided secret testimony about the embezzlement. According to Tolks, Angel Falls was abuzz with "wild speculation" that a vengeful Weber, angry at Perris for having ratted him out to the grand jury, ran him off the road that night. And yet, as with most busybodies, Tolks, when pressed, had no solid proof, only innuendo and vague rumor.

"Nobody's gonna talk to you, either, not in this town," he said. "They're all too scared of the sheriff."

There was, however, another, he said, who purportedly knew all about Sheriff Weber's nefarious dealings. Like Weber, the man had grown up in Spruce County and also had fought in Vietnam. They'd remained friends until recently, when they'd had some sort of falling out.

"It's a small town," Tolks said. "You hear things."

"You mean, when you're not opening their mail and reading it," Sterling said.

The clerk glared at her. "You can't prove that."

"You got a name on this guy?" I asked him.

"Yeah," Tolks said. "His name's Cyril Tomasello."

Two hours later, having escaped detection in Angel Falls, Sterling and I were parked opposite each other at a table near The Basilica's front windows. Candlelight refracted off the glass as outside the snow landed and wetted the panes. I thought of something inspirational Francis Bacon wrote that I'd read when I was at the academy: "Begin doing what you want to do now. We are not living in eternity. We have only this moment, sparkling like a star in our hand—and melting like a snowflake."

"We need to find Mr. Tomasello sooner rather than later," I said, "before he winds up down some mine shaft."

"Good call, Captain Obvious," Sterling said, dipping a crust of sourdough bread in a plate of vinegar and olive oil.

I liked her smile, the gentle way she teased me, her self-confidence. At what point, I wondered, does liking someone start to add up to something more than that? I was about to do something I've rarely done—share with a woman what I was starting to feel for her—when the waiter showed up and interrupted the moment. He was a tall, chiseled twenty-something, with long sideburns, carefully cropped stubble, and an arrogant air that suggested little trouble with the ladies.

"We have some outstanding special starters tonight, including one of my personal favs: fresh mushroom caps stuffed with cream cheese, spinach, and a touch of herbs, and topped with melted fontina-provolone cheese. Second, we—"

"Stop right there."

He looked down at me, blinking, not used to being interrupted in midspiel.

"I'm sorry?"

"You should be," I said. "First of all, unless you're from Ye Olde London Town, which it sounds to me like you're not, it's not pronounced 'herbs,' like a bunch of guys named Herb. It's pronounced 'erbs,' The H is muted. Secondly, there's a reason why it's called 'waiter.' You don't come barging in like that on people's conversations. You *wait* politely until they pause and they give you a cue that they're ready to hear the specials, or to have their orders taken. I guarantee, the end result will be a bigger tip. It ain't rocket science. Understood?"

"Yes, sir."

We went with the mushrooms as an appetizer. I ordered spaghetti and meatballs. Sterling opted for puttanesca, a glass of chianti, and, after our server left, a healthy dose of criticism.

"I waitressed when I was in college," she said. "I dealt with my share of obnoxious customers too. I can only imagine the secret flavor ingredient he'll be adding to those mushrooms back in the kitchen."

"I wasn't being obnoxious. I was being educational."

"Educational? You didn't have to chew him out like that, Logan. There's a right way to talk to people, and there's a wrong way."

"There's also a right way and a wrong way to wait tables."

Silence ensued. Our romantic evening, along with any notion of sharing with Sterling what I was feeling for her, melted like the snow on the windows. Our server was right: the stuffed mushrooms were beyond outstanding. I detected no secret sauce.

I was deep into my spaghetti and meatballs, making short work of my last meatball. "We need to find Tomasello."

Sterling nodded and finished her wine. There was no sarcasm this time. She said she needed ten minutes to touch base with her bosses back in Langley, so that they could pass along what we'd learned about Sheriff Weber to her fellow case officers in Arizona who were investigating the death of Joe Zyra. After I insisted on paying the bill—this was, after all, a date—she went out to make her calls in the car.

I figured I'd take a walk in the snow, burn off some pasta, and check in with Buzz, but the call went to voice mail, so I dialed Mrs. Schmulowitz. She was watching an infomercial on natural male enhancement pills.

"I didn't realize at your age that you were still interested in such things, Mrs. Schmulowitz."

"What, you think because my birth certificate is in Roman numerals, I'm no longer a sexual animal?"

"That's not what I meant, Mrs. Schmulowitz."

"Look, bubby, I may happen to have Adam and Eve's autographs, but that doesn't mean I don't periodically crave male companionship—or, as we used to call it growing up in Brooklyn, 'churning a little butter?'"

Uncomfortable, I quickly changed the subject, walking faster to keep warm. "How's Kiddiot doing?"

"Are you kidding? Never better. He won't stop eating, this cat. So listen to this: I'm watching *Dancing with the Stars* tonight—you know how much I love that show, right?"

"I was not aware of that, Mrs. Schmulowitz."

"One of the greatest shows ever. Right up there with *Ed Sullivan*. Now, *that* was a show. I loved the plate twirlers and that funny thing he did with his hand, the little Italian mouse, with the lipstick. Anyhoo, the point is, I'm watching my show, OK, and this *shmaltzy* cat of yours, he walks past the television set. Blocks the screen. He keeps walking and walking and what happens? I miss the entire first half!"

"I believe that's called exaggerating, Mrs. Schmulowitz."

"Exaggerating? Bubby, I don't know how to break this to you, but your cat is getting so fat, he could sell shade."

She went on about how Kiddiot had started making little chirping noises whenever she started cooking, when I noticed a black pickup drive slowly past, its tires crunching in the snow. Tinted windows prevented me from seeing the driver, but the hair on the back of my neck told me I was being eyeballed. I watched it drive down the street and disappear around the corner.

"When are you coming home, bubby?"

"As soon as I can, Mrs. Schmulowitz."

"Well, just be careful, OK? Take care of that beauteous face. I worry."

"Don't. I'm fine."

Sterling was just getting off the phone when I returned to our rented Subaru. The engine was idling. Exhaust vapor curled up from the muffler and hung in the frigid air. I didn't tell her about the truck. Maybe I should've.

It was plenty toasty inside. I held my hands to the warm air blowing from the passenger vent.

"Man, this feels good."

Her lips were pursed. She didn't look over. Something was amiss.

"Unless we can definitively establish a national security connection by tomorrow night," Sterling said, "my orders are to disengage and head home."

Though we hadn't discussed it before I'd agreed to work with her, I understood that our mission was effectively illegal. The CIA is prohibited by law from spying domestically or conducting any active intelligence-gathering operations in the United States, but its "foreign collection mission" can be conducted anywhere. It was through that small loophole and under the aegis of the CIA's National Resources Division that Sterling's section, the Casualty Assessment Matrix, functioned. The division's ostensible task is to debrief US residents, typically scientists and business people, returning from travel to hostile countries like Iran and North Korea, with potential intelligence to be gleaned. If Congress or the press were to ever learn CAM's true purpose, that CIA case officers were engaging in what amounted to domestic espionage, heads might roll.

"Then we'll just have to get to the bottom of this bad boy by tomorrow night," I said.

Sterling nodded halfheartedly, staring down at her lap. "I don't like the idea of leaving any assignment unfinished," she said.

"Be honest. You don't like the idea of saying good-bye to me."

That got a smile out of her. "Thanks for dinner, Logan."

"Anytime, Sterling."

"It's Layne."

"Layne it is." I liked the way her name felt on my tongue.

"You don't look much like a 'Cordell,'" she said.

"Then let's just go with Logan."

"Logan it is."

At her behest, she said, Langley had done some digging on Cyril Tomasello and come up with a new lead about where we might find him. Federal income tax records showed that Tomasello worked part-time at a Home Depot, not far from the VFW post in Denver where he and I crossed paths in the men's room. Our plan was to head back to Denver in hopes the highway remained open, and do whatever it took to find him. I offered to drive.

"What," Sterling said, "you think you can drive better than me in the snow?"

"I didn't say that."

"No, but you implied it. FYI, in case you haven't noticed, Logan, I've *been* driving in the snow this entire time and, correct me if I'm wrong, but we haven't been killed yet, have we?"

"No. Not yet."

Frigid air blew in through the broken back window. Layne gave me a smirk and put the Subaru in reverse. "Besides," she said, "the rental agreement's in my name."

Sand trucks and snow plows were out in force, but the snowstorm appeared to be winning. We got on I-70 eastbound, lucky to be doing fifteen miles an hour. Somebody behind us had their high-beams on. I squinted at the head-lights reflecting in my side-view mirror. Sterling glanced up in her rearview and squinted too.

"That guy's coming up awfully fast," she said.

Too fast.

I was turning in my seat to get a better look at whoever it was when he slammed full-force into us.

FOURTEEN

The tinkling of glass breaking, air bags exploding, then darkness and the howl of the wind. That's all I could recall afterward. The rookie Colorado Highway Patrol officer I'd flagged down after crawling up the embankment credited me with having pulled Layne Sterling out of the wreckage and covering her with my coat to prevent her from going into shock, but I don't remember that part. I surmised, though I couldn't be certain, that it had to have been a full-size pickup or SUV that hit us, something big, given the force of the impact. The front of my head hurt like I'd smacked into a wall. Other than that, I felt fine. Layne didn't. She was woozy and bleeding from a deep gash over her left eye.

"She's gonna be OK," the cop assured me while paramedics worked to stabilize her.

I was hardly reassured by his words. I've seen death. I know how fragile life is. I also know it's the nature of first responders to say such things, as if a badge or a firefighter's helmet somehow carries with them a greater potential for comfort.

"Is she going to be OK?" I demanded of one of the paramedics, as if a second opinion mattered at all.

He said it looked to him like she might've broken her left arm. He was unwilling to speculate whether she'd sustained a skull fracture or internal injuries, but she was breathing on her own and her pulse was strong—both good signs, he said.

I leaned in and kissed her on the check as they loaded her into the ambulance.

"Don't worry, Layne, you're gonna be fine, you hear me?"

If the weather had been more cooperative, they would've helicoptered her to the nearest Denver-area trauma center, which was Saint Anthony's Hospital in suburban Lakewood. They would have to drive her there instead. The Highway Patrol rookie was willing to drive me there too. I told him I was happy for the ride, but said there was one thing I had to do first.

"Hey, come back here!"

Disregarding the cop, I slipped and slid my way back down the embankment, about twenty meters, reached through a broken window to extract Sterling's shoulder bag and backpack before collecting a scraping of paint from an obvious transfer low down on the crumpled hatchback.

"What are you doing down there?" the patrolman yelled from above, shining his flashlight through the snow. "C'mon, we gotta go. It's cold out here!"

In the light from my cell phone, the paint shone flat black.

A RUMPLED ER doctor who looked like he'd just been rousted from a nap said I had a concussion. He wanted to run additional tests. I declined.

"I never take any test without properly preparing."

He yawned. "It's your noggin," he said and left.

Layne was wheeled into surgery within minutes of her arrival. The paramedic had been right: X-rays showed her arm had been broken and would require surgery. Her spleen had ruptured and also needed to be removed. I found the hospital cafeteria, bought myself a cup of burned worm dirt that passed for coffee, and called Buzz to tell him what had happened.

"You sure you're OK?"

"I'm fine, Buzz. Still functional, more or less."

"Who do you think did it?

"Unknown."

"Well, when *will* you know? This ain't the civilian sector, Logan. This isn't some gravy train. We work for Mr. and Mrs. America. Time is money."

"I'm doing the best I can, Buzz. Look, I nearly died tonight. So, for once, why don't you stop trying to bust my chops?"

He exhaled long and slow, then apologized. "I'm just worried about you, Logan, that's all."

I told him I appreciated his concern and to look for the sample of the paint transfer I'd scraped off the back of the Subaru that I'd be expediting to him via FedEx first thing in the morning. He gave me contact information for a forensics lab in Arlington, Virginia, and told me to forward the sample directly there. He said he would take care of the wrecked Subaru and brief Layne's chain of command on her condition.

"Just so you know," I said, "I'm not disengaging. I will find this bastard. And I will make him pay."

"I'm not saying let it go. No one's asking you to break contact, Logan. Yes, this is a Christians in Action production and, yes, you're just the hired help, but we're all trying to get along in the community these days—no more firewalls, interagency cooperation, all that happy horsepucky. All I'm saying is, don't let your emotions get the best of you. We both know too many good operators who stopped thinking. They started reacting and ended up getting dead. You copy?"

"Yeah, Buzz. I copy."

I wasn't about to let it go. As the Buddha once said, "I do not dispute with the world; rather, it is the world that disputes with me." I was angry and needed no encouragement to press on alone. I would hunt down whoever it was who'd hurt Layne and I would hurt them in return. Badly.

I was cooling my heels in a second-floor waiting room about an hour later, thumbing through a year-old copy of *Sports Illustrated* and growing increasingly more anxious by the minute. I couldn't find anyone to give me an update on how she was doing. Was she still in surgery? Was she out? The nurses were apologetic, but none had any answers. I decided to take a walk and burn off some caffeine. Rounding a corner in the corridor outside the hospital's cardiac care unit, I nearly collided with a physician. Her head was down. She was reading something on a clipboard. The name stitched in blue cursive thread on her white lab coat read, "Samantha McBride MD."

The woman who'd rescued me from the icy clutches of the Champ River looked as surprised to see me as I was her.

"What are you doing here?"

"I was in a car accident."

"Were you injured?"

"My partner was."

She narrowed her eyes like she was jealous. "Your *partner?*"

"My colleague. She's in surgery. She had to have her spleen removed."

"I see. Well, I hope she's all right."

"I don't know yet. Maybe you can find out for me."

"Sure, I can probably do that for you."

I spelled out Layne's name for her. She jotted it down on her clipboard, then stood there for a long, awkward moment, shifting her weight from one foot to the other, unwilling to make eye contact.

"So," she said, "you're not interested in going out?"

"It's not that I don't appreciate what you did for me, Sam. I do. Big time. It's just that I kind of have a lot on my plate right now."

"Oh, well," she said, smiling like it was no big deal, even though I could see that it was.

She told me she'd meet me in a few minutes in the waiting room. I went back to the room and hunkered down for another hour in the same well-worn easy chair on which I'd sat earlier. Dr. Sam McBride never showed.

Somewhere in the night, I dozed off. I awakened shortly before 0600 to someone's gentle hand on my shoulder.

"Mr. Logan?"

White hair sticking out of a blue surgical cap. Kind eyes behind round, rimless glasses. Salt-and-pepper goatee. Blue surgical scrubs. He told me his name but all I caught was "doctor."

"She did fine," he said. "We're just about to move her out of recovery. She'd like to see you."

✈ ✈ ✈

LAYNE STERLING's left arm was wrapped in a soft cast. Her forehead was bandaged. She was tethered to an IV drip and a nasal oxygen cannula. Her eyes were closed.

"You look like you just went ten rounds with Hulk Hogan."

"You're dating yourself, Logan," she said softly, barely moving her lips.

She seemed skeptical that I hadn't been injured. I assured her I was fine, and that I would find whoever it was who'd put her in the hospital.

"Just promise me you'll be careful."

"I'm always careful."

"Somehow I find that hard to believe."

I asked her what, if anything, she remembered of the crash. Any details of the vehicle that had rear-ended us? She shook her head. Nothing. I wondered aloud if it had been Sheriff Weber or one of his deputies acting on his behalf.

"I guess you'll just have to work on that yourself until I can get out of here," Layne whispered. "Where's my backpack?"

"With your clothes. Don't worry. They put all your things in a locker. I made sure it's secure."

"Have them bring me all my stuff. I'd feel better with it next to me." She reached out and took my hand. "Dig out my phone. The security code—it's three seven three six. There's an app. The Weather Channel. Open it. Press your phone against mine."

"Then what? Our mobile phones make a baby?"

She barely had the strength to smile. "I can track your location."

"Sounds extremely James Bond-ish."

"*Jane* Bond-ish," Layne said, correcting me.

There was another, even more 007-ish app on her phone, she said, one that could be easily transferred to mine. I won't get into the operational specifics of it for security reasons; virtually every modern phone offers the same capacity. What I can say is that my phone, when so modified, after rubbing up against anyone else's phone, even for a second or two, could then monitor that person's calls and text messages. All I had to do was remain within a range of about a quarter mile. Illegal? Probably. Awesome? Without question.

I assured her that I'd be back later to check on her, softly stroked her cheek, and told her to go back to sleep, but she already had.

A nurse escorted me to a locker room down the hall the size of walk-in closet and got out a plastic bag containing Layne's clothes. He also removed her backpack and shoulder bag.

"I'll give you a minute," he said.

"Thanks."

I waited until he stepped out, found Layne's phone, and dug mine out of my pocket, whereupon I established eavesdropping and tracking connections as Layne had instructed. As I put her phone back, I came across her Glock. The untraceable .380 she'd loaned me was up in the mountains, presumably still in the Subaru, which meant I was unarmed. Not a good thing when you're hunting for humans. I needed a weapon. I figured she wouldn't mind loaning me hers.

I ejected the magazine to make sure there were bullets where they were supposed to be. There were. A full load. They were bonded rounds rather than jacketed, the kind that stay intact when penetrating hard objects, like bones. The kind that improved the odds of doing knocking-down and debilitating damage to a human target. I reseated the magazine, racked the slide, chambering a round, and stashed the pistol in my coat pocket. I hoped I didn't have to shoot anybody.

Nobody enjoys that kind of paperwork.

A block south of the hospital was one of those pack-and-post places that charges you up the wazoo to ship anything. I filled out the necessary forms, slipped the paint sample I'd collected from the Subaru into a flat-rate box, and paid for overnight shipping to the forensics lab in Arlington. As my landlady, Mrs. Schmulowitz, might've said of the expense, "No big whoop." I presumed the government would reimburse me.

Then it was off to find Cyril Tomasello. Only there was a problem: I lacked transportation. Here I was, on loan to the Central Intelligence Agency, revisiting the assassination of John F. Kennedy, and pondering the possibility of having to catch an Uber. Even with the federal deficit, I figured that Uncle Sugar under the circumstances had sufficient resources to spring for another rental car. I called Enterprise. A pleasant young man from Ethiopia came and picked me up. Unfortunately, he said, the only vehicle he had available was a white Toyota minivan.

Blizzard conditions remained in effect. The roads in north Denver were a slick, snarled nightmare. The minivan handled them like an alcoholic on hockey skates.

Tomasello wasn't home and appeared not to have been there all night—no tire tracks in the snow on the street out in front of his unit; none in the driveway leading to his carport out back.

I drove to the Home Depot where he supposedly was employed, but he wasn't there either.

"Dude hasn't worked here in weeks," said the assistant manager, a spindly little man with major-league ears. He was typing and focused intently on a computer monitor behind the store's special orders counter. "Dwayne" was scrawled in black marker pen under the "Hi, My Name Is" area of his filthy orange work apron.

"Any idea where I could find him?"

"Nope."

The guy didn't have the common courtesy even to look at me. I didn't like that. I didn't like that at all. I'd already unsheathed the threat of federal sanction in the form of the

EPA on another unwilling witness—coroner Jed Jones up in Angel Falls. I had no problem getting blustery again and vowing to unleash other federal investigators on this bozo. "OK, Dwayne," I said, "here's how this is going to go down. I'm going to ask you, politely, if you would be kind enough to share with me any information that might help us find Mr. Tomasello. He happens to be a party of interest in a federal inquiry of major importance. You, in return, are going to be equally polite and fully cooperative. It's either that, Dwayne, or I'll have a platoon of investigators here from the Occupational Safety and Health Administration first thing tomorrow morning. And I can promise you, they'll comb this store for even the slightest employee health and safety violations. Ladder safety. Forklift signage. Not enough hand sanitizer in your lavatories. You've seen the way bargain-hunting housewives go berserk, swarming the mall the day after Thanksgiving? It'll be like that in here, Dwayne, only ten times worse, with really stiff penalties. The store will get shut down and you'll be out of work. You really don't have time to deal with all that, do you, an uncooperative anal cavity such as yourself?"

His eyes shifted from the computer to mine. His Adam's apple bobbed. I knew I had his full attention.

"Check out The Rehab," Dwayne said.

"*The* rehab?"

"It's a cocktail lounge. Twenty-Ninth and Humboldt. Used to drink his lunch over there. Didn't come back half the time. It's why he got canned."

✈ ✈ ✈

WEDGED BETWEEN a taqueria and a Vietnamese nail salon, The Rehab brought new meaning to the term, "dive bar." The decor was cave-like. Dim lighting. Walls splashed with graffiti. A floor covered in sticky linoleum that sucked at the treads of my shoes. A massive antique jukebox took up the far end of the joint. Taped to it was a handwritten sign: "Not working." The same could've been said of the scruffy regulars perched at the bar.

Tomasello was sitting at a small pedestal table next to the jukebox with a blousey older blonde with a big bouffant and even bigger cleavage. The two of them were laughing too loudly at something.

"Hello, Cyril, remember me?"

He looked up, bleary, trying to focus. "Donald Trump?"

The blonde cracked up.

"No, Cyril. Not Donald Trump. We met at the VFW a couple of days ago. I asked you about Rico Perris, remember?"

Without taking his eyes off me, the drunken smile melted from his face. "Take a hike," he told the blonde.

"But, baby—"

"I said, get lost."

She offered him her middle finger—"Up yours, you freakin' loser"—and got up unsteadily to go find a spot among the other lushes at the bar.

I took her seat and sat down. "You're quite the ladies' man, Cyril."

Tomasello's phone was sitting on the table next to his nearly empty beer glass. He twirled it around and around, glaring at me.

"What do you want?"

"The truth."

I walked him through how we'd talked to Maureen, his estranged honey. I recounted the dust-up he'd had with Rico Perris shortly before Perris's death and how he'd driven up to the mountains the day Perris was killed. I explained that we knew all about his driving demolition derbies, which made him an expert in crashing into other cars. Then I told him that body filler we'd recovered from Perris's Porsche matched the chunk of filler I'd seen embedded in the mangled fender of his Jeep. That last part, if you've been following along, was a lie. But when you're trying to determine whether you're dealing with a good guy or a bad guy, nobody ever said you must be George Washington.

"You got it all wrong, man," Tomasello said. "I didn't kill Rico. Rico was a buddy."

"We know you met with Alessandra in Angel Falls. Rico died that night."

He blanched and looked down at his phone, spinning it with one hand.

"What were you doing up there, Cyril?"

"None of your damned business."

"Wrong answer. You want me to rephrase it? Because I know you used to be a marine, and I think we can all agree that marines tend not to be the quickest bunnies in the forest."

The slight flew over his head. "A marine's never *not* a marine," he said woozily. "Once a marine, always a marine."

"Not exactly a badge of honor from what I've observed. You guys are overrated. For one thing, you're terrible marksmen. I once saw a marine throw himself on the ground—and miss."

"You better shut your mouth, mister, unless you're planning to eat those words."

I continued provoking, pummeling him with every dumb marine joke I could remember. *What has eighty-two legs and an IQ of forty-two? Forty marines and their lieutenant. Why are marines allowed to ride on navy ships? Because sheep can't swab a deck. How do you knock out a marine while he's drinking water? Slam the toilet lid on him.* With each zinger, I could practically see the steam building between his ears. He withstood the barrage as long as he could before he finally blew, exploding out of his chair and lunging wildly at me over the table. Exactly what I wanted him to do.

The table pitched over and so did I. It was an Academy Award-winning performance on my part, if I do say so myself. Patrons came running, screaming, "All right, OK, break it up, break it up!" A couple of guys held Tomasello at bay while he kicked at me and flailed and threatened to rip my head off and use it as a bowling ball. Underfoot, in the middle of all that yelling and chaos, I found his phone where it had fallen and quickly swiped it against mine.

Mission accomplished.

"You dropped this," I said, getting to my feet.

He snatched the phone from my hand and called me names you won't hear on Saturday morning television.

The Rehab's paunchy, thickly bearded owner, who spoke in a Middle Eastern accent, emerged from his tiny office in the back and instructed me never to show my face in his establishment again if I knew what was good for me. The blonde suggested I might want to buy the house a round for all the trouble I'd caused. I declined.

"Call me," I mouthed to Tomasello, making my hand like a phone.

He flipped me off.

Snow was blowing off the rooftops outside. I'd parked the minivan a half block down the street. The engine was still warm. The heater fired right up.

So did Tomasello.

Fewer than two minutes after my dramatic departure, while he was still inside the bar, he placed a call to Sheriff

Harlan Weber in Angel Falls. I listened in on their conversation, courtesy of cutting-edge, CIA technology. Even though the reception was static-filled to the point of being mostly unintelligible, I caught the gist:

Weber had a secret and appeared willing to silence anyone who threatened to uncover it. Including, apparently, me.

FIFTEEN

The snippets of conversation that I gleaned from my rented minivan, listening in on Sheriff Weber and Cyril Tomasello conversing telephonically, left more questions than answers.

It was apparent in their comparing notes that both men now realized I was no glorified insurance agency employee. They knew I was an investigator, but for whom or what remained a mystery to them.

Weber reiterated what he'd said in the flesh when Layne Sterling and I last crossed paths with him, that I was sticking my nose in places where it didn't belong (I apparently have a nasty habit of doing that), and that something "big time" would have to be done about me. "They're (static, unintelligible) of a witch hunt," I heard him say, but what the subject of that witch hunt was, I couldn't pick up.

"Rico was (static, unintelligible)," Tomasello responded. "The guy was way too smart for (static, unintelligible) . . . happened up there that night was, you know (static, unintelligible) . . . tell you right now, there is not a jury in this whole entire country in their right (static, unintelligible) conviction, guaranteed."

"I appreciate that," Weber said. "The only thing I know is that if (static, unintelligible), I'm looking at (static,

160

unintelligible) protective custody. I'm a cop. No way a cop (static, unintelligible) out of there alive."

He said something about driving to New Mexico but, again, the reception was too filled with static to make out much.

I'd parked on the same side of the street at a meter five spaces up from where Tomasello had parked where, courtesy of the van's passenger side-view mirror, I could maintain eyes-on of both his Jeep and the bar itself. It took less than five minutes before he emerged. Bundled up and head down, squinting the way somebody does when snow or rain is falling in their eyes, he made a beeline to his vehicle and quickly climbed in. I was careful to slump low in my seat and look away as he pulled out and drove past me. I waited for three other cars to pass by, their rear tires spitting rooster tails of snow, then pulled out and followed him.

Tomasello never saw me—or, if he did, pretended not to. I debated at first whether he was playing dumb and drawing me into a trap; he certainly took no countersurveillance measures like speeding up or taking sharp, unannounced turns. This diminished in my mind the possibility that his military training had included anything remotely secret squirrel-like. Either way, mindful of not underestimating his capabilities, I hung back with my headlights off, carefully maintaining separation, careful to keep at least three other vehicles between us. I hoped he might make other calls that I could intercept, but he didn't.

Cars were slipping and spinning out. Conditions were white out. A UPS driver slid sideways through a red light on Colfax, nearly tagging me as I turned south onto Colorado Boulevard. He mouthed a heartfelt "Sorry" as I maneuvered around him.

Down Colorado Boulevard Tomasello accelerated. The pavement was snow and ice under my tires. Tomasello's Jeep had four-wheel-drive. My minivan didn't. I had to drive faster than the conditions and prudence dictated or risk losing sight of him. Somehow I kept up and kept back without being observed. He turned right on Alameda Avenue, crossed University Avenue, and turned south onto Gaylord Street. He was headed, I realized, back to the home of his ex-girlfriend, cocktail waitress Maureen Spencer. To maintain cover, meanwhile, I continued westbound on Alameda. I knew, after all, where I could find him.

I drove the neighborhood, then circled back and parked down the block, on the same side of the street, obscured by four other parked vehicles but with an unobstructed sight line of Tomasello's vehicle. The Jeep was right where I thought it would be—directly in front of Maureen's house.

Then I shut off the ignition and waited. There were no calls.

One hour turned into two, then three. It was like sitting in a meat locker. Ice collected inside the windshield. I had to scrape it off periodically to see out. To say I was tempted to fire the engine and crank up the heater goes without saying, but that would have produced an exhaust plume, and the exhaust plumes from idling vehicles attract attention. And so I sat, my arms wrapped around me, watching the house and trying to think warm.

I was reminded of what Buzz had once said on a Middle Eastern snatch-and-grab to which Alpha had been assigned. Our high value target du jour was a 300-pound Saudi zillionaire with jihadist leanings and reputed ties to Osama bin Laden—or more simply, "Bin," as we called him back then. It was mid-June and 110 degrees in the shade. Our hideout, a Bedouin tent pitched just south of the Kuwaiti border, afforded little coolness. The industrialist was expecting to rendezvous with an A-list Hollywood actress known to have a thing for Arab men (sex, we found, was always a big draw when hunting bad guys) but this bad guy was late. Posing as nomadic shepherds, we sat broiling under that sun for most of the day, waiting for him. I worried that I might stroke out and die. Buzz wasn't even perspiring. Lounging on one elbow, munching dried dates, listening to some opera in his earbuds, his MP-5 submachine gun at the ready under the folds of his tribal robes, he looked over at me and snorted derisively.

"Any swinging crank on a sunny Sunday afternoon thinks he can be a special operator, Logan. *This* is what being an operator's all about, OK? The heat. The cold. The rain. Sleet. Snow. The zombie apocalypse. Toenail fungus. Crabs up your exhaust pipe. Being forced to watch endless reruns of *Gilligan's Island*. This here is why we're special, Logan. Because we suck it up and take it. Because we can take *any*thing, and it don't affect our ops."

And so I sucked it up and took it without complaint, just as I had in countless other hell holes around the world that nobody's ever heard of. Because that's what special means, because freedom isn't free. And all of that.

My stroll down memory lane was abruptly cut short when Tomasello emerged from the house with his supposed ex-girlfriend hard on his heels.

They stood on the front porch, jabbing fingers at each other and arguing animatedly. I couldn't hear what they were fighting over, but their dustup didn't last long. She shoved him off the porch, into the snow. He got up, brushed himself off, fired an obscene gesture at her, and left in his Jeep while she stormed back inside and slammed the door behind her.

Whatever he'd said or done that had angered her, I didn't care. What mattered was that she was angry. Often as not, angry ex's have an almost compulsive need to dish, to get revenge. I had ample reason to think Maureen Spencer would reveal much about Cyril Tomasello I did not know.

She would not disappoint.

"You want some ice cream or something. I know you cops prefer doughnuts, but . . ."

Outside, it was colder than a mother-in-law's kiss, and she was offering me *ice cream*?

"Ice cream's great," I said, leaning against her kitchen sink. Anything to establish trust and rapport.

Maureen rummaged through her freezer. She'd traded her robe and slippers, since I had seen her last, for blue jeans, Ugg boots, and a heavy alpaca wool sweater. I didn't disabuse her of the notion that I was a police officer.

"I got chocolate strawberry swirl. Is that OK?"

"That'll work," I said.

"So, where's your partner, the Asian lady?"

"She took the day off."

"Nice. Wish I could. I go to work at five."

I watched her spoon the ice cream into two chipped earthenware bowls.

"You know, I've been thinking a lot about it since last night," she said. "To be honest, I'd just as soon drop the charges. Cyril didn't really punch me. I fell. Ran into a doorknob."

"A doorknob, huh? How does that work?"

"I don't know. It just did."

"Why did you tell the officers he hit you?"

She set one of the bowls in front of me, unwilling to meet my eyes. "Cyril's been seeing somebody else on and off. I got jealous, OK?"

"Somehow I don't think you're telling me the whole truth, Maureen."

"Think whatever you want. I really don't care."

"What was Cyril doing here for three hours?"

She grunted, feigning offense. "What?"

"I followed him here, Maureen. I sat outside for three hours, waiting and watching. I watched the little tiff you two had on the porch. I watched you push him. I watched him drive off. Something's not adding up here, so why don't we just cut to the chase."

"Look, I already told you. I fell. I was jealous, OK? I called 911 and I shouldn't have." She licked her lips and rubbed the back of her neck, growing more nervous by the moment. "Can't we just let this whole thing go?"

"No, Maureen, we can't."

Sometimes, you go with your gut. In military parlance, it's called "indirect fire." You aim in a general direction, take a shot, and hope you hit something. In this case, I more than did.

"Tell me about Sheriff Weber," I said.

I watched the blood drain from her already wan face. Then she said something I didn't anticipate:

"We're done here." She snatched my bowl away before I'd taken a single bite and said she wanted to talk to an attorney.

"Attorneys are for people who've done something wrong, Maureen. You filed a false police report. What else have you done wrong?"

"Nothing."

"Right."

"Listen, I know my rights, OK, and I refuse to answer. Under the Sixth Amendment or whatever. Now, get out. I should've never let you in to begin with."

The beauty of people believing that you carry a badge, as I've discovered, is that you can get away with stuff a real cop never could. Including, for example, combining your make-believe authority with that of any number of other real authorities. All of a sudden, you're no longer just a cop. You're the prosecutor. You're the judge and jury. In truth, you are little more than a con artist preying on the gullible. As Einstein put it so eloquently, "The difference between genius and stupidity is that genius has its limits." As long as it's all for a righteous cause, in my book, so what?

"I am prepared to offer you forthwith and in perpetuity," I told her, trying to sound as official as I could, "complete and total immunity from any criminal charges, whether they be federal, state, or municipal. All you have to do is cooperate with me."

"Is this for real?"

"Just tell me the truth, Maureen."

And so she did.

My phone buzzed. The caller ID said, "Steve Weiss, Denver PD."

"I have some information for you on your man, Cyril Tomasello," he said. "How soon can we meet?"

I told him what had happened to Layne and that I was on my way to Saint Anthony's to check in on her. I said I'd call him back as soon as I could. He said he'd be standing by.

The hospital had moved her into a semiprivate room, a contradiction in terms if there ever was one. A wizened old woman was in the other bed with her mouth open, snoring. You could hear the wet death rattle in her chest. Her television was tuned to the History Channel. I wondered if she'd been watching to see if she was on it. Across the room, Layne Sterling was looking vastly better than anyone had the right to after having undergone major surgery mere hours earlier.

"I have every intention of getting out of here by tomorrow morning," she said.

"This isn't the decathlon, Layne. Let's just take it one day at a time, OK?"

I made sure her roommate was still asleep, then told her what Maureen had told me: That Maureen had, indeed, struck her face on a doorknob while she and Tomasello tussled. The reason for the fight was that Cyril Tomasello had been seeing another woman—none other than Rico Perris's girlfriend, Alessandra Munoz. But that wasn't the real stunner. The real stunner was the identity of a third man who, in addition to Tomasello and Perris, according to Maureen, had also bedded Alessandra.

"Go on," I said, "take a wild guess."

"Bart Tolks, the guy at the post office."

"Negative, though I will say, that guy is most certainly on my radar. Guess again."

"That bartender at the Molly B?"

"Nope."

"Frosty the Snowman, the Jolly Green Giant. Hell, I don't know, Logan. *Who?*"

"Harlan Weber."

"Sheriff Harlan Weber?"

"One and the same."

She looked away and nodded to herself, like things were starting to make sense. "That would explain why Alessandra behaved the way she did when she left the bar. She's afraid of Weber."

"He's apparently one scary guy," I said, "for the world's greatest grandpa."

I told her about the call I'd intercepted between Weber and Tomasello, and the reference Weber had made over the phone to New Mexico. At a minimum, Sterling said, the call established a potentially incriminating connection between the two men, assuming it was eventually determined that either had contributed, for whatever reason, to Perris's demise or Joe Zyra's fatal hit-and-run in Phoenix.

"Agreed," I said, "but it still doesn't explain whether Tomasello or Weber had anything to do with either man's death."

"Or had any connection to any CIA activities."

Layne's ancient roommate made a wet snorting sound and her chest heaved. For a second, she seemed to stop breathing—a monitor started beeping—then her respiration returned to normal.

Layne asked me if Maureen had offered any other relevant information. I shared with her everything I could remember of our conversation.

Perris and Tomasello had enjoyed what Maureen described essentially as an often strained friendship, one predicated on heated political debates and, occasionally, jealousies over shared interests in the same women including, apparently, Maureen herself. They had belonged, however briefly, to the same book club, she said, one made up of mostly aging military vets who usually met online every month or so and whose reading tastes gravitated to nonfiction—history, particularly war, biographies, and the like. They talked about buying a project car together someday, an old Triumph or a GTO, and fixing it up, but it was just talk.

"Why did she lie initially about not knowing who Rico Perris was?"

"She told me she didn't want to cause any more conflict with Tomasello than there already is," I said. "She claimed she didn't even know that Rico was dead. She was shocked."

"And you believed her?"

"I don't believe in anything, with the possible exception of Superman pajamas, which make you as powerful as Superman when you wear them. I totally believe in that."

"You don't look like the pajamas type to me, Logan. You probably don't even own any."

"True. But if I did, they'd be Superman pj's."

I made like the Caped Crusader—biceps flexed, smiling faster than a speeding bullet.

Sterling rolled her eyes and suppressed her own smile, the way women do when they're reminded that men remain boys, only larger.

An economy-sized nurse wearing purple scrubs and an Afro that would've made Angela Davis proud, entered. "OK, player, party's over. Scoot. My patient needs her beauty sleep now."

"Then I shall return first thing in the A.M."

"You'd better." Layne yawned and closed her eyes. "Just be—"

"Yeah, I know. Careful. My middle name."

No response. She was already asleep.

✈ ✈ ✈

FINDING CYRIL Tomasello and getting him to come clean was my imperative. I would scour the snowy streets of Denver to find him. I would stay up all night if I had to.

It was now dark outside. Detective Weiss was standing outside the main entrance of the hospital. I'd spotted him as soon as I got off the elevator, hands shoved into his coat pockets, shivering.

"How's your partner?"

"She'll live. Sorry I didn't call you back. I was just about to."

"I need you to take a ride," he said, falling in beside me as I hurried to the parking garage before I, too, began shivering.

"Why? Am I under arrest?"

"What makes you think you're under arrest?"

"Every cop movie ever made, the detective says, 'I need you to take a ride with me,' then the guy goes to jail. It's a standard trope."

". . . A *trope?*"

"Forget it. You said you had some information for me?"

"Look, Logan, I don't know who you are or *what* you are, and I don't know who you *think* you are, but I don't like your attitude, OK? And just so we understand each other, I don't owe you any favors."

"Then what're you doing here, Detective? Because I'm a little busy at the moment."

"Look, if you could just stop for one minute so I could talk." He grabbed my arm.

In my more violent past, if you were male, grabbing me without prior approval would've likely been the last thing you did that day. The new me didn't react instinctively as I once might've; I didn't bend his wrist back until it snapped. The new me slowly looked down at his hand in a way that let him know I would tolerate it being there for only so long.

He quickly realized his error and let go of his grip.

"What can I do for you, Detective?"

"Somebody found a body in an alley. We think it's Cyril Tomasello."

SIXTEEN

Yellow police tape cordoned the alley. Police cruisers were positioned at either end, guarding the approaches, their revolving red and blue lights affording the only color in a whitewashed winterscape.

The body lay curled on its left side next to a dumpster outside the back door of a pool hall in lower downtown Denver. The gray sheet that had been placed over it was dusted with a fine coat of fresh dry snow, like powdered sugar on pastry.

"We don't think at this point that there was any foul play involved," Detective Weiss said. "Looks like he had The Big One and checked out."

"I can think of a few worse ways to go," I said, wishing I was back inside and somewhere warm. Living in California had thinned my blood big time.

Two other detectives stood aside, jaws tight, bitching about the lousy weather, as Weiss stooped from the waist and pulled back the sheet. Cyril Tomasello's legs were drawn up to his chest, his left hand pillowing his head, his right clutching his stomach. He looked like he was sleeping.

"Is this the man you asked me about?" Weiss aimed a flashlight at the body.

The snow swirled. The cold cut straight through us.

"That's him," I said.

Tomasello appeared in death even plumper and more out of shape than he'd been in life. I didn't test his limbs for stiffness, but they didn't appear contorted. Rigor had not set in.

"There's no outward indication of trauma," Weiss said. "No blood, no gunshot wound, no knife wound. We're going with natural causes."

"Not everybody bleeds out, Detective. Ambient cold— the weather—can affect blood loss. Things shrink. Sort of like when you jump into an unheated swimming pool, if you catch my drift."

Weiss looked over at me with a smug, superior expression. "I take it you've seen dead people before?"

It served no purpose sharing with him how many I'd seen or personally dispatched in the name of national security.

"Roll him over," I said.

"Can't," one of the other detectives said. "Gotta wait for the coroner to release the body."

"The victim is holding his stomach for a reason," I said.

Weiss hesitated, then knelt beside the body. He brushed some snow off the corpse, gently pried back Tomasello's hand, and peered closely with the flashlight.

"Shit," was all he said.

The ivory hilt of what looked to be a small folding knife protruded from Tomasello's belly, obscured by his overcoat, his hand, and the snow.

Weiss looked up at me. "How'd you know?"

"Lucky guess."

My face was numb from the cold. I walked back to Weiss's idling, unmarked Ford Crown Vic and climbed in. He followed me. Doors shut, heater blasting, we sat in silence for a good ten seconds, not looking at each other.

"Tell me you didn't kill him," he said finally.

"OK, I didn't kill him."

"OK, I'm not saying you did. But you can appreciate the timing of this, right? I mean, you ask me to check this guy out for you and now he's dead. I find that a little curious, don't you?"

"If you're looking for an alibi, Detective, I can vouch for my whereabouts."

"I just want you to tell me what the hell's going on here," Weiss said.

"I wish I could. I'm sure you understand."

"Actually I don't. I don't understand at all."

You've seen that sad face your dog makes, those eyes? Weiss had that look. I found myself feeling sorry for him. Here he was, with a new homicide on his hands, and here I was playing spook, struggling to maintain operational cover and, from his perspective, being an evasive jerk.

I realized in the same moment that I was spinning my wheels and getting nowhere fast on an assignment that was probably unlawful to begin with, considering the CIA's charter. Had I not found myself drawn to Layne Sterling as intensely as I was, I probably would've quit right then and there. I would have found a way back to Arizona, retrieved my hope-fully repaired airplane, and returned to my plodding if not stable flight instructor's life in Rancho Bonita with my cat and my meshugganah landlady. But I knew I was too vested in Sterling and her mission for any of that. As I'd vowed, I would find whoever put her in the hospital. I would find who or what was responsible for retired CIA analyst Rico Perris's demise. To achieve those objectives, however, what with Layne laid up and our primary lead sleeping the big sleep, I needed reinforcements, more boots on the ground.

"OK, here's the deal," I told Weiss. "I'll share with you what I can without compromising operational security, but anything I tell you goes no further than this car. If you pass on any of what I'm about to tell you to anyone, you'll find yourself in very short order checking in at the Graybar Hotel in Leavenworth for an indefinite stay. In exchange, you're going to help me do my job. Are we clear, Detective Weiss?"

"Crystal. But can I just say one thing first?"

I waited.

"I feel like I'm in a spy movie or something."

I told him about Rico Perris's secret life, about the death in New Mexico of his fellow former CIA analyst, Joe Zyra, and how the two men had once investigated the Kennedy assassination. I told him about the classified documents that had been kept under wraps for decades at the National Archives and were set to be unsealed, and how some had inexplicably vanished. I told him about Spruce County Sheriff Harlan Weber's reputed connections to the Florida mob when he was a young man fresh out of the Marine Corps, about the mob's connection to the JFK assassination, and about ex-marine Cyril Tomasello's apparent ties to Weber. I told him about recovering the black paint transfer from the rear bumper of Perris's vintage Porsche, about how Tomasello had driven a black Jeep, and how Perris and Tomasello had nearly come to blows over their apparent interests in the same woman.

"You're saying Cyril Tomasello had motive to kill Rico Perris?"

"I'm saying that's one possibility," I said.

"How does Perris spell his name? Like the city?"

I spelled it for him.

Weiss jotted it down in a reporter's notebook. "OK," he said, "here's what I can tell you. I ran Tomasello through our records after we talked, and the national computer too. The guy was no saint. Multiple arrests. Some jail time. He also shows up on the membership rolls of the Posse Comitatus.

They're a right-wing extremist group. They hate the government, minorities, anything that—"

"—I'm familiar with Posse Comitatus, Detective," I said. "You're not telling me anything I don't already know."

"Fine. OK. What if I told you I'm very familiar with Sheriff Weber? I have a buddy with the Colorado Bureau of Investigation. CBI's been investigating Weber for two years. He's dirty as the day is long. No question about it."

"Again," I said, "that doesn't get me where I need to go."

"OK." Weiss closed his notebook and tucked away his pen. "I could go to jail for what I'm about to tell you," he said somberly, "so, just, you know, don't snitch me off, OK?"

"Deal."

I prefer it when people divulge sensitive information without me having to threaten them or stress any of their anatomical parts. Cooperation and nonviolence. The Buddha, I'm certain, wanted it that way. It's why the Buddha was the Buddha. I shook my head to myself, wondering what he would've thought of our current crop of political leaders.

For the next ten minutes, until Detective Weiss's pregnant wife called to tell him that her water had broken and that she was on her way to the very same hospital where Layne was laid up, he proved himself to be a font of relevant information. None of it got me where I needed to go in ferreting out a killer, but it got me closer.

I TOLD Layne what Weiss had told me: The Colorado Bureau of Investigation regarded Sheriff Harlan Weber as a suspect in not one, not two, not three, but count 'em, four unsolved homicides.

According to Weiss's source, the first two dated back to the 1960s. Both victims were low-level, south Florida mob associates suspected by the Trafficante organization of being police informants. One wiseguy's body was never found. The other turned up in the Everglades. Investigators at first believed that he'd died after being mauled by an alligator, but that was before an autopsy revealed a .22-caliber slug buried in his partially digested head. A .22-caliber handgun later was found in Weber's car and some witnesses placed him in the area at the time of the murder, but a forensics examination of the weapon proved inconclusive and Weber's alibi held up: his first wife swore he was home that day in suburban Miami, repairing a fence that had blown over in a hurricane. She would later disappear from a cruise ship off the coast of Nassau while the couple vacationed. One crew member said he thought Mrs. Weber might've been pushed. Prosecutors, however, concluded there was not enough evidence to bring charges.

Weber's fourth victim was believed to have been the drug courier who Tolks, the postal clerk in Angel Falls, had told Layne and me about, but there was a twist in Detective Weiss's version of the story. Tolks's version had Weber happening on the scene when the courier supposedly already was dead, then stealing dirty money to help finance his dream casa in New Mexico. Weiss's version of the tale had the courier and Sheriff Weber in partnership. The two men had arranged to meet down a lonely dirt road and split profits. Weber instead shot his partner dead and made off with the dough.

One bit Tolks did get right that squared with what Weiss told me: a grand jury in Spruce County was investigating Weber for stealing vast sums of money from the Boy Scouts of America.

"It's one thing to rip off a drug dealer," I said to Layne, "but the *Boy Scouts of America*? I don't know if I believe in hell, but if there is one, I guarantee you, he'd be on the first bus."

She was sitting up in her hospital bed, wincing, trying to get comfortable. Her ancient roommate was gone, the other bed empty and freshly made. Someone that old, I didn't ask what had become of her.

"Why hasn't the CBI arrested him?" Layne asked me.

"They're apparently still working the investigation. You want me to fluff your pillow or something?"

"I'm good, thanks."

She sipped some water from a straw and wanted to know whether Weiss knew anything about the sheriff's possible involvement in the death of Rico Perris. I shook my head.

"He said he'd do some sleuthing and get back to me. It might be a day or two. His contact's out of town, and he's off-duty for the foreseeable future. His wife's in labor. He did, by the way, run Weber's name through Colorado DMV while we were sitting there. Weber owns a Chevy sedan and a Ford F-250. The Chevy's white in color, the F-250's gold."

"What you're telling me is that the sheriff didn't ram Rico that night."

"Maybe not with his own personal vehicle, but that doesn't rule out the possibility of his having used a company car to get the job done. A lot of sheriff's department vehicles are black."

"I wouldn't put anything past Weber," Layne said. "The more we learn about him, the more gnarly he sounds."

"Gnarly. Must be Hawaiian for 'menace to society.'"

"*Shaka, brah,*" she said, smiling, shaking her left hand with her thumb and pinkie outstretched.

I smiled too. "Not to get too corny, but I got you something."

"Hopefully not cheese enchiladas."

I produced a single red rose in a simple glass vase that I'd been hiding under my coat since stopping in at the hospital gift shop downstairs on my way up to Layne's room.

"Sorry it's a little smushed," I said. "The thorns have been stabbing me in the gut. I hope it makes you feel better."

Layne stared at the rose and said nothing.

"I know it's not much, but it's all I could afford."

"No, it's fine. It's beautiful. Really. It's just, honestly, I can't remember the last time anybody bought me flowers."

"I think you mean *flower*," I said. "It's not exactly a bouquet."

She smiled. "Regardless. You're very sweet. Thank you."

"You're welcome. And we're even. I can't remember the last time anybody referred to me as sweet."

She told me the doctor had said that she could expect to remain hospitalized for another three days at a minimum.

"I told him where he could put his three days. I'm busting out of here tomorrow. I can't stand it. This place reeks of illness."

"You're being a bad patient, Layne. Just go along with the program."

"Talk about the pot calling the kettle black. When did 'going along with the program' ever benefit you, Logan?"

I had to admit, she had a point.

Her cell phone began vibrating on the bed stand with an incoming call. "Lex Mutual," it said on the screen. I handed her the phone and watched the smile drain from her face as she listened.

"From Colorado," she said to whoever was on the other end. "Are you sure? . . . Priority overnight. It should have gotten there the next morning . . . Yes, I'm positive . . ." She let out a long slow breath. "OK, we'll see what we can do on this end."

She hung up and slowly lifted her eyes to mine.

"That paint sample we sent in from Angel Falls," she said, "the one you scraped off the Porsche? It never made it to Langley."

"Check the tracking number."

"My people already tried. Postal inspectors said the tracking number doesn't exist. They have no record of me ever mailing anything from Angel Falls."

"Houston," I said, "we have a problem."

VENTURING OUT onto the icy Champ River in hopes of retrieving another sample from Rico Perris's car invited suicide. The only thing left to do was to drive back up to Angel Falls, confront postal clerk Bart Tolks, and force him to spill his guts. That strategy carried its own risks. Sheriff Harlan Weber was in Angel Falls. Were he or one of his deputies to spot me, I'd likely be arrested or, worse, end up down some mine shaft like his alleged accomplice in the coke trade. To avoid being shot down, I'd have to avoid getting caught in his crosshairs—the "kill circle," as we used to call it when I was in the air force. It wouldn't be easy.

Layne was adamant that I not go alone and that I had no idea what I was getting into. The risks, she said, were too great. But the way I saw it, with Tomasello dead, there wasn't much choice. Somebody had murdered him. Somebody had tried to murder us. Any prudent person under similar circumstances would have concluded that that same somebody had murdered Rico Perris and, for all I knew, Joe Zyra, the retired analyst in Phoenix. How many others would die? I didn't want to wait around to find out, or let the killer take another crack at us.

"If you poke a stick at a rattlesnake," I said to Layne, "you *will* get a response. Unless you're prepared to kill the snake immediately, the snake may kill you."

She didn't disagree with me, but again insisted that I wait until she was out of the hospital so that she could back me up.

"You're not getting out of here anytime soon, Layne. You just had surgery. You're in no shape to go chasing bad guys. Relax and get well. I'll see you when I see you."

"What about this detective? He can go with you."

"He'd lose his job. Besides, his wife's having a baby."

"Logan, please, don't do this."

"I'll be OK."

Impulsivity is not usually part of my DNA, nor are spontaneous demonstrations of affection, but there was something about her that begged to be kissed. I leaned over the bedrail, avoided her nasal cannula, and did just that. Layne's full, soft lips were as warm as I'd imagined them to be.

"You still owe me a decent dinner when I get out of here," she said.

"Consider it done."

She was right, of course. I had no idea what I was getting into.

None.

SEVENTEEN

Even I recognized that returning to the mountains and harm's way in the middle of a snowstorm, in the dead of night, as tired and hungry as I was, was asking for trouble. I needed food and sleep. A mile or so away from the hospital on Sixth Avenue, I found a forty-nine-dollar-a-night flophouse called the Capri with an illuminated vacancy sign and three discarded shopping carts out front. Across the street from the motel was a greasy spoon called Eat Me that was still serving. I should have deduced by the name what to expect by way of clientele and menu choices but, like I said, I was tired and hungry.

The restaurant was a collection of Formica-topped, graffiti-carved tables with molded plastic patio chairs and some worn, fake leather banquettes the color of baked beans. Strips of insect paper thick with dead flies hung from water-stained ceiling tiles. Framed prints of the Eiffel Tower and other Parisian scenes hung incongruously from the walls.

The lone waitress on duty was an anorexic punker with a long chin and blue streaks in her spiked hair. She was leaning on her elbows on the counter behind the cash register, engrossed in a copy of the *National Enquirer*. "Anywhere you like," she yawned without looking up at me.

I was the only customer in the joint.

I took a seat at a four-top table facing the entrance and close to the kitchen, where I could exit the building in an emergency if I had to.

She brought over a laminated, one-sheet menu. "Hello, welcome to Eat Me, my name is Bree, I'll be taking care of you this evening," she said in a rehearsed monotone, like it had been beaten into her by management. "Would you care for something to drink?"

"Water, please."

Bree hovered over me with her pen and notebook poised, shifting her weight impatiently from one pencil leg to the other, wearing an expression that suggested she would've rather been anywhere but working at Eat Me.

"Are you ready to order?"

"How's the chili tonight?"

"Fine, if you're planning to commit suicide."

"Thanks for the heads-up. I think I'll have a tuna melt."

She pursed her lips and subtly glanced back at the kitchen, as if to make sure she wasn't being watched. "I'd have to advise against the tuna melt."

The table was sticky, like the menu. "I'm open to suggestion," I said.

"Cheeseburger. It's the only thing that fool back there knows how to make that's halfway any good."

"You know what? I have an excellent idea. I'll have a cheeseburger and fries."

She sighed and went to go place my order.

The burger wasn't bad. I was on my third bite when Sheriff Harlan Weber walked in, accompanied by what I gathered were two of his deputies. All three of the men were out of uniform.

"Anywhere you want," the waitress said, again without looking up from her reading.

Like they knew I'd been there all along, they strolled over and sat down at my table.

"You're a long way from Spruce County, Sheriff. Are you lost?"

He ignored the question and glanced down at my plate, smiling thinly. "Looks tasty," he said, helping himself to some of my fries. "Nothing like a good cheeseburger, eh?"

"This one's a tad overcooked. I've had worse."

I didn't have to ask whether Weber and his boys had tailed me. Clearly they had. I silently cursed myself, my inattention. That would've never happened in my prime.

"You've been running around, asking a lot of folks a lot of questions about me," Weber said. "I don't like it. I don't like that at all."

"What you like or don't is of no interest to me, Sheriff. What interests me is determining how Rico Perris died. That's number one."

". . . Rico Perris?" He furrowed his brow, pretending not to know the name.

"Your assistant scoutmaster. The one who caught you with your hand in the cookie jar."

"I don't what you're talking about."

"I think you do."

He glared. Our waitress showed up.

"Can I start you gentlemen out with something to drink?"

One of Weber's deputies slowly turned his head toward her. He had a crewcut and dark, reptilian eyes.

"Beat it," he said.

"Excuse me. I work here. You can't talk to me that way."

"He said beat it," Weber said.

"OK, that's it. I'm calling the cops."

The other deputy flashed his badge. "We *are* the cops. Now go sit down." He had a long Doberman nose and tiny Doberman ears.

Weber waited until the waitress had taken refuge behind the cash register. "Now, where were we? Oh, yes, right. You were explaining to me what was of interest to you. I believe you were on number two."

I wiped my mouth with my napkin and folded my hands in my lap. "Number two, Sheriff, is putting you on ice if I find out you or any of your people had anything to do with putting my partner in the intensive care unit."

"Are you threatening me, Mr. Logan?"

"Not threatening. Just telling it like it is."

Weber leaned forward on the table and glared at me, his voice low and menacing. "You do realize, don't you, that I could haul your ass outside right now and nobody would ever see you again?"

"You don't want to do that, Sheriff."

"Why don't I? I'm the *law*. I'm the beginning and the ending."

"As well as a movie star." I nodded toward a small digital camera mounted near the ceiling and aimed in our general direction. On the wall below the camera was a sign:

"These premises protected by video surveillance."

The world's greatest grandpa flushed red with rage.

"I want to know who you work for," he said, his jaw clenched, "and I want to know right goddamn now."

"Who I work for doesn't matter. What matters is you doing some soul-searching and coming clean. Things are gonna go a lot easier on you if you do."

"The sheriff asked you a question, asswipe," Deputy Bullet Head said. "Who do you work for?"

He reached for my throat, but not fast enough. I grabbed him under the table by his chicken tenders and squeezed like I was milking Ol' Bessie. He stifled a pathetic choking sound while his eyes bulged.

Deputy Doberman drew his semiauto and leveled it at my head. "Let him go."

"I'm calling 911!" the waitress yelled from behind the register.

My eyes never wavered from Weber's.

"Let's not waste each other's time, Sheriff. The smart play for you would be to confess your crimes—graft, vehicular assault, multiple murders. That way, when they interview me for the federal sentencing report, I could say you were cooperative. But I've got a hunch you're not going to be cooperative this evening, are you?"

"You've got a pair of balls on you, Logan. I'll give you that."

"I'll take that as a compliment."

I squeezed Deputy Bullet Head's pair even harder, until he started to heave.

Weber ordered his other deputy to holster his weapon, pushed back, and stood up. "I would advise you, Mr. Logan, to cease and desist posthaste with all these questions you're asking. I can guarantee you, nothing good will come of them, especially to you. Enjoy the rest of your meal."

He walked out into the snow with Deputy Dobie close in trail. I feared Deputy Bullet Head might pass out as soon as I unsqueezed his acorns, but he didn't. Coughing and wheezing, he somehow got to his feet and staggered out into the night after his boss.

I walked over to the front windows and watched them drive away in a Suburban, black in color.

The waitress was crying and cowering on the floor behind the register with her knees drawn up to her chest.

"They're gone. You OK?"

"Really? You have to ask me that? I thought they were gonna shoot you in the face or something, then me. I've never been so scared in my life. Jesus."

"Crisis averted. C'mon, you're OK."

I helped her up, fished a double sawbuck out of my wallet and told her to keep the change—but not before requesting a box for the rest of my cheeseburger.

Bedding down across the street at the Capri was a no-go. Weber and his crew had likely watched me check into the motel. Who knew if they'd be back? I needed to find more secure quarters, catch a few hours' sleep, and regroup in the morning. I also needed a new rental car considering the minivan had been made.

I drove through the snow around west Denver, making frequent turns without signaling, pulling over and stopping suddenly, constantly checking my mirrors. Nobody was following me. Midnight had come and gone before I found a place to hole up for a few hours. The place wasn't much of an improvement over the Capri, but at least there were no shopping carts out front. The shower had plenty of hot water and the bed springs didn't squeak loud enough that they kept me awake. I found myself thinking of Layne Sterling as I climbed under the sheets and closed my eyes.

MORNING BROKE cold and clear. I let myself doze on and off until close to 0800, a rarity for me, and took my time waking up. I thought about checking with Layne to see how she'd fared in the night. Maybe if the opportunity presented itself

again, I would find some way to tell her that I missed her
and that I wondered if I was starting to have feelings for her.
I didn't want to alarm her with news of my dinner meeting
with Sheriff Weber and his goons. I'd check in with her later.

I showered and dressed. Following a complimentary motel
breakfast of viscous, thirty-weight coffee and a cherry-filled pop-
over whose primary ingredients were chemical preservatives—the
names of which I couldn't pronounce—I set off to exchange
the minivan for a vehicle in which I wouldn't be recognized.

I drove in aimless circles, running yellow lights and stopping every so often on side streets to see who would pass by.
Nobody was following me. The Enterprise office was in a
decidedly working-class business district on West Colfax, next
to a liquor store and across the way from a cannabis shop.
The customer service rep who waited on me appeared to frequent neither. She was a polite young brunette in a dark skirt
of modest length and matching jacket.

"Was there any particular reason you'd like another car,
sir?"

*Yes, actually. I'm hoping to avoid being detected by a suspected
killer up in Angel Falls, where I intend to confront a postal clerk
and find out what happened to an evidentiary paint sample he
was to have mailed to the CIA. Would you, by chance, happen to
have any cars that are bulletproof?*

I didn't say that, of course, even though it would have
been the truth. I laid some line on her about how ancient I
felt driving around and how I preferred a vehicle better suited
to my more sporty nature. This seemed to satisfy her; she
asked no more questions. Ten minutes later, I was back out on
the road, behind the wheel of a metallic gray Dodge Charger.
Not the most snow-friendly car Detroit ever produced, but
without question more sporty and speedier than a minivan.

I knew I needed to beef up my operational cover—to look less like a guy freelancing for an alphabet agency with a borrowed Glock pistol wedged in the small of his back, and more like, well, just a guy. What I needed was a disguise. I found what I was looking for a couple of miles west at a costume shop named, appropriately enough, "Disguises." The store opened at 1000 hours. I was the first customer through the door.

Entire rows were devoted to super hero costumes, monster masks, Halloween decorations, and bags of Halloween candy, even though October had long come and gone. The place was cavernous.

"Can I help you find something?" The clerk was cleverly disguised as a friendly, middle-aged woman with sparkly half glasses and a lopsided smile.

"Yes," I said, "I'm in the market for some facial hair. Beard, moustache, the whole enchilada."

She didn't ask why.

From werewolf to Wolf Blitzer to the "Saddam Hussein Hiding in a Rathole" look, my beard/moustache choices were many. I quickly settled on a neatly trimmed brown number with a distinguished hint of gray. The clerk said I looked as if I'd grown the beard, which hooked snugly over my ears. She said I resembled the actor Hugh Jackman in *Wolverine*. I took it as a compliment anyway.

To enhance my undercoverness, I added a red-and-blue-striped Colorado Avalanche knit ski cap and a pair of Una-bomber-style aviator sunglasses with mirrored lenses, before finishing off the look with a small, clamp-on, fake diamond ear stud. The entire get-up would cost the federal government something slightly south of $100. I made sure to keep the receipt. The clerk was so pleased with having made such a big sale so early in the morning, she threw in a couple of granola bars, which I tucked into my coat pocket.

I'd worn beards and/or moustaches a few times in civilian life, slave that I am to fashion, and shaved them off when I grew bored with the look, or when small animals began finding sanctuary in my whiskers. I'd also grown them in preparation for deployments abroad as accoutrements of going native. *Dishdasha* tunics in Saudi Arabia and Iraq. *Khet partug* and *Sindhi* caps in Afghanistan. More than once in the Middle East, I had needed to pass myself off as female, piously cloaked in a burka and veil. With the exception of those missions where I was compelled to be in touch with my feminine side, growing out my own beard and moustache was part of the deceit. For adult males in many parts of the world, facial fur is *de rigueur*. To be clean-shaven is to stand out. However I'd never had to wear a fake beard before, and this one itched almost as much as my toes had.

I began scratching my face almost as soon as I left the store. I couldn't see out of my new sunglasses to save my life, while the clip-on stud I'd purchased quickly cut off circulation to my earlobe, which began throbbing painfully. The Avs cap, though, did keep my ears plenty toasty, a good thing considering temperatures with the wind chill were hovering in the low teens. I kept the cap in place and removed everything else. I would put the beard and sunglasses back on just before heading into Angel Falls. The torturous ear stud I tossed over my shoulder onto the back seat of the car.

THE PLOWS and sand trucks had done a good job on the highway while the snowstorm faded. Traffic moved at a solid thirty miles an hour. Many of the cars and SUVs that passed me toted skis and snowboards in rooftop racks, their occupants anxious to hit the slopes. I was not without my own anxiousness. In disguise or otherwise, I was aware that spending more time on Sheriff Weber's turf, especially in daylight, invited disaster. My goal was to get in, confront Tolks, the postal clerk, recover the paint sample that I suspected he'd never mailed, and get out. But as with all well-intentioned strategies, this one veered from the expected.

On my previous visit to Angel Falls, Tolks had been alone at the post office. No townsfolk had braved the snow to come in while Layne and I were there. Now, under cold but sunny skies, the building was all but mobbed—a virtually unbroken string of customers dropping off and picking up mail.

I sat on the street in my rental car wearing my Unabomber shades and clawing at my itchy Hugh Jackman beard while pretending to read a copy of the *Denver Post* I'd picked up in the motel lobby. The stream of postal customers never let up.

After nearly an hour, a Spruce County sheriff's Suburban rolled slowly past. My cheap sunglasses and the sun glaring off its windshield prevented me from seeing who was driving, but whoever it was kept going. Whether I'd been taken note of I couldn't say, but I figured better safe than, well, you know. I cranked up the ignition and left.

Confronting Tolks at his place of work had been, in hindsight, a dumb idea. Plan B was to confront him at home. The only problem was, I didn't know where he lived. I jumped on the interstate, removing my sunglasses and that stupid beard, and drove west about twenty minutes until I passed a sign that said, "Now Entering Karius County." Immediately west was the small, Victorian Era tourist trap of Luft, Colorado. Safely out of Sheriff Weber's jurisdiction, I got off the highway and found a café called "Never Close." The sign out front said it offered free Wi-fi service. A booth in the corner afforded moderate privacy. I ordered coffee from a flirty, big-boned waitress with pretty green eyes. After she left, I called Buzz.

I told him I needed him to run an address for me. He said he would, but that he first wanted to pass on the lab results from the paint scraping I'd shipped him the day before.

"Wow, that was fast."

"We're not playing around here, Logan. Langley's wanting updates on this op every ten minutes. Your partner, she's doing OK?"

"Still in the hospital but it looks like she's going to pull through OK."

"Good deal. Losing a skirt that hot would be a bummer. The intelligence community's not exactly known for its good-looking babes, am I right or am I right?"

I said nothing. There was little point in reminding him that he was now a resident of the twenty-first century and that such remarks were considered sexist. Buzz was a relic, a dinosaur. He wasn't going to change.

Lab analysis showed that the transferred paint I'd scraped off the back of the wrecked Subaru could have come from any one of a dozen General Motors-built vehicles. GM did not manufacture Jeeps, which ruled out the likelihood of Cyril Tomasello having been the driver who slammed into Layne Sterling and me. It didn't, however, rule out the possibility of our assailant having piloted a GM-manufactured Chevrolet Tahoe, the type of which I'd seen Weber and company drive away the night before.

I briefed Buzz on my most recent interaction with the sheriff, if only to put the encounter on the official record should anything bad happen to me. He cautioned again about what he said was my impulsivity and sticking my neck out too far. I assured him that wouldn't happen. I knew he didn't believe me.

"I just need that address, Buzz."

"I need a name."

I spelled out "Bart Tolks" for him. He put me on hold.

At the lunch counter across the café, I watched two senior citizens cooing and trading love eyes over steaming mugs of coffee. Her lipstick matched the color of his "Make America Great" baseball cap. They couldn't keep their hands off each other. I was reminded of something Mrs. Schmulowitz once said wistfully while observing a similar scene at the beachside restaurant where I'd taken her for lunch on her birthday: "Oh, to be eighty again."

"You still there, Logan?"

"Still here."

"Your man Tolks shows a post office box in Angel Falls, Colorado."

"No street address?"

"Negative."

"You checked the big data center in Utah?"

"What does this look like, amateur hour at the Bijou? Yes, Logan, we checked. Everything. What do you want me to do, make up an address? The guy shows a PO box."

My only option was to return to downtown Angel Falls and establish a surveillance outside the post office, blocks from the sheriff's office, then follow Tolks home. Every minute I waited there in the open would up the chances of my being discovered and confronted by a corrupt, morally bankrupt civil servant who, if various accounts were to be believed, would stop at nothing to keep hidden his dark secrets. Part of me said don't go. A bigger part of me, however, welcomed the challenge.

The Buddha believed that one should not shrink from but squarely confront the prospect of death. Only then can we truly begin to appreciate the beauty of life and the great cosmic rhythm of the universe. In short order, faced with the end of my own life high in the Colorado Rockies, I would come to know again precisely what that wise man had been talking about.

EIGHTEEN

The Angel Falls post office closed at 1700 hours. The winter sun would set a few minutes before then, with darkness coming soon after that. I would arrive in the gathering twilight, ten minutes before the end of Bart Tolks's workday, thus minimizing my profile and time in Angel Falls as I tailed him home.

With time to waste, I thought I might go skiing. Then I remembered: I don't ski, not with a surgically reconstructed knee held together with more screws than a nightstand from IKEA. But that didn't stop me from finding the nearest ski lodge, another ten miles or so up the highway, and chilling in front of a nice crackling fireplace until duty called.

The central lodge at the Loveland Ski Area was pretty much like every other lodge. A-frame. Big windows with a view of the slopes. I shed my coat, settled into a big comfy armchair, and read my newspaper in earnest. "The World is Coming to an End," was the message every story seemed to convey. So what else was new?

A petite blonde garbed in pink ski bibs and a white turtleneck had just plopped down into the chair next to me and struggled to unbuckle her left ski boot.

"Would you mind doing me a favor? Would you mind helping me get this thing off? I think I really messed something up in there."

"Sure."

She gritted her teeth and grimaced as I pulled with both hands. The boot refused to come off without a fight, but it did eventually.

"Thank you," she said, massaging her ankle.

"No problem. Hope it feels better soon."

I sat back down and returned to my paper.

"You don't look like a skier," she said, "or a snowboarder."

"Could be because I'm neither."

"Do you work here?"

"I don't."

"Then what're you doing here, I mean, if you don't mind me asking?"

I couldn't think of anything to tell her but the truth, which I knew she'd never buy anyway.

"I'm working freelance for the Central Intelligence Agency. We're investigating the recent death of a retired analyst that may or may not be related to the assassination of John F. Kennedy who, by the way, was president long before you were born. I'm just waiting for the sun to go down so I can begin tailing a party of interest in the investigation."

"Cool."

She looked at me the way people do when they think you're nuts, with that kind of disingenuous little nod and half smile that would have you believe they believe you, when in fact they don't believe you at all.

"Well, anyway," she said, getting to her feet, "guess I should go find somebody who can take a look at this ankle. Thanks again for the help."

"Good luck."

Ski boot tucked under her arm, she was hobbling away as quickly as her injury would permit when my phone buzzed in my pocket. Layne Sterling was calling.

"You're still alive."

"Last time I checked," I said. "And you?"

"Coming along."

I didn't tell her about my little set-to of the previous evening with Sheriff Weber. I didn't want to alarm her. I didn't have to tell her where I was—that, she said, she already knew: My location showed up on her phone thanks to the tracking software she'd installed on mine.

"What are you doing at a ski resort? You'd better not be screwing off, Logan," she said, half seriously. "You're still on assignment, you know."

"Thanks for the reminder. I completely forgot."

I told her that because I was in a nonsecure location, I couldn't get into operational specifics, but that I intended to return to Angel Falls that night to confront the postal clerk Tolks.

"We definitely need that paint transfer," Layne said, "unless you're willing to go swimming in that river again."

"Your employers aren't paying me enough."

She didn't disagree.

Her doctors had told her that she could expect to remain in the hospital for another two days at a minimum. She wasn't happy about it.

"Think of it as a vacation," I said. "You've got room service, unlimited access to happy drugs, abundant reading time, and you don't have to worry about anything other than getting back on your feet."

"Smooth. You should be selling used cars. You really should."

"I'd be making more money than I am now."

"Call me in the morning, first thing. I want to know you're OK."

I promised her I would.

I ate a chili dog. Miraculously I managed not to get any on me. I watched skiers and snowboarders riding the slopes down and the chairlifts back up. I napped in front of the fire and dreamed of Savannah. She was still alive and we were lying side by side on some white sand beach under a tropical sun, impossibly iridescent blue waves frothing on the shore. My ex-wife, pregnant with my child—our child—was more radiant than I could ever remember. She was smiling contentedly. Slowly her eyes opened and stared into mine, only they were not her eyes. They were those of a goat, yellow and alien. I gasped awake, my breathing fast and shallow, my heart thumping high in my chest. I blinked the image of her away, rubbing my forehead, and tried to forget.

At 1605 hours, I set off for Angel Falls.

One half hour is what I calculated it would take to get there. I allowed myself forty-five minutes to be on the safe side. That would give me ten minutes on station, waiting for senior postal clerk Bart Tolks to get off work and hoping Sheriff Weber didn't happen by and notice me. Then I would tail Tolks home, crossing my fingers that he lived off alone deep in the woods somewhere, where no one could hear him scream if it came to that. As per usual, however, things didn't go as planned.

An accident—I never did learn the details—had reduced traffic on the highway to a one-lane, stop-and-go crawl. If there were any alternative routes to Angel Falls, they didn't show up on the Dodge's GPS display. I was stuck.

The old me may have fantasized about thumping whoever the idiot driver was who'd caused the accident, who'd knocked me off my schedule along with every other motorist similarly waylaid on that parking lot of a highway. But I didn't. In my albeit thin, Zen-like calm, I turned on the radio and searched for one of those all-news stations that broadcast traffic conditions every few minutes, so that I might know how long I could expect to remain trapped. I quickly found a station out of Denver that reported the conditions of virtually every road in Colorado, with the exception of the one on which I was trapped. I was about to go looking for another station when the announcer reported the following:

"In other news, Denver police have identified the body of a man found stabbed to death last night in an alley behind a lower downtown pool hall as Cyril Tomasello, age sixty-six. Authorities said that Tomasello, back in the early eighties, had worked briefly as a deputy with the Spruce County Sheriff's Department. No suspects have been identified."

Had I been writing a book about it, which I wasn't because, believe me, the last thing I am is a writer, this is the part where I would have said, "The plot thickens." *Tomasello had once worked as a Spruce County sheriff's deputy?* Why hadn't Layne picked this up in the background check she had run on him? What had Tomasello known that had gotten him killed?

Over my back, the sun was departing the day. Traffic inched along. I tried calling Buzz to get him to drill deeper into Tomasello's employment history, but there was no cell signal. Coverage in the mountains could be spotty that way. I took long, slow breaths and remained calm. The Buddha would've been proud.

Twenty-one minutes past closing time, I finally reached the exit for Angel Falls and donned my scratchy bogus beard. I figured I'd probably find the post office closed, but I drove past it anyway because you never know.

Guess what? It was closed.

When I played football, no one ever accused me of being the swiftest receiver on the field, or having the best hands. But few disputed my nose for the ball—that ephemeral quality some guys just have where they somehow *know* the spot where the quarterback is going to heave the pass and find a way to get there. That same innate skill helped me on innumerable occasions sniff out and vaporize often camouflaged ground targets as an A-10 pilot flying close-air support missions in Iraq. As a special operator assigned to Alpha, I came to tap into and trust that same instinct. Now I trusted it again to find Bart Tolks.

He went grocery shopping after work.

I checked the Safeway, the only grocery store in Angel Falls. He wasn't there.

He's having a drink at the Molly B.

I pressed my bearded face against the saloon's front window and peered inside, knowing I also was pressing my luck, a stranger in a strange town. The faces of those few patrons in the bar glanced my way. None of them was Tolks.

He stopped off for a bottle of booze.

Third time's a charm, I told myself as I climbed back into my car, glancing around for any sheriff's vehicles, and headed for the liquor store on the east end of town. I parked out front and made a quick pass inside.

Tolks wasn't there either.

Damn.

The lights were on next door at the Conoco filling station where I'd met Nepalese mechanic Ram Bhattarai on my previous visit to Angel Falls. I could see him sitting inside his office, hunched over his little television set.

I pulled off my beard, shoved it in my pocket, and walked across the street.

"How're you doing, Ram my man?"

"Hey, my man." He pried himself away from the *The Housewives of Whatever* he was watching and gave me a gap-tooth grin. "What's the haps? Flat tire guy, right? How's that thing holding up for you?"

I didn't tell him the car was wrecked. We bumped fists.

"Holding up just fine," I said. "Hey, I need a favor. I'm trying to find a buddy here in town and I think I lost his address."

"Yeah? Who that be, your bud?"

"Bart Tolks. He works over at the post office."

"Yeah, I know that dude real good. Good guy. I work on his piece-of-crap VW all the time. He knows everyone in town, you know?"

"Believe me, I know."

Ram slipped on a pair of reading glasses with black frames and sifted through a desk drawer, thumbing through a stack of repair receipts until he found one with Tolks's name on it.

"Here you go, man," Ram said, handing it to me. "Tell him I said howdy."

BART TOLKS lived in the Dogwood RV & Mobile Home Park along Colorado State Highway 107, about a mile south of Angel Falls. His shiny aluminum Airstream trailer was a noticeable step up from his neighbors' decrepit double-wides, converted buses, and glorified camper shells. The Airstream was dark. He wasn't home.

I pulled in down the road, turned off the ignition, and waited, though not for long. Five minutes later, Tolks's Volkswagen Beetle came putt-putting past me, backfiring like a snare drum. He parked, got out with a stack of magazines under his arm, spit tobacco juice, and hurried inside. Through the parted gingham curtains of his kitchen window, I watched him set the magazines down at his kitchen table and fire up a giant doobie.

He was reading the latest issue of *Motorcycle Mama* when I walked in without knocking.

"*Que pasa*, Bart. We meet again."

"You can't come in here. This is my house. You get out right now!"

He tried to stand. I shoved him back down in his chair. His table was a mess of unopened bills, empty and half-empty pouches of Red Man chewing tobacco, and many magazines. All of the magazines were addressed to other residents of Angel Falls.

"Not until I get a few answers," I said. "First you get high on federal property. Now I find out you're stealing other people's mail? Oh, Bart. I'm so disappointed."

"It's not stealing. It's borrowing. There's a difference, OK?"

I swept the magazines and the bills and the tobacco pouches on the floor to let him know I meant business, pulled out a chair, and sat down uncomfortably close to him, purposely violating his personal space. I could smell the fear on him. It was almost as strong as the Red Man and the marijuana.

"If you recall the first time we met a few days ago, my partner and I came in and mailed a box off to Langley, Virginia. 'Home of the world-famous CIA,' as you so astutely put it. Remember?"

"No."

Spoiler alert: Violence is never condoned except when it is. I grabbed him by his windpipe and squeezed hard enough that he began to gag. "How about now, Bart? Are you starting to remember now?"

He gagged and nodded frantically. I let go. He doubled over, coughing and wheezing.

"Sonofabitch. You didn't have to do that."

"Tell me what happened to the box, Bart."

"I threw it away."

"Why would you do something like that?"

He looked away, nervously rubbing the tops of his thighs with both hands. "I don't know, man. I just did."

"That's not good enough, Bart. 'I don't know' is not an adequate answer. Let's try it one more time, shall we?"

"Can't you please just go?"

I reached for his throat again.

"Yeah, OK, OK," he sputtered, terrified. "I was afraid, all right? Jesus."

"Of who?"

"Who do you think?"

"Sheriff Weber?"

"You don't live here, man. You don't understand."

"Did Weber tell you to throw the box away?"

Tolks shook his head no, staring at the floor. Tossing the box, he said, was his decision alone. He'd made us for federal authorities. The only reason for the feds to have been snooping around Angel Falls, he figured, was if they were probing Weber's activities. Whatever it was we were sending to Langley had to have contained some bit of incriminating evidence. Weber would owe him big time if he knew that Tolks had thrown it away, thus impeding an investigation without ever even having been asked.

"Did you look inside the box?"

"No."

There was little more to be said. I'd run the string. The prospect loomed of having to go back out to that river, onto that ice, and take another paint scraping—assuming the water hadn't swallowed Rico Perris's Porsche whole.

"We're done here, Bart," I said. "Enjoy the rest of your evening."

"You're not gonna arrest me?"

"Just make sure all those nice people get their magazines."

I was nearly out the door when he said, "It's still out in the dumpster, you know. Behind the post office."

"What is?"

"The priority box you mailed. Trash guys don't come for another couple days."

I wanted to kiss him. Well, not really. But you get my drift.

"If you're lying to me, Bart . . ."

"I'm not. I swear. It's in there. You'll need this," he said, getting up and removing a key from a fat chrome ring hanging on a hook near the stove. "Thanks for cutting me some slack."

"No problem."

BEFORE PAPER shredders came along, dumpster diving was intelligence-gathering standard operating procedure. More than a few big league bad guys have been located over the years and neutralized because of actionable leads developed after literally sifting through trash. I've engaged in a few such missions myself. The more desirable ones were always in winter, when the overpowering stench that comes with immersing oneself in someone else's pile of garbage was not nearly as bad as it was in summer. In Angel Falls that night, the temperature was well below freezing, which meant that I didn't have to worry much about the smell.

Tolks had referred to the dumpster in the singular. There were actually two, both overflowing with stacks of newspapers, heaps of bulk advertising flyers, miscellaneous crushed cardboard cartons, and what I assumed were random, undeliverable pieces of mail. I couldn't have asked for a better, more obscured location to dive in. To have seen me, one would've had to walk or drive through the post office parking lot, all the way around the rear of the building, and entered a chain-link enclosure secured by a sturdy padlock, which I had opened. Even then, in the dark, it was all but impossible to see.

Ten minutes is what I estimated it would take to search each dumper for the errant Priority Mail box, but the going was much slower than that. I had to toss out myriad pieces of trash with one hand to survey the refuse below in the faint light of my cell phone. Close to half an hour went by before I finally reached the gunk-encrusted bottom of the first dumpster.

No box addressed to Langley, Virginia.

I exited and returned all the trash I'd thrown out onto the ground because, hey, I may be many things, but no one will ever accuse me of being a litterbug.

As I walked over and began picking through the contents of the second dumpster, I heard the roar of an automobile engine approach at high speed. Standing there, I was illuminated in the blinding high beams of an onrushing vehicle. It drove straight toward me, veering away at the last second and skidding to a stop to avoid the chain-link fence that surrounded the trash enclosure. I could see "Spruce County Sheriff's Department" and the department's logo emblazoned on the Chevy Suburban's passenger door.

I ran for my car, expecting a bullet in my back at any second.

NINETEEN

Americans are fascinated by police pursuits. TV networks break into their regular programming on a regular basis to broadcast them live. We stop what we're doing to watch, even when the pursuit is playing out 2,000 miles away, in places we've never been and never will go. Though most of us are reluctant to acknowledge our species' innate lust for violence, the fact is we watch to witness somebody crash in truly spectacular fashion or, even better, to see them gunned down. But it's a different story, I'm here to tell you, when you're the one being chased.

Note to self: the next time you decide to lead local law enforcement officials on a chase in the dark over the wintry back roads of Colorado's High Country, make sure you do it in a rental car with all-wheel drive, not one that slips and crabs on the snow like a school kid going down a waterslide. The Dodge Charger was all over the place. Every icy curve boded disaster.

I didn't know whether Sheriff Harlan Weber himself or one of his deputies was behind the wheel of the Suburban riding my tail—all I could see when I glanced up, squinting, into my rearview mirror were the vehicle's blinding high beams and its roof-mounted lights pulsating red and blue. What I was certain of, though, was that the pursuit would end badly for me if I didn't shake him, and soon.

That I'd been schooled in evasive driving tactics while enjoying my previous occupation proved of little benefit. My pursuer exhibited consistently excellent reflexes and anticipation. When I slowed down, he slowed down. When I accelerated, he did, maintaining two car lengths between us.

I knew he was waiting for me to lose control, to spin out and hit a tree, or maybe plunge off the edge, the way Rico Perris had met his end. I also knew I was running out of time. He would not wait indefinitely. At some point, when rage got the better of him, he would accelerate and ram me from behind. Or maybe he would move in closer, roll down his window, and open fire. Take your pick. For a lawless cop, either option worked well. Out there in the deep dark forest, miles from civilization, there were no witnesses—the human kind anyway.

As I fishtailed around a sharp bend, carrying too much speed and with too little warning, the beams of my headlights picked up the eerie red glow of wild animal eyes. Standing his ground defiantly in the middle of the road, mere meters ahead, was a massive bull elk and three of his cows.

I spun the wheel reactively, hard right, and somehow managed to avoid hitting any of them, but lost control of the car. I could feel the front end start to wobble as the tires lost contact with the road surface. At that point, I was no longer the pilot. I was a mere passenger, along for the ride. I won't repeat the irreligious idiom I blurted out at that moment, but let's just say it wasn't, "Cheese and crackers."

The Dodge rotated 180 degrees, trading ends, and slid down a shallow gully going backward before coming to rest unscathed against a cushioning snowdrift.

That's one I owe you, Buddha.

Whoever was driving the sheriff's vehicle wasn't so fortunate.

As he rode my bumper, my car apparently blocked his view of the elks. When I spun out evasively, he'd had even less time to react and less distance to avoid slamming into the herd. Reflexively, my pursuer cut his wheel sharply as I had—only too sharply given his vehicle's high center of gravity. His left front tire gripped the snow laterally and the SUV rolled—three times by my count—coming to rest on its roof. Spooked but otherwise unharmed, the big bull and his harem bolted for the safety of the pines.

A true humanitarian would've rushed to render aid. I wasn't exactly looking for a Nobel Prize, however. As far as I was concerned, this guy or guys (I still couldn't see from where I was sitting how many people were in the SUV) had just tried to kill me. Besides, help already was on the way. I could hear multiple sirens approaching from the direction of Angel Falls. Those cops would do to me what dirty lawmen have always done when they catch criminal suspects who've run from them. Away from the public's prying eyes, adrenaline and testosterone pumping, they would beat me like a tambourine.

I slammed the gear shift between drive and reverse, rocking the Dodge out of the snow, and got the hell out of there.

The road hugged the side of a mountain. I wasn't sure exactly where I was, though I knew I was moving west, away from Angel Falls, and roughly paralleling the Champ River. I could periodically make out its icy path below me as patches of clouds gave way to moonlight. The landscape began to look familiar. I was not far from where Rico Perris had gone over the edge.

I wasn't worried about whatever manufactured criminal charges might arise from my having gone dumpster diving behind the post office and run from local law enforcement. Buzz and Uncle Sugar would resolve all that behind the scenes. Of that I was convinced. First things first: I needed to continue heading west, get out of Spruce County, and ditch the Dodge. After that, I'd regroup and find a way to nail Sheriff Weber, with or without an evidentiary paint scraping from Rico Perris's Porsche.

Nobody was behind me or on my nose. For about thirty seconds I breathed a little easier—until I caught sight of flashing red and blue lights reflecting off the mountainside, just beyond the bend, about a mile ahead of me—more cops coming my way.

A side road appeared on my right. With no other options, I slowed down, flicked off my lights and took it, rumbling across a steel cattle guard. Soon I was into the pines.

Lucky for me, the road had been freshly plowed. Snow was heaped on either side higher than the door handles of my car. Without headlights, the sensation was of negotiating a darkened bobsled run. I stayed off the brakes for fear of illuminating my taillights, ricocheting off piles of snow to manage my speed, glancing up every couple of seconds in my rearview mirror. I fully expected to see those red and blue flashers coming after me, but they didn't.

That was two I owed the Buddha.

I passed by a couple of ranch houses with lights on inside. Wood smoke rose invitingly from their chimneys. Beyond those outposts, the mountains slumbered dark and tomb silent under their white blanket. There was something comforting in it, surrounded by all of that *nothing* when so many people were after me.

One road gave way to another, and another after that. Barbed-wire fences. Trees. Snow. I drove aimlessly, without landmarks. Occasionally roads would intersect and there would be signs indicating route numbers, but I could find little value in them, nothing that distinguished east from west, north from south. The night sky could've easily turned me in the right direction—the two outer stars of the bowl of the Big Dipper pointed straight to Polaris and true north. But hidden from view by clouds and the granite peaks that towered around me, not a single star appeared.

I was lost.

Then, just like that, I wasn't.

Ahead and to the right was yet another road, perpendicular to the one on which I was driving. A wrought iron sign mounted on two telephone poles hung over the road, connoting the entrance to "Rocky Ridge Ranch."

Dr. Samantha McBride's place.

Florescent "Private Property, No Trespassing" signs were nailed to each pole. I ignored them.

I drove around behind her weathered, oversized barn and parked. No one would see the car there, even from the road. She didn't appear to be home, but, Cuddles, her dog, was. I could hear him barking angrily inside the cabin, even before I stepped out.

"Good job, Cuddles. Way to defend the fort."

The dog continued barking while I found an unlatched window next to the front door, which was locked, removed the screen, and climbed in.

Cuddles backed up, baring his teeth and growling, low and mean.

"Relax, big guy, we're buddies, remember?"

He didn't remember. Not at all. His ears were back. His fur was up. He looked like he was giving serious thought to taking a big chunk out of my leg. Not until I tossed him one of the granola bars that had been in my coat pocket since visiting that costume shop down in Denver did he seem to recall our relationship. Immediately we were best friends.

I sat down on the sofa and watched him chew. His tail never stopped wagging. Granola, I decided, is wasted on people.

"WHAT IN the world?"

Sam McBride wasn't happy to see me. I can't say I blamed her. Nobody likes coming home and finding an uninvited guest in her living room, clutching a dish rag and engaged in a spirited game of old sock tug of war with her guard dog.

"I happened to be in the neighborhood. Thought I'd drop in."

"You don't expect me to believe that, do you?"

"Cuddles did."

He trotted over to greet her. She ignored him.

"How'd you get in?"

"Opened a window. Then I bribed your furry friend."

"C'mon, boy." She let the dog outside to relieve himself. A chill wind whistled in as she stood in the open doorway. "I take it that's your car behind the barn?"

"It is."

"You must've done something."

Cuddles hustled back inside. McBride closed the door, then slipped off her woolen scarf and shearling coat and hung them on her hall tree. She was wearing green surgical scrubs underneath.

"I'm not sure what you mean," I said.

She dumped some cordwood into the fireplace and struck a match to it. "What I mean is, it's night, it's late. I just drove

home from work through Angel Falls. There's sheriff's deputies all over down there, stopping traffic with their guns out.
You show up at my house unannounced and park behind my
barn, like you're running from something. I'm thinking maybe
you need to tell me what's going on, the truth, or maybe I'm
just going to have to call those cops and have them come
up here."

"Have a seat," I said. "This could take awhile."

We sat on either ends of her sofa. I told her about Rico
Perris and Sheriff Weber. Not everything, but enough. Her
eyes got a little wider when I got to Weber's questionable connection to the Kennedy assassination and the long-classified
documents that had gone missing from the National Archives.

"This is amazing," she said. "You're telling me that this
guy who died in the Porsche, Perris, he used to be a CIA
agent?"

"Not an agent. Agents are typically foreigners who freelance. If you're a full-time agency employee, you're either a case
officer forward-deployed, gathering intelligence and recruiting
agents for spying purposes, or you're an intelligence analyst
back at headquarters, standing watch and riding a desk. Perris
was an analyst. A good one, by all accounts."

She grunted enigmatically. I followed her into the kitchen
and watched her remove a blue ceramic baking dish of lasagna
from a yellow, 1950s-era Frigidaire refrigerator.

"So you're a case officer?"

"Not me. I'm just hired help."

"I knew the minute I met you that you didn't work for
any insurance company," McBride said. "You see too much."

She slid the dish into a cast iron oven that more than
matched the age of her refrigerator. Cuddles came over and
sat on my shoes.

"Thanks for not turning me in," I said.

"You're going to love my lasagna," she said. "It's the best in the world."

A GLOPPY, tasteless, meatless mess is perhaps the only way to describe what came out of the oven forty-five minutes later. I didn't complain. Food is food when you're in the field, even when you have to convince your stomach that it is, in fact, food.

We dined by candlelight. The napkins were linen and matched the placemats. The silverware was, indeed, silver and the dinnerware was Wedgewood china. Samantha McBride, MD, may have been no Julia Child, but she did set a mean table.

"Delicious," I said, forcing down another bite.

"You don't like it, do you? What's wrong with it?"

"Nothing's wrong with it."

"You're lying. I can see you don't like it." She snatched my plate away.

"It's not that I don't like it. It's just . . ."

"It's just *what*?" The muscles in her jaw were pulsating. "I don't mind criticism. What I can't stand is when somebody is just mean for the sake of being mean. Do you have any idea how hard and how long I worked on that lasagna?"

"You're misunderstanding me, Sam. It's good. Very tasty."

". . . You're not just saying that?"

"Not at all."

"My mother's recipe," she said.

"Nice."

Slowly I reached over, took my plate back, and forced down another horrid bite, hoping my expression didn't let on how horrid. I didn't want her kicking me out into the cold.

"I've always been fascinated by President Kennedy," she said. "Because my mother was."

"Kennedy loved lasagna. It was his favorite."

"Is that true?"

"Well, if it's not, it ought to be."

I waited for her to smile, but she didn't. More uncomfortable silence followed. If this was supposed to be some sort of first date, as I suspected McBride believed it was, it clearly wasn't going well.

"So," she said, "Sheriff Weber worked for the mob in his younger days, the mob killed Kennedy at the behest of the CIA, and Weber killed Rico Perris because Perris held secrets that would verify what was in these documents that have gone missing? That's got national best seller written all over it."

"I didn't say that," I said.

"Then why would Weber have killed Perris?"

"I don't know."

"I do," she said. "It makes complete sense."

"What does?"

"The connection to Kennedy."

When I glanced up from my plate, Sam McBride was smiling.

She wouldn't tell me at first what she knew or how she knew it, only that the answers I was seeking could be found at the Dumont County Courthouse, located in Draperton, some thirty miles up Interstate 70.

"It's all right there," McBride said. "Everything you need to know."

"Help me out here, Sam. I'd need a little something more to go on than that."

"Look up a file on Aideen Fitzgerald."

"OK, Aideen Fitzgerald. What about Aideen Fitzgerald?"

"She took out a restraining order against Sheriff Weber about a year ago. There was a big write-up about it in the local newspaper."

Sam McBride was staring at me expectantly, like light bulbs should've been going off in my head. They weren't.

"You don't get it," she said.

"I'm afraid I don't."

What, I wondered, was so relevant about *Aideen Fitzgerald*? Then it hit me: Fitzgerald—the F in John F. Kennedy.

"She was President Kennedy's cousin," McBride said. "Harlan Weber tried to kill her too."

TWENTY

After helping with the dishes, I bunked with Cuddles that night on Sam McBride's sofa. The cabin quickly turned cold when the flames petered out in her fireplace, but I was plenty toasty with only a top sheet and thin cotton blanket. Who needs a down comforter when you have a ninety-pound mutt that insists on using you as a mattress, one that you have to fend off periodically because he keeps trying to lick your face? How Cuddles got his name was no longer a mystery.

I worried that McBride was going to invite me to share her bed, and how I would diplomatically decline, but the offer never came. She intuited that my romantic interest in her was nil and retired for the evening at 2200 with a terse, "Good night." I was relieved. With the Spruce County Sheriff's Department on the lookout no doubt for my rental car and me, I would need her Volvo if I hoped to make the drive undetected the next day to the courthouse in Draperville, or have her chauffeur me there. I'd wait until morning to make the request.

Even with a dog on top of me, sleep came surprisingly easy. Outrunning the police can tucker a man out.

Morning arrived all too quickly with the clacking of an electric typewriter. I opened my eyes to find the dog sleeping on the floor, the fireplace roaring, and a frustrated McBride at her desk, even more taciturn than usual. She was struggling to make progress on her current writing project, she said, a sequel to her last. I should've asked what it was about, but I didn't. I was still exhausted.

"There's coffee in the kitchen."

"Any chance I could borrow your car today?"

She stopped typing and looked over, surveying me coolly. "Typical male. All you do is take, don't you?"

"I'm happy to pay you."

"You mean the government's happy to pay me."

She huffed a sigh, got up from her desk, and tossed me a key ring from a peg near the door.

"It's out front," she said, returning to her desk. "My other vehicle's in the barn. I can take it to work this afternoon."

"Thanks, Sam. I appreciate it."

Zero response. I got up and pulled on my coat. When I left, she was still typing.

COLD, BRILLIANT sunlight bathed the Rockies. But for sporadic patches of snow and ice that clung stubbornly to its shadowed curves, the highway was wide open. Traffic was light. I observed no cops along the way.

The Dumont County Courthouse dominated a small public square ringed by ornate wrought iron fencing at the west end of downtown Draperton. The courthouse itself featured three stories of cut gray granite blocks braced by two handsome turreted spires. A pair of Civil War-era howitzers flanked the entrance. Inside, a grandmotherly type wearing a hand-knitted sweater adorned with snowmen raised her eyebrows knowingly as she handed me the file I'd requested. Her desk plate identified her as Jean Rousseau, Deputy Clerk of the Court.

"Some good reading in there," she said. "Enjoy."

"Thanks."

There was nowhere to sit. I stood at the counter, opened the manila file folder, and read.

The records detailed how Fitzgerald, single and twenty-five years Weber's junior, had entered into a brief and tumultuous relationship with the sheriff, who'd wooed her with false promises of a high-level, well-paying administrative job within his department. The affair, she alleged, soon turned violent. Weber grabbed and slapped her when they argued, which was often. Sometimes he'd punch her with a closed fist, leaving bruises and once breaking teeth. After she ended it he'd allegedly come storming into Premier Mountain Estates, the Draperville real estate office where she worked as a sales agent, and, gun drawn, he threatened to kill her.

Despite at least one witness who confirmed Fitzgerald's version of events, Dumont County Sheriff Todd T. Linhart refused to arrest his Spruce County counterpart because of what Aideen Fitzgerald complained was professional courtesy. A district court judge in Draperville with no such allegiances subsequently granted her request. It mandated that Weber have no contact with Fitzgerald and that he remain at least 1,000 feet away from her at all times or risk immediate arrest.

Sam McBride had said that "everything" I needed to know would be found in the file. She was wrong. I derived nothing of use from it. I slid the file back across the counter.

"Can I ask you a quick question?"

The deputy clerk smiled. "Sure."

"Somebody told me that the woman who was granted this restraining order, Ms. Fitzgerald, is a cousin of John F.

Kennedy. You wouldn't happen to know anything about that, would you?"

"May I ask what your interest is in the case?"

To be an effective operator, I learned early on, is to sometimes play fast and loose with the truth. Never let the facts stand in the way of finding and neutralizing a high-value target. So it was during my visit to Draperville, Colorado. I made up a story on the fly because the truth of my assignment only would have frightened townsfolk like Jean Rousseau while blowing my cover in the process.

"I'm an independent television producer from Los Angeles. We're doing a documentary series called, *Relatable.* The show is about people who lead ordinary lives and are related to famous individuals in history."

"From Los Angeles. A TV show. Wow, how exciting."

"We hope so."

Jean Rousseau didn't know much more than what I'd already gleaned from the file. Aideen Fitzgerald, she said, was long-rumored to have been a blood relative of the late president—she certainly *told* people she was—but whether she actually was, nobody in town could be certain.

"Nice gal. I will tell you this, though," Rousseau said, leaning her elbows on the counter and lowering her voice, like she was letting me in on our little secret. "She used to joke about how everybody in her family knew who *really* killed the president but were too afraid to go public because they thought they may be next."

"You say she *used* to joke. You make it sound like she's no longer around."

"Aideen? Yeah, I really couldn't tell you what happened to her. Haven't seen her around here for a while. She used to sell a lot of houses. You might want to check Premier Mountain

Estates. It's just across the way. Gloria Gatley's the receptionist over there. Nice lady. Been there forever."

Satchel Paige, the great baseball player, once said, "Don't look back. Something might be gaining on you." It's precisely for that reason I make a habit of looking back. Walking out of the Dumont County Courthouse that morning, I saw that Jean Rousseau had picked up the handset of a green desk phone and was speaking somberly to someone with her hand cupped over her mouth. Her nonsmiling glance directed my way gave me pause. Was she calling Gloria to give her a heads-up that a famous television producer was in town and wanted to interview her? Or was she calling men with badges and guns, alerting them that I was in town.

I would find out soon enough.

A COMMEMORATIVE brass plaque mounted near its front door stated that Premier Mountain Properties was once the home of Draperton's first haberdashery that had opened for business in 1888, before all the gold and silver ore played out. Displayed in the front windows were color collages of real estate for sale in the surrounding hills, from raw land to timbered estates.

Jean Rousseau was right. Friendly didn't begin to describe receptionist Gloria Gatley, who could've passed for the actress Betty White's twin. "Chatty" and a "tangential thinker" were other words that also applied.

"I was sitting right here because, let's face it, I love my job. I saw the whole thing. The gun. The look on his face. Oh, he was so angry. I'll tell you what, my heart was going a mile a minute. She calmed him down though, Aideen did. Such a sweet lady. Deserved better. Some women have such

bad luck with men, you know? My younger sister, Velma, she
married this crazy Brazilian who secretly liked dressing up in
her clothes. She came home from work one day and he—"

"I don't mean to interrupt you, Gloria," I said, which was
exactly what I meant to do because I would've been there all
day otherwise, "but I'm wondering if you know where I could
find Aideen? It's very important."

"And you say you're from what show? I just love *Dancing
with the Stars*, by the way. I could watch that show all night.
Not too crazy about *America's Got Talent*. Some of those
people, whew, they—"

"It's called *Relatable*. It's not on the air yet."

"I see. OK, well, so anyway, you want to know about
Aideen."

Conversing with Gloria was like keeping a sailboat on
course in a stiff crosswind, but I did eventually glean some
relevant details. Aideen Fitzgerald, she said, was indeed JFK's
second cousin in the labyrinth of a family tree so root-bound,
it defied untangling, even as Gloria tried her best to explain
who was related to whom. More significantly, she also revealed
that Aideen had left Draperton shortly after the bust-up with
Harlan Weber and at last report was living somewhere down
outside Angel Falls with her new boyfriend, a "very nice"
retired federal worker named Rico Perris.

"Sorry, what did you say her boyfriend's name was?"

"Rico Perris."

I asked her what Aideen looked like: Tall, brunette,
refined, high cheekbones—the woman she described could've
just as easily been Alessandra Munoz.

"Wait, hold the phone, if I'm not mistaken," Gloria said,
swiveling in her chair and rummaging through her desk, "I
do believe I have a picture of her here somewhere. Realtors
convention down in Denver last summer. You can't believe

the buffet table. Shrimp. Crab. These little toast thingies with
goat cheese. All you can eat. *So* delicious. We both must've
gained twenty pounds. Yes, OK, here we go."

She handed me a glossy copy of *Colorado Realtors* magazine, opened to a page of several photographs of various par-
tyers under the headline, "Rockin' It Realtor Style!" One of
the photos showed two women lounging poolside flaunting
margarita glasses and half-snockered grins. One of them was
Betty White's lookalike, whose desk I was standing over.

The other woman without question was Alessandra Munoz.

"You don't look too good," Gloria said.

My head may not have been spinning, but my gut was.
I'd been on a snipe hunt, running in circles, chasing my tail.
I was, I realized, no further along in determining who killed
retired CIA analyst Rico Perris—if, in fact, he was killed—
than where Layne Sterling and I had started.

"Would you like a glass of water? Some crackers maybe
to settle your stomach? We have some saltines around here
somewhere. I personally prefer Ritz even though they do stick
to my dentures, but you know, most people, they don't—"

"I'm good, thanks."

I handed Gloria back her magazine, thanked her for her
time, and left.

The air outside was bracing. It helped clear my head.
What I concluded was hardly inspiring: I didn't need this. I
didn't need any of it. Yes, I wanted to find and punish whoever had put Layne in the hospital, but the ultimate explanation of Perris's fate remained of little concern to me. I would
call Layne Sterling and tell her I was done, that her people
needed to put somebody fresh on the case who was smarter
than me and who truly gave a damn. With or without her
in my life, I would return to Rancho Bonita, back to my
unappreciative cat and my decrepit airplane, back to teaching

bored housewives and spoiled rich kids how to fly. Anything had to be less vexing and frustrating than this.

And yet I knew in the same breath I could never do that and still look at my unpleasant mug in the mirror. If I learned anything on the football field and the field of battle, it's that you don't quit. Ever. Not until the mission is complete. Especially when a woman like Layne was depending on me.

I would find Aideen Fitzgerald aka Alessandra Munoz or whatever name she was now going by. I would extract the truth from her.

✈ ✈ ✈

"It's about time," Layne said over the phone. "You said you were going to check in with me first thing, Logan. Or did you forget?"

I was sitting in Samantha McBride's borrowed Volvo outside the Dumont County Courthouse. I could hear hospital noises in the background over the phone. Monitors beeping. Doctors being paged.

"No, I didn't forget, Layne. Things got somewhat busy, that's all."

"Did you at least find out whatever happened to the box we mailed from a certain location?"

"It's gone," I said.

"What do you mean, it's gone?"

"I mean, we'll have to figure out a way to get another paint sample."

Her disapproving silence was followed with a sigh. "Well, what progress *have* you made?"

"Tons. I'll brief you on everything when I see you."

I won't dispute that I was misleading. But the woman was recovering from surgery. What else was I supposed to say?

She was more forthcoming with me than I had been with her. She'd spoken, she said, with Jason Brannigan, her fellow CAM case officer who had been assigned to investigate the death in Arizona of Rico Perris's former CIA colleague, Joe Zyra. Brannigan had run into his own roadblocks. He'd been unable to link Zyra's death to anything associated with the JFK assassination or the Red Lancer task force. Those close to him, his widow and adult children, his friends and neighbors, to a person were unaware of his having received any threats of violence in the weeks leading up to his death. And he had no known enemies. By all indications, he'd taken an after-dinner stroll and been the victim of an unfortunate accident.

"I've apparently developed some sort of minor infection," Layne said. "They want to keep me in here another day at least, until they can get whatever it is under control."

"That's good. You just can't rush these things."

"Easy for you to say."

I forced a chuckle. I wanted to tell her something, but I couldn't.

"What is it?" she asked me.

"What'd you mean?"

"I mean, you sound like the cat's got your tongue."

"It's just that . . ." I cleared my throat. "I miss you, that's all."

"Are you just saying that to make me feel better?"

"Good call. Exactly."

She laughed. "Thank you. I feel *so* much better."

"You miss me?"

"Yeah, Logan, I do."

"Good. That's definitely a start."

"Yes, it is. Listen, I've gotta go. The vampires are here. They want to draw more blood. Every six hours. Ridiculous.

You'd think they would use the old stuff. Just be safe out there, Logan, OK?"

"You be safe too," I said.

"Roger that." The line went dead.

Who can say where love begins? Not me. I'm the last guy to articulate those kinds of feelings, let alone be in touch with them. But I did know that I felt something deep for this woman.

And that was a definite start.

CHICKENS AREN'T the only animals that come home to roost. You can count people too. It's one of the first rules of human behavior you learn when hunting humans. Those on the run tend to gravitate toward comfort and shelter. When it comes to either or both, Dorothy Gale, she of *The Wizard of Oz* fame, was correct: There's no place like home. Operating on that basis, I returned to Rico Perris's cabin in the woods above Angel Falls in search of Aideen Fitzgerald, or Alessandra Munoz as she apparently preferred of late.

It was snowing again, lightly, but the interstate had been plowed, and I made good time from Dumont County. Again I encountered no sheriff's cars. From about 300 meters, I observed an old, brown, rust-bucket Olds 88 negotiating the narrow private road that led perpendicularly from the cabin. It stopped before it reached the two-lane county highway. The driver got out to shut the gate behind her. My timing could not have been more perfect. As the Buddha said, sometimes it's better to be lucky than good.

It was Alessandra.

I floored the gas pedal. The station wagon accelerated like a cinder block. My plan was to swing in and block her from getting out on the highway, but she seemed to sense me coming. She glanced over her shoulder, quickly forgot all about the gate, jumped back in behind the wheel of the Olds, and took off.

Down the highway we raced.

I couldn't help but wonder. Fifty miles an hour turned into sixty, then seventy. Even on dry roads, such speeds would have been imprudent. On snow and ice, they were damn near suicidal.

Suddenly she fishtailed off the county highway, busting through barbed wire and onto a ranch road that led higher into the mountains. I stayed right with her as we twisted through what quickly became a canyon flanked on either side by steep walls.

I never saw the avalanche coming.

TWENTY-ONE

The jostling felt like severe turbulence in the air, only the roar was louder and it seemed to last forever, even though it was no more than a few seconds. The violence ended as quickly as it began and I found myself floating in black silence. I could hear my heart pounding in my ears. I could feel the panic rising. I had no idea how many feet of snow the Volvo was buried under. I had no idea which way was up or down. All I knew was that I was in deep trouble.

Think, Logan. Focus.

First things first, I told myself. Practice your combat breathing. Suck in some air for four seconds, exhale for four seconds. Send some extra oxygen to the old mainframe. Slow your pulse rate down and take command of your situation.

Had my circumstances been less dire, I might've laughed. How often in my academic and military lives had I sat in some classroom or attended some field training course and paid zero attention because I thought I'd never need to apply whatever it was I was ostensibly being taught? Avalanche survival had fallen squarely in that category.

Any number of instructors had spent weeks seeking to battle-proof my fellow special operator wanna-bees and me on how to live through any number of improbable catastrophes:

Tornados, hurricanes, floods, lightning strikes, runaway trains, bear attacks, venomous snake bites, the zombie apocalypse. OK, maybe not the zombie apocalypse, but just about every other disaster imaginable. I thought back then what a giant, pointless time-suck most of it all was, how my day would've been better spent on the shooting range honing my marksmanship, or learning the fastest way to kill someone with a knife. But it's amazing what can come bubbling back up to the surface in a moment of crisis, the obscure lessons you thought you never absorbed but apparently did.

I somehow remembered that snow makes an excellent insulator. Lest I die of trapped carbon monoxide, which will kill faster than a lack of fresh air, I located the ignition and turned off the Volvo's engine.

I remembered to spit and felt the saliva drool down my chin. This told me I was sitting upright and that the station wagon was still on its wheels. A good thing.

I remembered that unless you're being shot at in the dark, there is no better assessment tool than *not* being in the dark. I reached up and switched on the dome light.

The good news was that the windows had remained intact. The bad news was that all of them were completely covered over with snow. Opening one and digging my way out, I knew, invited instant death. Real avalanches aren't like movie avalanches. The snow isn't fluffy powder. It's got the consistency of wet cement that can pour in and suffocate you.

Sitting there, entombed in that Volvo, was not an unpleasant experience, as odd as that might sound, nor even unfamiliar. In some ways, the sensation was of instrument flying, when your airplane is in the soup and the entire universe is cocooned within the interior of your cockpit. There's something womb-like in the feeling, even comforting. Once I determined that I was in one piece and had not yet met my immediate expiration date, I started to relax a little.

But not for long.

Like an earthquake, more roaring and a second round of violent shaking rocked my world—the weight of the snow settling around the station wagon, I assumed, or more falling on top of it. All I could do was hold on and ride it out. The roar faded quickly as the shaking subsided. Once again, I was immersed in silence.

Any competent military tactician knows that inaction is the worst action. The worst thing you can do in a crisis is to do nothing at all. My training and my field experience had taught me the value of a three-pronged battle plan—the "Rule of Three," as we used to call it when I was with Alpha. Establish a list with the most viable solution first, then run through your options.

Option One: My phone. I tried but could get no cell service.

Option Two: I tapped out an SOS on the Volvo's horn repeatedly but heard nothing in response. This brought me to my third option:

Saving myself.

Waiting for help was a nonstarter. Whether I lived or died, I now realized, was up to me. I undid my shoulder belt and went rummaging through the station wagon, crawling over seatbacks, in search of anything that might help me get out.

A shovel, I knew, would've been too much to ask for. Suffice it to say there was none. What there was, I discovered, was a forty-pound bag of dried dog food and several petrified french fries—at least I wouldn't starve to death before I froze or suffocated. There was a plastic snow scraper, snow chains, some old medical text books, a laminated road map of the

Desert Southwest, and a pair of women's hiking boots embedded with what looked to be cactus needles. In the storage compartment under the carpet, behind the rear seat, I found a spare tire jack. The accompanying crank handle was about two feet long and solid steel.

Bingo.

Ever so slowly, I rolled down the right rear passenger window about three inches. Some snow fell into the car, but not enough worth mentioning. To my great relief, the walls of my tomb didn't collapse in on me. The glass held against the outside pressure of the snowpack.

I extended one end of the jack handle through the opening and began probing out and up, gently pushing snow aside, carving a channel about as wide as the barrel of a baseball bat.

At first the effort seemed beyond futile. I had no way of knowing whether I was under five feet of snow or fifty. But then, faintly, the snow at the far end of the channel I'd carved began to brighten.

You're imagining things, Logan.

Wishful thinking, I told myself. Only I wasn't.

I could hear muffled yelling. And a dog barking.

"Down here!" I yelled.

I hit the ignition and beat out a drum solo on the station wagon's horn.

The yelling and barking grew louder, closer. Something metallic began clanging on the roof. Then another jarring bang and several more after that—the blades of shovels and spades, digging frantically. Twenty minutes later, with enough snow cleared, I rolled down the driver's window as far as it would go and crawled out.

Waiting for me on the surface, about three feet above the roof of the station wagon, were two lanky cowboys in their early twenties and their extremely excited Australian shepherd. One of the men extended a hand and helped pull me out.

"I can't thank you enough, fellas."

"Bodie was the one who found you," the shorter of the two said, removing his battered Stetson to wipe away the sweat. He nodded toward the dog. "He was the one who sniffed you out."

"Thanks, Bodie." I got down on one knee and tried to pet him but he kept running around in circles and wouldn't stop barking.

Alessandra Munoz was standing there, fingers clasped anxiously to her mouth as if she'd been praying.

"Thank God. Are you OK?"

I told her I was.

She had glanced up in her mirror, she said, just as the snowslide came rumbling down the mountain behind her, sweeping me under. The two ranch hands, who'd been branding cattle in a corral just up the road with their dog, had also witnessed the slide. They were already coming on the run to save me, shovels in hand, before Alessandra turned around and doubled back.

Grateful for their help, I tried to slip them each twenty dollars—all the money I had left in my wallet—but they refused to take it.

"Just leave the keys in the ignition," the shorter one said, spitting tobacco juice.

They needed to go finish up their work in the corral, the shorter one said, then they'd be back to make quick work of digging the Volvo out of the snow. His partner suggested that rather than standing around and getting cold after having endured such a traumatic experience, Alessandra might want to drive me down into Angel Falls where I could enjoy a beer or three at the Molly B while soothing my jangled nerves.

I wasn't about to tell him that Angel Falls was an extremely bad idea.

"You sure I can't pay you guys for your time and trouble?"

"No, sir," said the taller one. "Not a penny. You'd do the same for us."

I'd like to think I would've. We all would. I shook their leathery hands and watched them return to their corral. Bodie never stopped barking.

The sun was shining but the air was cold. I shoved my hands in the pockets of my coat and shifted my weight. I could feel Layne's Glock still wedged in the small of my back. Carry a gun long enough and you sometimes forget it's there.

"Why'd you run, Alessandra?"

"I thought you were him. Then I saw you weren't. He's a monster. You know that, right?"

"You mean Sheriff Weber?"

She nodded.

"I don't work for an insurance company," I said.

"So I'm not getting any money, am I?"

"I'm afraid not."

Again she nodded, this time to herself, like she knew all along it was a lie. "So, then, if I might ask, who do you really work for?"

"I can't tell you that. All I can tell you is that I really need to talk to you, and I really need you to be honest with me. It's important. Lives depend on it."

When I glanced over at her, she was staring at me hard.

"This is about when Rico worked for the CIA, isn't it?"

✈ ✈ ✈

SHE'D LIED about not knowing her late boyfriend was a spook. She had also lied about not having anywhere to stay. We took back roads to what she described as her "safe haven"—a ski condo some ten miles outside of Draperton that she said was owned by a childhood friend who was out of state and for whom she occasionally house-sat.

"Rico never told me specifically what he did, his actual job," Alessandra said as we parked and walked in, "but he did tell me he was a spy. He was proud of it. He just told me to not ever tell anybody else. There's a fine line between the good guys and the bad guys, and you never know who's who on any given day. That's what he used to say all the time."

I couldn't disagree with his thinking.

The condo sat just across the Spruce County line, a studio on the second floor of a twelve-unit complex that looked like a converted roadside motel, the kind that used to offer free color TV back when everything was black-and-white. The interior was dorm-room sparse. A double bed. A plaid recliner. Table and chairs. Framed color photos of alpine scenes on the walls. She made sure the door was securely locked, turned up the thermostat, and asked me if I was hungry.

Food is a unifier. Sharing a meal builds trust, trust builds rapport, and rapport is the cornerstone of any productive human intelligence-gathering effort to learn the truth.

"I'm starving," I said.

She made me a peanut butter and honey sandwich, which I happily accepted. She also offered me a banana which I politely declined because bananas always bring back memories of a jihadist financier I neutralized while on assignment once in the Azores. He was lounging on his ocean-view veranda when I drilled a 168-grain, .308-Winchester round through his mouth from a sailboat anchored 200 meters offshore. The banana he was munching on went everywhere, along with his brains.

"Here," Alessandra said, handing me the sandwich on a green plastic plate. "I'm afraid it's all I have."

"It's all I need."

We sat at the table. I ate quickly. "Should I call you Alessandra Munoz or Aideen Fitzgerald?"

Her eyes were downcast.

"You're not related to the Kennedys, are you?"

She stared at her hands. They were trembling.

"It's OK, Alessandra. You can tell me."

"No. Not that I don't wish I were."

"Aideen Fitzgerald" had been a ruse, she said, initially concocted to avoid a bill collector before taking on a life of its own. Being related to America's one true royal family, Alessandra discovered, came with built-in social standing.

No longer was she a twice-divorced loser who'd failed at virtually everything she'd ever done. She was a Kennedy, a far-distant resident of that shining city on the hill once known as Camelot. People looked at her differently, treated her differently. Sometimes she told them that her name was really Alessandra because she was tired of the expectations that came with being a minor celebrity. Sometimes it was impossible to keep the story straight in her head, her pretend past and her real one, all the little lies. She knew it was inevitable that it would all come crashing down. Part of her, a big part, she said, was relieved all of it was finally over.

Hearing about Cyril Tomasello's murder on the radio had left her fearful for her own life. She'd returned to Rico Perris's cabin only long enough to retrieve some personal possessions and was planning to hit the road when she saw me coming, thought I was Harlan Weber, and freaked out.

"He knew I'd moved in with Rico," Alessandra said. "He knew Cyril and I had been intimate. Harlan went nuts when he found out. He couldn't take the thought of me being with another man. He can't let it go. He thinks I'm his property. That restraining order, it's just a piece of paper to him. He knows nobody'll arrest him no matter what he does because he's the damn sheriff. It's like he's the king of that county and everybody else, they're his servants."

"So Weber becomes so consumed by jealousy over the woman he can't have, he murders her two lovers?"

"You make it sound like I'm all that or something. I'm not. He would've had other reasons, believe me, not just me."

"Such as?"

"Rico knew about how Weber had been stealing money from the Boy Scouts for years. He built a house down in New Mexico with that money. I hear the state's after him. He's under investigation, big time. He was afraid Rico was about to talk. At first I thought Rico just went off the road in the snow. An accident, you know? But now, I mean, you know?"

"Why would Weber have killed Tomasello?"

"I don't know. They were in Vietnam together. Maybe Weber did bad things there too. Maybe Cyril knew. I can't believe this. I can't believe they're both dead. Oh, my god. I wish this would all just go away."

She covered her eyes and cried. There was nothing contrived in her tears. I reached across the table and took her hand. I wasn't trying to be manipulative in the way I once would have been, to get her to trust me more so she'd be more forthcoming. I was only trying to be decent.

"I'm sorry, Alessandra."

"I'll be OK." She grabbed a paper napkin from a stack on the table and blew her nose.

"What did you and Cyril used to talk about?"

"Other than his being a marine? We didn't." She dabbed the wetness from under her eyes. "It wasn't that kind of relationship, if you know what I'm saying."

"Did he ever talk about President Kennedy?"

"I don't get it. You keep asking about President Kennedy. Why? What's so important about Kennedy?"

"We found a copy of a book in Rico's cabin about the JFK assassination. We found the same book in Tomasello's place. And you're running around the mountains, passing yourself off as a member of the Kennedy clan. I mean, I'm sure you can certainly appreciate how weird that looks."

"Look, I already told you, Rico and Cyril were in a book club. I don't read books. We never talked about what they were reading or not reading. Either one of them. It was their thing. And as far as me pretending to be related, I wasn't, OK? I don't know what to tell you. It is what it is."

She admitted to having been distantly "related" over the years to other prominent individuals as a means of masking her identity, always staying one step ahead of the people to whom she owed money. The Rockefellers. Bill and Melinda Gates. Once she passed herself off as the third cousin, twice removed, of the British royal family. But she swore she was done with all of that now.

"All I want," she said, "is to get the hell out of Dodge and go somewhere far away, where nobody will ever find me again."

She took my plate and was putting it in the kitchen sink when the front door blasted open.

I'd like to say that instinct kicked in, that I drew my weapon and rolled off my chair to the left because most shooters are right-handed and hitting a target that's moving left-to-right is slightly harder for even the most adept right-handed gunman. But I never got the chance. I had absentmindedly, inexcusably, stupidly let my guard down and committed an operator's cardinal sin: I'd sat down facing away from the entrance.

As I turned in my seat, I heard Alessandra scream and, in my peripheral vision, glimpsed a man in a green sheriff's uniform. Simultaneously I heard a muffled shot that I knew had come from a Taser, and was instantly consumed head-to-toe by blinding pain.

I could feel my eyes rolling back in my head as Alessandra's screams faded to nothing.

TWENTY-TWO

I came to while sitting on Alessandra Munoz's couch. I'd lost consciousness for maybe a minute, long enough for Deputy Doberman to pull my wrists behind my back and slap on the cuffs. He was standing over me, his impressive arms folded across his chest, his Taser returned to its holster. The pistol I'd been carrying was now tucked in his gun belt.

Alessandra was sitting at the table, eyes downcast, trembling. Sheriff Harlan Weber was perched on a kitchen chair drawn close to me. His legs were crossed at the knee, his hands folded placidly in his lap. He was smiling, while his left foot twitched like a rattler's tail, giving away how tightly wound he was.

"Edison's medicine," he said. "Hurts like hell, doesn't it, getting Tased?"

"Beats a bullet."

"That it does." Weber chuckled, but there was nothing mirthful about him.

He turned to Alessandra and asked her in a saccharine, skin-crawling way, if she wouldn't mind making him a cup of coffee. He called her "honey." She got up and filled the pot as if her life depended on it.

"We put a tracking device under her car," Weber said, "just in case you were wondering how we found you."

"Thanks for enlightening me."

"The least I can do." Weber unfolded his legs and leaned in closer. His smile faded, replaced by a face that was anything but friendly. "So now that I have your undivided attention, Mr. Logan, perhaps you can tell me who you really work for."

"I'm afraid that's considerably above your pay grade, Sheriff."

His smile returned, then he backhanded me hard across the face. I'd just been shot in the back with two gas-powered darts and zapped by 50,000 volts of electricity. The slap was a mosquito bite.

"I happen to know you work for the CIA," Weber said. "Alessandra told me. Didn't you, honey?"

She stood over the coffee maker, eyes downcast, and said nothing.

Weber turned back to me. "You think I killed Rico Perris. I didn't. I've never killed anybody in my life. That's the god's honest truth. Anybody who says I did is a liar."

"Not even down in Florida?"

". . . Florida?"

"When you were working for the mob. C'mon, Sheriff, you remember that, don't you? Carlos Trafficante and boys? Breaking kneecaps? Good times, am I right?"

"Where the hell did you hear that?"

"Same place I heard about that dead drug mule, the one who helped you swing the financing on that little vacation casa of yours down in New Mexico. And let's not forget the Boy Scouts. They helped out too. It's only too bad they don't give a badge out for embezzling."

Weber traded a glance with Deputy Doberman before his eyes returned to mine. "You've got it all wrong," he said. "I'm one of the good guys."

"Right. Just keep telling your grandkids that."

Jaw tight, nostrils flaring. You could see he wanted to slap me again. Somehow he controlled his temper.

"You're under arrest," he said.

"On what charge?"

"It doesn't matter. I'll find something."

He nodded to Deputy Doberman who promptly grabbed my left arm and yanked me off the couch to my feet.

"Not to keep second-guessing you, Sheriff," I said, "but you really do need to rethink this. FYI, my people are aware of everything I'm aware of in real time. They know exactly where I am at this very moment. In fact, they're listening in on us right now. Say hello."

I turned the right side of my head toward him, like my ear was equipped with some kind of super-sophisticated listening device, which, in a manner of speaking, you could say it was.

The deputy paused and looked over at his boss who looked back at me like he wasn't sure whether I was shining him on or not.

"He's full of it," Weber said. "Let's go."

We headed toward the door.

"OK, fine," I said, "let's say for argument's sake that I do, in fact, work for the CIA. You have no notion, none, of what the agency is capable of these days technologically. It's mind-blowing stuff. Puts Jason Bourne to shame, believe me. We know everything there is to know about you, Sheriff. And then some."

Anyone who has ever ventured inside Langley's cubicle farms or lunched in its vast food court, with its security-cleared Subway and Burger King franchises, knows that Jason Bourne has never set one foot inside the place. A more bumbling, bureaucratic, risk-averse intelligence organization would be hard to find on this or any other planet. But the only version outsiders these days know is the high-speed, high-tech Hollywood one. Deputy Doberman appeared to be among them. He paused, his hand still on my arm, uncertain how to proceed.

Harlan Weber apparently was no longer sure either.

"I didn't know Rico worked for the CIA," he said.

He looked me square in the face when he said it, which is neither here nor there. Most liars know enough to maintain eye contact.

"And Joe Zyra?"

"I don't know who that is."

"But you did know Cyril Tomasello."

"I had nothing to do with what happened to him."

"You're a liar," Alessandra said, grabbing a wood-handled carving knife out of a drawer. "You murdered him, you son of a bitch, just like you did Rico."

She raised the knife over her head and charged, growling like some wild animal.

Reflexively, Deputy Doberman released his grip on my arm and pulled back his green sheriff's jacket to draw his semiautomatic.

But not fast enough.

I spun and dropped him with a roundhouse kick to the groin, then pivoted and body slammed Alessandra into the wall just as she rushed past me. Staggered, she slumped to her seat and dropped the knife.

For an older man, Weber was as surprisingly quick as he was strong. He picked up the blade, tossed it across the room, and held her down face-first on the carpet. She never stopped growling and squirming.

"You're in violation of a restraining order, Sheriff," I said. "You're also out of your jurisdiction. And one more thing: I assume you're familiar with the CBI, also known as the Colorado Bureau of Investigation?"

"What about it?"

"Nothing—other than they're on their way. They'll be here any minute. If I were in your shoes right now, I'd be leaving."

"You're bluffing. The CIA. The CBI. It's all bluff."

I smiled. "I suppose we'll soon find out."

Deputy Doberman was scraping himself off the floor, clutching his groin and grimacing in pain. The nervous glance he and Weber exchanged told me I had them precisely where I wanted them.

"Get these handcuffs off of me," I said.

Weber hesitated, deliberating, then nodded to Deputy Doberman, who unhooked a key ring from his belt and unshackled my wrists while Alessandra wriggled free from Weber.

"Listen to me," he said to her. "I'm no choir boy, but these things you think I did, I didn't."

"Get the hell out of here," she said.

Weber tried to touch her.

"Now!" Alessandra screamed.

The sheriff followed his deputy toward the door, pausing to offer me a menacing smile before leaving.

"I'm sure we'll see each other again real soon, Mr. Logan."

It was less a prediction than it was a threat.

"Can't wait," I said.

I helped Alessandra up—I tried to anyway. She didn't want my help, she said. She didn't need any man's help.

She walked over and inspected the front door where it had been booted. The frame was splintered, but the door itself remained on its hinges and essentially intact. She peeked outside to make certain Weber and his deputy were gone, then managed to close and lock it. Only then did I realize they'd taken Layne's pistol with them.

"I need a drink," Alessandra said.

The cupboard nearest the refrigerator held a quart of Wild Turkey. She got out a juice glass, poured it half full, and asked me if I wanted to join her.

"No, thanks."

She downed the bourbon like it was water, standing at the counter with her back turned to me, and promptly refilled the glass.

"I can't believe I ever got involved with that man. I despise him."

"This does not exactly come as a bulletin," I said.

"He has friends all over that town who do a lot of his dirty work for him, you know. 'Henchmen,' I guess you'd call them. You should check them out too. There's one guy at the post office. Complete dirt bag. He's the dirtiest of them all."

"Bart Tolks?"

Alessandra turned, clearly surprised. "You know Bart?"

"We've had the pleasure of meeting," I said.

"I want to show you something," she said.

She gulped down the rest of her drink, walked over to the dresser, pulled out the middle drawer, and dumped its contents—socks and underwear—on the floor. Taped to the underside of the drawer was an envelope. Alessandra peeled it off. Inside was a section of a green dog-eared topographic map bearing a US Geological Survey stamp. A mountainous ravine on federal land about four miles northwest of Angel Falls was circled in faded red ink. Written in the circle, in a woman's careful hand, were the words, "Quarry Creek Mine."

"He'd had too much to drink. Got to running his mouth one night. Started telling me about some big drug courier who ended up dead over in Spruce County."

"Sheriff Weber, you mean?"

Alessandra nodded. "I don't know. Maybe I got it all wrong. He didn't come straight out and say he killed the guy, but that was the impression I got. He was almost bragging about it, like he'd done the world a favor. I probably should've told somebody a long time ago, but I was scared. I figure someone else should know, in case something happens to me."

"I don't understand." I glanced down at the map. "The Quarry Creek Mine?"

"If you're looking for where the body is buried," she said.

THE TWO ranch hands who volunteered to dig Sam McBride's old station wagon out of the snow for me after they had finished their chores had made good on their offer. I could see from a half-mile away as Alessandra drove us toward it that the station wagon was good to go. The cowboys had moved it onto the roadside. They and their herding dog were gone.

"Where can I find you?" I asked her.

"You won't," Alessandra said, "not if I can help it." She handed me the map. "If you ask me, I think you should get out of here, fast as you can, but I can tell you're the kind of man who's gonna do what he's gonna do, no matter how screwy or ridiculous it is, or what anybody else says."

"Screwy and ridiculous. Among my many character flaws unfortunately."

"Rico didn't have too many flaws," she said. "He was a sweet man. Maybe the sweetest ever. He didn't deserve to go the way he did."

"No, he didn't."

I climbed out of the car. She rolled down the passenger window.

"Not getting any insurance money when I thought I was going to." She fought back tears. "That's kind of rotten, you know?"

"I'm sorry we led you on."

"Yeah, well, not as sorry as me."

"You take care of yourself, Alessandra, OK?"

"I'd tell you the same, but I don't think you'll be alive much longer."

She drove on.

It would be dark in fewer than three hours. Ahead of me I had what I estimated was forty-five to fifty minutes of drive time over mountain passes and no less than an hour's hike through snow to the Quarry Creek Mine where, depending on Alessandra's version of events, Sheriff Harlan Weber had dumped the body of the cocaine dealer he'd either murdered or ripped off post mortem.

No one had to tell me that the smarter, more prudent move would have been to call the Colorado Bureau of Investigation down in Denver and alert them to the situation. But I knew that in the middle of winter, getting investigators who were eighty or ninety miles away and no doubt already overworked, mustering that kind of cavalry, could take days. Weber was aware that he was being hunted. I had no doubt he was feeling the walls closing in. I worried that his next play would be to return to the mine and dispose of whatever incriminating evidence he may have inadvertently left behind. I intended to get there first.

I didn't care about any drug dealer. What I cared about was leverage. Establishing any association between Weber and the dealer's death could compel the sheriff of Spruce County to tell us what he really knew of Rico Perris's demise, as well as Joe Zyra's.

That was all the incentive I needed.

✢ ✢ ✢

During summer, the rutted dirt path that connected the county road to the mine shaft a half-mile away would've been a walk in the park. Literally. But summer was long distant. This was fifteen degrees, just below timberline, and nearly two miles above sea level.

Fresh deer and rabbit tracks were etched in the snow leading in from the road. So were two sets of prints left by waffle-sole hiking boots. The width at the ball and heel of the prints told me in no uncertain terms that these humans were undeniably male, as did the depth of each tread—most men sink deeper into snow than women. Instinctively I reached behind me for the pistol wedged in my belt. Then I remembered: oh yeah, I was no longer armed.

Should I have heeded the bullet-pocked, "Posted Private Property, Do Not Enter" sign tacked to the trunk of a blue spruce, turned around, and gotten back in Sam McBride's Volvo? Driven to someplace down below where I could've gotten cell reception and contacted the appropriate state authorities? Probably. But Alessandra was right. Maybe I am a little screwy. Or maybe a lot.

Through the tops of the pines, mountain peaks loomed above me, glistening white in the late afternoon sun like giant shark teeth. A plump Steller's jay ruffled his blue and gray feathers and hopped from tree to tree, cawing as if trying to warn me of the danger that lay ahead. I ignored him—or tried to. When birds grow ominously silent in a forest or jungle, you know the situation's about to get real.

"Don't you have anything better to do, buddy?"

Caw, caw, caw.

I pressed on, higher and deeper, tracking the footprints left in the snow by the two men who'd preceded me.

Land navigation. That's the fancy term the military uses for what outdoorsy civilians call "orienteering"—the ability to find your GPS-less way through unfamiliar terrain using little more than a rudimentary map and compass. I may not be Magellan, but I always thought I was pretty adept at it, considering all the survival, evasion, and escape training I'd received with Alpha and, before that, with the air force. However, in this case, either the map was off, or I was.

A hike that I'd anticipated taking at least an hour required nearly twice that. Twilight was encroaching as the trail came to an end and I got to where I was going—or *thought* I was going. There was nothing there. No mine shaft. No mill tailings. Only dark, silent forest.

And a mountain lion, stalking me.

TWENTY-THREE

*K*a-bang!

The heavy-caliber gunshot seemed to come from somewhere close behind me and echoed off the mountains. Terrified, the puma ran.

A pair of bearded, shabbily dressed African American men emerged from the tree line behind me. The heavier of the two and, as I would soon discover, the more slow-witted, lowered a World War II-era, Russian-made, Mosin-Nagant rifle from his shoulder. His partner wore horn-rimmed glasses and was carrying an AR-15 carbine, the civilian version of the military's standard-issue M4 battle weapon.

"You suck, dog," the guy with the AR-15 said with a trace of Louisiana Cajun in his accent. "You couldn't hit the broad side of a guddamn barn if the barn was three feet away and you were driving a guddamn tank."

"If I wanted to hit him, Zion, I would've hit him," the big man with the Russian rifle said. "I was just trying to scare him off. Not many of those big cats left, you know, not that you care."

Both wore thick-soled hiking boots. I figured them for the sources of the tracks in the snow I'd followed to where

I thought the mine would be. The heavier guy asked me if I was hurt. I said I wasn't, and that I appreciated the two of them being in the right place at the right time.

"This ain't the right place," Zion said. "You're on our claim. Now, who the hell are you and what the hell you doing up here?"

"My name's Logan. I'm looking into a murder."

"We didn't have nothing to do with no murder."

"Shut up, Malik," Zion snapped. "Keep your mouth *shut*. I'll do the talking, you feel me?"

Malik outweighed Zion by fifty pounds or better, but he lowered his fleshy head and stared submissively at the snow.

Zion refocused on me, dangling the shotgun at his side with his finger resting lightly on both triggers. The pistol grip was wrapped with black electrician's tape to minimize fingerprints. A cheap thug tactic for a cheap thug firearm.

"You ain't no Hawaii five-zero, I can tell you that much," he said, looking me up and down. "Looking into a murder for who?"

I told him I worked for a newspaper in Denver. I was seeking "truth, justice, and the American way," I said, not to mention the location of a dead drug dealer whose remains the corrupt sheriff of Spruce County was rumored to have dumped down the Quarry Creek mine, wherever that was. While my reference to Superman appeared to have been lost on him, Zion seemed to spark to the notion of me being a reporter.

"Long as you ain't no cop," he said, uncocking his shotgun and shoving it barrel first over his shoulder, into his backpack. "We heard about that sheriff. He's a bad man."

"We thought maybe you was a claim jumper," Malik said. "That or parole."

"Shut up, Malik."

Zion pointed. They lived just over there, he volunteered, in what had once been a trapper's cabin. The two of them panned and dug for gold on a leased, twenty-acre claim of federal land. They also were married.

"Husband and husband," Malik said, "legally bound under the laws of Colorado and the eyes of the lord."

The two of them looked at me like they expected indignation or disapproval, but that's not me. Adam and Eve or Adam and Steve, I couldn't care less who swears to love and cherish until death do them part, so long as everybody's of legal age and nobody starts tossing haymakers over who gets to control the television remote.

"Mazel tov," I said.

That appeared to go over both of their heads too.

They didn't need to tell me they were ex-cons. The teardrops tattooed below the outside corners of their right eyes said as much, as did the letters, "EWMN"—short for "Evil, Wicked, Mean, Nasty"—inked on the knuckles of Zion's ungloved right hand. I'd seen identical tats on a few American-born jihadists, ex-cons who'd converted to a warped and violent view of Islam before traveling overseas to fight for Allah. I'd been only too happy to help facilitate their dreams of martyrdom.

"I'm looking for the Quarry Creek mine," I said.

"Then you'd be looking in the wrong place, Clark Kent," Zion snorted, "because the Quarry Creek mine's straight up that-a-way." He gestured toward the tall peaks to the north.

"How far on foot?"

"In the snow? 'Bout fifteen minutes, I'd say."

"Make it twenty," Malik said.

Dusk was turning rapidly to darkness. In the fading light that bled all detail from the alpine landscape and turned every color gray, I could barely make out the narrow pathway through the pines to which he pointed. My topo map was of little use; the trail wasn't even on it.

"Alrighty then," I said, folding the map away and setting off, up the mountain. "Catch you guys on the flip side."

Zion was incredulous. "You crazy? You can't go up there."

"Why not? You just said it's only fifteen minutes."

"Yeah, but, it's almost dark, you got no gat on you cuz you would've used it on that cougar who was about to chew on you. Plus that mine's all boarded up. Plus it's getting down below zero tonight. You go up there all by yourself, reporter man, you ain't coming back down, I guar-on-tee."

"Then you'll just have to come with me. Besides you know where the mine is. I don't."

Zion laughed as if accompanying yours truly deeper into the wilderness on a winter's night was the last thing he wanted to do. His husband saw things differently. Some old-timers down in Angel Falls whom Malik said they'd had beers with one night were convinced that the Quarry Creek mine was anything but played out. Deep inside could still be found the mother lode, a gold vein they said ran as thick as your wrist. All you had to do was look. Here was a chance to do some potentially profitable spelunking with impunity.

"If we get caught," Malik said, "we blame it on this guy. It was his idea, not ours. We were just helping him out."

Zion was sold. "Forget what I said about keeping your mouth shut."

He slugged Malik in the arm, who beamed.

"The only problem," Zion said, "is that if we *do* find gold, we're probably gonna have to shoot this guy to keep it secret."

His straight face made me wonder if he wasn't kidding.

✈ ✈ ✈

ZION LED the way with his flashlight, me in the middle, Malik bringing up the rear, lifting our knees through the snow. Somewhere far off, an owl hooted to its mate without response. It was a lonely sound.

He and Malik had it all figured out, Zion said. The hills may not have been what they were in 1859, when a man could stick a shovel blade into the ground and haul nuggets out by the bucketful. But back then, he said, gold traded for twenty dollars an ounce. Today an ounce went for upward of $1,300. All they had to do was find a small amount, and they'd soon be leading the good life. Zion intended to use his share to buy a top-of-the-line Lexus and a mansion in Beverly Hills with a custom air-filtration system for his allergies; Malik wanted to get his teeth fixed.

I thought about explaining the economics of annual inflation rates, how twenty dollars back then was probably closer to $2,000 today for all I knew, and how they'd have to discover a fair amount of gold to go the route of swimming pools and movie stars, but all of that, I knew, would've been counterproductive. They were armed and I wasn't. And if, by some remote chance, a spooked Sheriff Harlan Weber decided that night to revisit the scene of his alleged crime, to further cover his tracks, I was going to need reinforcements, no matter how shallow their ambitions, or how long their rap sheets.

We rounded a bend. Looming at the end of the trail, about as far from civilization as one can get in the Centennial State, was a mine.

"This is it," Zion said. "Quarry Creek."

There were no signs indicating such. The portal, dug into the mountainside, was cave-like and considerably smaller than what I had envisioned. Hand-hewn timbers framed the opening like a doorway, which was about five feet across and low enough that even the average-sized man back then would've had to crouch to step inside. Two-by-eight-inch boards had been nailed top to bottom across the framing, forming a complete and solid barrier. Zion smacked his palm on one of them.

"Ain't gonna be easy getting in there," he said.

"Do me a favor and let me borrow your flashlight."

"What for?"

"The man wants to borrow your flashlight," Malik said. "Let him borrow the flashlight."

Grudgingly Zion handed it over.

A closer inspection of the boards showed that while they were old and weathered, the nails were modern—round galvanized heads, not square-cut or rusting. This suggested to me that while the boards may well have been installed when the mine was shuttered, whenever that was, they had been subsequently removed, then put back in place.

"Somebody's been in there," I said. "They've been inside. Recently."

"How recently?"

"Hard to say. Do me another favor. I need to borrow your shotgun."

"Ain't no way," Zion said.

"Fine. Then let me borrow your crowbar."

"Ain't got no crowbar, man."

"Well, then unless you have a better idea as to how to get these boards off, so that we can get inside to see if there's a dead body in there and/or the Treasure of Sierra Madre, I suggest you letting me borrow your shottie. Believe it or not, I have some experience in this department."

Sawed-off, twelve-gauge shotguns can be wondrously diverse tools. In close-quarters battle, they can clear a room of enemy combatants as well as any weapon ever made. At close range, they also can put impressively large holes in a vast array of inanimate objects, including locked doors. At Alpha, in the hypermasculine, often misogynistic world of the special operator, we referred to our sawed-off shotguns universally as "The Bitch." No one that I can recall ever asked why.

"Nobody's touching my shotgun," Zion said, reaching back and pulling it out of his pack.

"Then at least let me show you where to aim."

I felt along the boards, starting from the top and working my way down, pushing with my fingertips until I found a section near the middle and close to the left side of the frame where the wood was spongy and gave way a little. Dry rot.

"Shoot here," I said, aiming the flashlight where I wanted him to fire.

"What if somebody hears us?" Malik asked. He looked around anxiously.

"Malik, we just shot at a mountain lion," Zion said, cocking both hammers. "Ain't nobody within five miles of us, man."

He squeezed the dual triggers. Flames spewed from both barrels, lighting up the night sky for a second, while the deafening report thundered across the Rockies before fading on the wind. The flashlight revealed that the buckshot had splintered one of the boards, ripping it virtually in half, while leaving a jagged opening the size of a grapefruit in the board above it. My accomplices and I kicked at the wood with our boots and pried off chunks with our hands.

We were soon in.

✈ ✈ ✈

HIBERNATING BROWN bats hung from the ceiling. We had to crouch to avoid them.

"Bastards give me the creeps, man," Malik said. "Suck your blood, like zombies. Give you AIDs and all that shit, you know what I'm saying?"

"Not AIDS, stupid," Zion said, "spinal merengue."

Telling them that neither had any idea what he was talking about would've been a waste of breath and minutes of my life I knew I'd never get back. Most bats ate bugs and generally minded their own business. They weren't exactly my favorite animals, either, but as long as we left them alone, I expected them to return the favor.

The shaft's rock walls were braced every three meters or so with beamed timbered posts, upon which rested crudely positioned wood planking intended to prevent cave-ins. Running parallel at our feet and deeper into the gradually descending black hole were two iron rails where wooden carts once rolled quarried ore out of the mine to be shipped on horse-drawn wagons to the smelter. The ground was littered with a few old crushed beer cans, a rusting pick ax, minus its handle, and what looked like condom wrappers. I saw no dead bodies.

"Freaky in here, man," Zion said, his flashlight playing off the walls and down the shaft. "Damn, dog, check it out."

A vein about two inches thick of iron pyrite glistened through the black rock like a layer of yellow frosting sandwiched between devil's food. Even Malik knew that it was fool's gold, but where the fake stuff was, he and Zion agreed, the real stuff can often be found.

We advanced at a crouch, deeper into the shaft, Zion leading the way with his flashlight, me in the middle, Malik bringing up the rear again. My anxiety grew with each step. Being unarmed in the company of two ex-cons who were locked and loaded only partly explained the apprehension I was feeling. I could never admit to being a tad claustrophobic when I was flying for the air force and, later, working with

Alpha, because I knew that even a mild case might disqualify me from duty. I was always able to control the fear when it came on, as I had hours earlier when I found myself buried in snow in the car. This felt different. Worse. It was cold enough in that mine to see your breath, but I was sweating like it was August in south Florida.

"What I wanna know," Zion said, "is what newspaper you said you worked at."

"I didn't."

"So how do we even know you is who you say you is?"

"I suppose you don't."

He reached under his coat and whirled back toward me, leveling his flashlight and an older .38-caliber revolver with a five-inch barrel, the kind cops carried before they went to semiautos.

"What're you doing, man?" Malik demanded. "Put that thing away."

"He don't work for no newspaper," Zion said. "He's a damn claim jumper is what he is."

"You don't know that. They gonna send us back, you pull this. Is that what you want? Because I don't. Now, you wanna be with me? You put that thing away."

Reluctantly Zion tucked the revolver back under his coat, gave me a look, and pressed on. Malik and I followed. There were no more questions about which newspaper I worked for.

After about thirty meters, the shaft curved to the left and came to a sudden end. The mine had collapsed into an impenetrable wall of rocks and dirt.

"Oh, hell no," Zion said.

There would be no going any farther, which was just as well.

"If anybody *had* dumped somebody in here," I said, "we would've found him already. Nobody would have dragged a dead body this far. Let's get out of here."

"What about the gold?" Malik asked.

Zion shook his head and lit into his husband, swearing at him like a trucker with a flat tire. Any idiot, he said, could plainly see that we had come to the end of the road and that if there was a pot of gold on the other side, you'd need a blankety-mother-blanking bazooka to get at it.

My fear for the future of their marriage was not misplaced. I couldn't get out of there fast enough. Literally.

From somewhere deep and low, the earth began to rumble. Dust fell on our heads.

"Cave-in!" Malik screamed.

We ran.

TWENTY-FOUR

Had it been a big-budget Hollywood feature production, we would've sprinted in slow motion toward the camera. We would have outrun tumbling boulders and a giant roiling dust cloud while the tunnel collapsed behind us, in the same way movie stars are always able to outrun the flames and shock-waves of large explosive devices, diving headfirst to safety in the proverbial nick of time. But that's not how it went down in the Quarry Creek mine. Yes, the ground quaked a little and grumbled audibly, as the earth is wont to do sometimes. Yes, some dust landed on our heads. The mine, however, didn't cave in on us. Mr. and Mr. Convicted Felon and I escaped into the frigid night and would live to tell the tale.

Zion drew his handgun once more and leveled it at my face. "Who are you, man, for real?" he asked, then started to sneeze. All that falling dust in the mine had triggered his allergies.

Disarming him was easy. In one fluid motion, I side-stepped left and out of his line of fire, wrapping my left hand around the revolver and torquing his gun hand outwardly with my free hand, nearly but not quite snapping the fine carpal bones in his wrist while twisting the weapon from his grip. Malik started to raise his rifle, then thought the better of it.

"Hand it over," I said, "by the barrel, nice and slow."

He did.

"You got a sidearm too?"

"No, sir."

I slung the rifle over my shoulder and did the same with the sawed-off shotgun I unsheathed from Zion's backpack as he doubled over, groaning and clutching his wrist.

"What the hell, man? You done busted my arm!"

"You'll be fine. Rub a little snow on it, take two aspirin, and don't call me in the morning."

"That was some nasty shit for a reporter, man, you know what I'm sayin'?" Malik said, like he was enjoying a little too much watching his spouse writhe in pain.

"OK, for the record, I'm not a reporter. What I am, though, is a guy who will swear to anyone who ever asks that I was never here tonight, and that the three of us never met. I'm also the guy who sincerely hopes you two lovebirds find the mother lode as soon as possible so that you can afford to get yourself some counseling. You'll get your weapons back after we get to my car. Now let's roll."

We descended the mountain trail in silence, under a canopy of stars. This time I was Tail-End Charlie. Meteors streaked across the sky every couple of minutes. I thought I could see vehicle headlights slanting through the trees ahead, but by the time we reached the trailhead and Samantha McQueen's Volvo station wagon, they were gone.

I ordered Zion and Malik to stop and get down on their knees.

"If you're going to shoot me, you can shoot me standing up," Malik said. "This mofo got bad news written all over him, dog. Bushwhackin', claim-jumping mofo is what he is. I could smell it the minute I first laid eyes on him."

"He ain't gonna shoot us, Zion," Malik said, "are you, Mister?"

"I may if your husband doesn't shut his big cake hole."

Zion gave me the evil eye and turned away. Malik offered me a smile and got down on his knees.

I unloaded the shotgun and flung it into the snow, as far away from them as I could. Ditto the rifle. Not the revolver. That, I said, I was keeping.

"That's bull," Zion said. "You said you'd give it back."

"My apologies for the inconvenience. Thanks for the escort."

Driving on, I could see him in the rearview mirror clawing frantically through the snow to recover the ammo and guns while Malik held his stomach and doubled over, laughing.

✈ ✈ ✈

TRUE TO its sign out in front, the Never Close café in Luft was open and surprisingly busy for that hour of the night—or early morning, as it were. Almost half the booths and tables were occupied, all by customers young and old who looked half drunk or half awake. The restaurant was overheated and smelled of bacon. I wasn't about to complain about either considering how chilly it was outside and how predisposed I am to processed meat products—in moderation, of course.

The green-eyed waitress who'd flirted with me when I'd stopped in before seemed happy to see me again. I followed her to a vacant table in the back, near the kitchen. She handed me a menu and poured me a cup of coffee as I sat without being asked.

"You're not from around here."

"Just passing through," I said.

"Too bad." She smiled. "Do you know what you'd like, or do you need a little more time?"

"I was thinking about a salad because, hey, my body's a temple, but I think I'll go with a BLT instead because you only go round once. And more coffee, black, thanks."

"A little bacon never killed anybody, right?"

"Tell that to Miss Piggy. You know, life expectancy in this country would grow by leaps and bounds if lettuce tasted like bacon."

She smiled again. "Would you like a dill pickle with your sandwich? It's a dollar extra, but I guarantee you, they're absolutely the best pickles in the world. I put them up myself."

"Sold."

"I'm Linda Adams, by the way. I own this place. If you need anything at all, please let me know."

"Thank you, Linda."

She picked up my menu and angled toward the kitchen, subtly glancing back over her shoulder to make certain I'd taken note of how snug her jeans fit.

I considered calling Layne Sterling and briefing her on what little progress I'd made, but it was both too early in the morning and too late at night to do that. She was still hospitalized. She needed her sleep. Likewise Mrs. Schmulowitz. Much as I wanted to know how things were faring back on the home front in Rancho Bonita, I knew she and Kiddiot would be snoozing at that hour. I sipped my coffee and rued what I knew my next move unfortunately had to be:

I would return at first light to the icy Champ River, back to the wreckage of Rico Perris's Porsche, where I would attempt to collect another paint scraping that might prove who, if anyone, had rammed the retired intelligence analyst. I wasn't exactly doing handstands at the prospect; I didn't want to fall in again. Those crazy idiots in New York, who belong to the Polar Bear Club and go swimming in the Atlantic off Coney Island every winter in their Speedos because they think it's fun and invigorating? That would not be me.

My voice mail showed three messages. The first, delivered nearly five hours earlier, was from Buzz, chastising me per usual for not checking in with him.

"How many times do I need to explain this to you, Logan? Langley is all over me. I got these idiots calling every ten minutes. They—"

Beep. Erased. Next message:

"Hello, bubeleh? Mrs. Schmulowitz here," she said, as if I, or anyone was incapable of recognizing who she was from the first word out of her mouth. "Anyhoo, thought I'd give you a jingle and see what's the haps in your neck of the woods. The big news on this end—hold the phone, stop the presses—is this kitty of yours? He actually caught a bird. True story. Personally, I didn't think he had the smarts to catch a cold, let alone another living creature. Anyhoo, the bird's fine. Some little sparrow. Flew away, no harm, no *fowl*, no pun intended. Tell you the truth, I don't know which one was more surprised by the whole thing, the bird or the cat. Call me back collect if you want and I'll fill you in on all the details. I get free minutes on weekends, just so you know. Hugs and kisses."

Beep.

"Logan, it's Layne. Check your e-mail. I'm forwarding some photographs my colleague down in Arizona put in the pipeline this morning. Shots of Joe Zyra's residence. Nothing jumped out at me or the analysts back at headquarters, but I'd appreciate some backstopping. A set of fresh eyes never hurt. I'm still hoping, by the way, to get out of here tomorrow. Let me know how it's going, OK? Talk to you later. Bye."

Fresh eyes? Mine felt like they'd been through a meat tenderizer. I sipped my coffee and waited while the pictures downloaded.

There were fourteen in all, both interior and exterior shots. Zyra had resided in one of those gated desert communities where every house looks like the house next to it, and the house next to that: terra-cotta-colored stucco, Spanish tile roof, three bedrooms, attached two-car garage, crushed gravel landscaping with a few cacti and a climbing red bougainvillea thrown in to distinguish the front yard from the surface of the moon. I could never understand why anyone would ever voluntarily live in a place like Phoenix. Each to their own, I suppose.

Inside the house was considerably more inviting. Tall ceilings. Color-coordinated, high-end furnishings. Silk flower arrangements. Persian rugs that looked handmade. Bookcases filled to overflowing in the living room and master bedroom. It all had a thoughtfully arranged look to it. Everything tidy and in its place. Perhaps a little too much.

Few of the individuals I ever investigated or hunted when I was assigned to Alpha were bookworms. That's what jumped out at me, studying the photos there. He'd been an avid reader, or maybe his wife was, or maybe they both were. The same had been true of Rico Perris and Cyril Tomasello. There were books all over their houses as well.

Whoever had snapped the photos had used a high-resolution camera. The interior shots were so clear that when I expanded them on my phone, I could easily make out the titles of the hundreds of volumes, both hardbound and paperback, organized by subject, alphabetized by authors' names, and lined up like soldiers on Zyra's shelves. The living room collection included books about psychology and philosophy, bird behavior, travel guides, interior design, and romance novels.

Arranged in the same precise manner on the five shelves of the six-foot-tall, freestanding bookshelf in Zyra's bedroom were sections devoted to spirituality, self-help, poetry, the Civil War, and historical fiction. The bottom shelf was devoted to mostly books about the Kennedy assassination, including *Lancer's Last Day: The CIA and the Murder of John F. Kennedy* by P.S. Plaissance, the same obscure title I'd observed in Perris's cabin outside Angel Falls as well as Tomasello's north Denver duplex.

The Buddha believed that our recognition of coincidences happens increasingly the more we advance spiritually through life. He was convinced that coincidences are, in fact, signs that we're following the right path. Whether that's true is not up to a spiritual fledgling like me to comprehend. What I did comprehend was that three men were dead. One was a former marine with a sketchy past. The other two had once held high-level, federal security clearances and had investigated the slaughter of an American president. However tenuously, all three victims held some kind of connection to the book and its author.

I Googled "P.S. Plaissance" on my phone—"the *Googles*," as Mrs. Schmulowitz insisted the search engine was called—but nothing came up beyond a handful of reviews of the book, all bad. Searching *Lancer's Last Day* produced many of the same negative reviews, along with various hits that had zero relevance, including a 2009 newspaper story about the final day of operations at a steakhouse in Cleveland called "The Lancer" that was closing after fifty years. I was able to glean the name of the book's publisher, Lipker & Kodrich, which showed a post office box in Wisconsin. Further digging revealed that the company had folded in 2015, due to what a business journal in Milwaukee described as a "short but memorable track record of releasing books that were consistently dubious in content if not quality."

"How're we doing, sweetheart? Top you off?"

I looked up to find Linda smiling down at me, coffee pot in hand.

"Actually," I said, "if it's not too much trouble, I could use a tiny favor."

I WOULD'VE called Layne Sterling, to have her people start turning up digital leads to help me hunt down P.S. Plaissance, but she needed her sleep. I'd wake up Buzz instead. Only I couldn't very well call him from the middle of the Never Close café. Too many customers around. I couldn't go outside and call him from the car either—too cold out there and no cell service. Which is why I stretched the truth a bit and told the waitress that I was a cardiac surgeon of international prominence. I need a quiet space, I explained, where I could consult immediately with other prominent surgeons in Europe who were about to perform a quadruple bypass on a famous international actor who lived in France and whose initials were Johnny Depp.

"I would've never guessed you for a famous doctor," Linda said. "You look more like a cop or something. And Johnny Depp? Heart problems? Little skinny guy like that?"

"Cigarettes and all that hollandaise sauce," I said. "The inside of the guy's ventricles look like tapioca."

She led me through the kitchen, past the time clock where she and fellow employees punched in, to a cubbyhole of an office adjacent to the café's back door.

"I very much appreciate this, Linda. I'll only be a couple of minutes."

"Anytime. Just don't forget my tip." She winked.

The office had room enough for a chair, a paper-strewn desk, and little else. Fifty-pound burlap sacks of potatoes and crates of economy-sized tomato sauce were stacked among other supplies in every conceivable space. I closed the door, sat down at the desk, and speed-dialed Buzz. He picked up on the second ring.

". . . Yeah?"

"Buzz, it's Logan."

"Why am I not surprised? Who else calls me in the middle of the night on a regular basis?" He hacked and coughed the way geezers do when they've been rousted from sleep. "What time is it anyway?"

"In Colorado? Just after one A.M."

"Not that you care, but I was dreaming about Raquel Welch, when she was Raquel Welch. We were on a catamaran off the coast of Acapulco, Mexico. She was in a bikini feeding me grapes. I'll spare you the rest of the details. You can use your imagination. All I can say is, this better be good."

I filled him in on P.S. Plaissance's *Lancer's Last Day*, and how the book dealt with the CIA and the Kennedy assassination. I reminded him how Perris and Zyra had worked on the CIA's Kennedy Red Lancer task force. I told him how we'd found a copy of the same book in Cyril Tomasello's residence, and how I was having little success in locating the author.

"We haven't been able to conclusively nail this down yet," I said, "but it looks like all three guys may all have been in a book club together."

"A *book* club? What the hell is that?"

"It's where everybody reads the same book, then they all get together and talk about it."

"Sounds like a total adrenaline rush to me. What is there to talk about? You liked the book? You didn't like the book?

I mean, what's next? Clubs for watching paint dry? Clubs for . . . 'Hey everybody, I got a fantastic idea. Let's all go down to the neighborhood barbershop and watch a few haircuts?' This is what passes for male entertainment today? I mean, Jesus."

"What I'd like," I said, ignoring Buzz's usual ranting, "is if you could help me track down the author of the book. He might have some insights."

"What about this crooked sheriff you've been targeting? What's the story there? He's out of contention?"

"You mean Weber? Negative, but I'm still working that end of it."

I let Buzz know of my plans to go back in the morning to the river, and to hopefully harvest another transferred paint scraping. He said he'd see what intel he could dredge up on P.S. Plaissance, and that he would pass along to Layne's superiors at the CIA what I had conveyed to him about three homicide victims owning copies of Plaissance's book.

"I gotta tell you, Logan, this sounds pretty thin to me," he said, yawning. "You want my opinion, you're getting nowhere fast. You've done what you could. If you wanna stand down, I won't lose sleep over it. I'll cable the agency first thing in the morning, if that's your call."

I may be many things, but I'm no quitter. So long as there were actionable leads to follow, I would follow them, as I had every investigation I'd ever undertaken. There was also Layne to consider and the prospect, however tentative, of a real relationship. This was her case. I didn't want her thinking less of me.

"I'm not finished here, Buzz. I need a little more time."

"We go way back, you and me, Logan, so I'm not gonna tell you no," Buzz said. "I'll try to hold off Sterling's people as long as I can, but you should plan on folding the tent pretty soon. Just do yourself a favor. Get yourself some sack time tonight. You sound like hell. I can hear the fatigue in your voice."

"Let me know what you come up with on Plaissance."

"Copy that."

I went back to my table. Linda refilled my coffee cup and asked me how the operation went. I must've blanched. For a moment, I thought she was referring to Red Lancer.

". . . Operation?"

"Johnny Depp."

"Oh, right, *that* operation. Sorry, it's been a long day. Yeah, the procedure went fine. Johnny's doing super great. We anticipate a full recovery."

She said she was relieved. She added that she got off work in a few minutes, that it had been a long day for her as well, and that she couldn't wait to get off her feet, into bed. I smiled and said I hoped she got some good rest. She left soon after. I never saw her again.

I sat alone at that table the rest of the night, sipping coffee, stealing five-minute catnaps, eavesdropping on the inane conversations around me, and trying not to think deep thoughts. At dawn, I set out for the Champ River outside Angel Falls.

What I found when I got there was not at all what I expected.

TWENTY-FIVE

$\mathbb{R}$ico Perris's Porsche had vanished.

Let me rephrase that: *Appeared* to have vanished.

Standing along the roadside, gazing down at the river where Perris had met his maker, I was convinced at first glance of Sheriff Harlan Weber's guilt. The murdering lawman had succeeded in having the sports car's wreckage towed so that he could destroy any recoverable evidence that might have implicated him in the retired spook's death. But when I looked closer, I realized that the Porsche hadn't been moved at all. It was exactly where I had seen it before, the same spot where I'd fallen in. Only now, the car appeared to have gone completely through the ice. Swallowed by the powerful currents swirling around and below it, it had settled lower into the water and been crusted over. If you looked hard enough, though, you could see a glint of sunlight on the tip of the Porsche's exhaust pipe—the only part of the sports car still visible above the Champ River's frozen skin.

So much for retrieving another paint sample.

And, also, so much for taking time to ponder my next move:

A half mile out, I caught sight of a Spruce County sheriff's SUV headed my way, up the mountain. He was negotiating a sharp switchback at a speed that I deemed considerably faster than one would maintain on routine patrol. What the cop's intentions were, whether he knew who I was and was coming to get me, or intended to pass me by on his way to another call, I didn't know, but I wasn't inclined to hang around and find out. I got back in the Volvo and split.

Not that I was speeding. I wasn't. No point in drawing any more attention to myself than I might have already. My prudence seemed to matter not at all, however. His strobes and siren came on within seconds.

I hit the gas.

To say the road was serpentine would be doing injustice to the word. Twists and turns galore. I was all over it—and nearly off it more than once—skidding and fishtailing on the snow, while the cop with his all-wheel drive steadily closed the gap. This, I knew, was probably not going to end well for me. But that was before that sort of karmic coincidence the Buddha talked about came visiting.

Two minutes into the chase, while rocketing along a section of highway flanked by pine forest and steep embankments, a Colorado Department of Transportation sand truck appeared out of nowhere, crossing behind me left to right, and appeared to stall on the road, blocking it completely.

The cop skidded to a stop to avoid a collision while I motored on, quickly disappearing from his view around a sharp bend.

Odds were he'd radioed his department's dispatcher that he was in pursuit—standard cop procedure. Other sheriff's patrol units were likely converging at that very moment to assist their fellow officer and join in the fun. They would block the road ahead and take me into custody, after which Sheriff Weber and I would have another little chat—assuming I lived that long.

First, though, they had to find me.

I was approaching an unmarked, ungated side road that led into a narrow, winding valley. Going off-grid had worked for me before. Why not again? I slowed and turned down the lane.

One thing I didn't have to worry about was leaving any tire tracks that Johnny Law could follow. Mine blended indistinguishably with several fresh sets already embedded in the snow, or so I hoped. The downside of such camouflage was it revealed that the road was well-traveled, probably by mostly area cattle ranchers. Rural people worldwide, I've found, tend to be more observant than city dwellers of their surroundings and more suspicious of individuals they don't recognize or know personally. They're also usually better armed. All of which posed potential problems for a guy wanting not to draw attention to himself and find a place to light for a few quiet hours until the heat died down.

Barbed-wire fencing ran along both sides of the road. I passed snowy, sun-drenched pastures of Herefords and a few black-and-white dairy cows grazing on dismantled hay bales. About three miles into the valley, up a side road, I chanced upon the out-of-the-way refuge I was seeking:

A century earlier, or longer for all I knew, it had been some hardworking farm family's home. The house was two stories, with a peaked roof, dormer windows upstairs, and a covered porch below. Hay barn. Storage sheds. All had been reduced by the elements and disuse to lifeless wooden hulks with stove-in roofs. I pulled the Volvo in behind a milking shed, as far off the road as I could find, rolled down the window, and cut the ignition. Blissful silence followed, punctuated only by the soothing, intermittent trill of a meadowlark.

The cloudless winter sun, magnified by the windshield, felt like a warm blanket on my face. I checked the revolver to make sure it was loaded. It was—all six chambers. I tucked the gun between my legs, hidden from view but within easy reach if I needed it, then sat back and closed my eyes. Buzz was right. I was exhausted. I must've been. Sleep came almost instantly. A minute later, or what felt like only a minute, I was wrenched awake by my own screaming.

Someone was shooting at me.

Bullets were shattering the windshield. I could hear the pop-pop-pop, pop-pop-pop of two AK-47s discharging three-round bursts. Somebody was shouting, "R-P-G, R-P-G!" and the tactical radio was alive with frantic calls for fire support. When I looked to my right, to the passenger seat, the man occupying it, a young Green Beret who'd recently joined Alpha and whom I barely knew, was casually glancing down and clutching the stump where his right forearm had been only moments before. I blinked disbelievingly at the surreal sight of his wound.

Only then did I shake free of the nightmare and come to.

The Volvo's windshield remained reassuringly intact. The air was not filled with incoming rounds. I was alone save for a crow perched on the Volvo's hood. He was cawing for the apparent sake of hearing his own annoying voice.

"Hey."

The bird recoiled, startled by my voice, then flew away. I heard no police sirens in the distance, saw no Spruce County sheriff's deputies. The dash clock showed I'd been asleep for more than four hours. That was long enough, I figured, for Harlan Weber and his boys to find better things to do with their time than chase me around the mountains of Colorado.

I was hoping Buzz might have come back with information on the author, Plaissance, but when I checked my phone for voice messages and e-mails, all I got was a black screen. The phone was dead. I'd forgotten to recharge the battery.

Great.

I cranked the key and drove back through the valley, the same way I'd come, passing on my way out an old rancher in a straw cowboy hat pulling a horse trailer in the opposite direction. He waved in a friendly way. I waved back. When I glanced in the side-view mirror, I could see that he'd stopped and stepped out of his truck. He was on his phone, looking back at me.

I drove faster.

THE VOLVO belonged to Sam McBride. She'd been more than kind to let me borrow it. I needed to get it back to her.

Prudence dictated that I minimize my presence on the county highway or risk encountering Weber or his minions. I navigated as many back roads as I could. Some were wrong turns, some dead ends. The nearer I got to McBride's cabin, though, the more familiar the terrain became. Soon the sign to her "Rocky Ridge Ranch" came into view. Turning down her long drive left me with a feeling of satisfaction. I'd run the sheriff's gauntlet, escaped detection, and reached a safe house where I could let down a little, if only for a while.

I parked the station wagon behind the barn, next to the Dodge I'd rented down in Denver, and had just opened the door when I heard movement in the barn. I glanced through a small, double-hung window. There stood Frou-Frou, McBride's horse.

"Thanks for saving my hide," I said. "You're a credit to your species."

She snorted and shook her head. I'd like to think she was saying, "You're welcome," but I don't speak horse.

The wind was starting to howl. Snow was beginning to fall again. I crossed the twenty meters or so to McBride's cabin. She wasn't home, but Cuddles was. As before, he barked and snarled viciously from behind the front door like I was Charles Manson.

"Chill out, buddy. It's me, the guy with the tasty face you can't resist. I'm coming in."

The barking and baring of teeth only intensified as I removed the screen and gained entry. Unfortunately this time I had no dog treat in my pocket to give him. Without it, Cuddles appeared to have no recollection of who I was. Agitated as he was, I thought he might lunge and take a piece out of me, but he didn't.

"All right, Cuddles, here's how it's gonna go down. You're going to move out of my way, and I'm going to go into the kitchen to get you something delicious to chew on other than my leg. It's not a bribe—I know that might offend a security professional such as yourself. Consider it a peace offering. OK, here we go."

I slowly advanced. He gave ground, doing his best vicious killer canine impersonation. Fur up. Ears back. Growling low and mean. As long as I didn't turn my back on him—he had that opportunist look about him—I figured we were cool. And we were.

Going through the cupboards, looking for dog food, would've only tried Cuddle's patience. I reached the refrigerator in one piece. Inside was a veritable trove of health-minded female-who-lives-by-herself grocery items: Cartons of yogurt, leafy greens and other salad stuff, more yogurt, half a pomegranate, a package of extra firm tofu. No hot dogs. No leftover chili verde burritos.

Is yogurt good for dogs? Beats me, but I do know there's nothing wrong with a little vanilla ice cream. I located a quart in the freezer, found a tablespoon in the silverware drawer, and offered Cuddles a heaping helping.

"Have at it, big guy."

He approached me warily, sniffed the spoon, then went to town when he realized it was his lucky day. Once again, we were best friends for life.

I looked for a charger and found one plugged in next to McBride's desk, but it didn't fit my phone. Her desk looked like a tornado blew through. Papers and files scattered everywhere. It reminded me of mine.

To be clear, I've never been one to go poking around in people's medicine cabinets or other personal effects, unless they were suspected terrorists and I was looking for insights that might help me hunt them down. What brand of hemorrhoid cream innocent civilians use as directed is their business. But I will admit to doing some snooping as I sat down at the desk, partly because I was looking for another phone charger, which I didn't find, and partly because her reading material was so bizarrely engaging.

In perusing the files on her desk and the unfinished proposal letter in her typewriter, it was apparent that McBride was hoping to write a feature-length article for a publication called *The Whole Truth!* Her story asserted that Gonzo journalist Hunter S. Thompson, who'd committed suicide in 2005 at his ranch outside Aspen, had instead been murdered. At the time of his death, Thompson was working on an exposé that would have revealed the US government's orchestration of the September 11 attack on the World Trade Center. That he was sixty-seven, in poor health after a lifetime of self-abuse, and had repeatedly threatened suicide to loved ones mattered not at all to McBride. Thompson had been shot dead, she claimed, in all probability by a Pentagon assassin.

The crux of her thesis was that Thompson's suicide had been staged. A spent shell casing was found close by, while the Smith & Wesson, Model 645 semiautomatic pistol which he allegedly had used to take his own life was found at his feet with its hammer cocked. Six unfired rounds remained in the gun, but there was no round in the firing chamber. This, McBride stated in a proposal to the magazine, strongly indicated that someone else had manually ejected the round in the chamber because Thompson could not have. He was already dead. Ergo a conspiracy.

I could have told her that the particular model of pistol Thompson used had a history of malfunctioning. It had failed to automatically seat a fresh round in the chamber, as semi-autos are designed to do until empty. Ergo, no conspiracy. But then I would've had to admit that I was going through her papers. Ten minutes later, I heard her pull in and drive over to the barn. I quickly put her files back where I found them and took a seat on the couch like I'd been there all afternoon.

She walked in wearing her shearling coat over surgical scrubs. Cuddles wagged his tail and moaned with happiness. She stooped to pet him.

"You're back," I said cheerfully.

"You said you needed to borrow my car for the day, not overnight."

"I ran into a few unexpected complications. The car did great though."

"Whatever." She disappeared into the kitchen.

I said I was heading back to Denver, that I'd waited until she returned home to thank her for all she'd done, and wished her well.

"Highway's closed to Denver," she said. "Giant truck over-turned on the pass east of Angel Falls. I had to take back roads. Took forever. Radio said they won't have it cleared 'til late tonight. Plus, you've got a big upslope condition moving in. It's already snowing down there. They're expecting two feet by tomorrow morning."

Negotiating heavy mountain snows in a Dodge Charger was, I knew, asking for trouble. Also, the Spruce County Sheriff's Department would be out in force, rerouting and monitoring traffic, upping the chances of my being apprehended. Better under the circumstances, I figured, to lay low until road conditions improved.

McBride said I could spend the night on her couch again if I wanted to and announced she was going to make supper. Had I been a praying man, I would've prayed it wasn't leftover lasagna.

THE WIND screamed. The cabin windows rattled. We spooned beef stew out of earthenware bowls. I've had worse.

"Excellent," I said.

McBride acknowledged the compliment with a glum nod, unwilling to make eye contact. She asked me what I'd learned in my search for JFK's cousin, Aideen Fitzgerald, aka Alessandra Munoz. I told her that the lead hadn't panned out. She nodded, refusing to make eye contact. Long silences punctuated dinner. Something clearly was bothering her.

"What is it about me," she said finally, "that you find so unattractive?"

"Nothing."

"You're lying." She got up and took her bowl into the kitchen. She'd barely eaten a bite.

Attraction is ephemeral, something no one can really explain, but you know it when you feel it. And, I'm sorry, Sam, I don't feel it with you. Besides, I'm interested in someone else. That's how I would've phrased it, had I been emotionally honest and willing to hurt her feelings more than they already were. I took the typical male route instead. I clammed up.

My offer to wash the dishes was refused. I considered bidding her adieu and taking my chances on the back roads to Denver, but the wind had strengthened to what looked like moderate gale force—more than thirty miles per hour—and the snow was falling like a solid curtain of white. I'd be spending the night.

I stoked the logs in the fireplace and played endless tug-of-war with Cuddles, who nearly pulled my arm out of its socket—he was one strong dog—while Sam McBride rinsed and dried. Afterward she sat down at her typewriter, ignoring me, and worked on what I assumed was her Hunter Thompson magazine proposal.

"You wouldn't happen to have another battery charger that would fit my phone, would you?"

"No."

"Fair enough. You think I could borrow yours? I'd like to touch base with my people."

"We don't get cellular service out here."

Further conversation was pointless. I found an old copy of the *American Journal of Cardiology* addressed in her name to a post office box in Angel Falls, and tried to read an article about the cardiovascular safety of Droxidopa in patients with symptomatic neurogenic orthostatic hypotension. It may as well have been written in Sanskrit for all the sense I could make of it.

After about an hour, McBride got up from her desk, threw on her coat, and said she was going out to the barn to check on her horse. I asked if she wanted company. She said no. Ten minutes later, she was back.

"I had a long day at work," she said. "I'm turning in."

"I may be out of here when you wake up."

She started to say something, staring at the floor, but didn't and turned to go.

"Sam?"

"What?"

"Thanks again for saving my life."

A smoldering grunt was her only response. I heard her bedroom door click shut and the lock turn.

"Well, Cuddles," I said. "It looks like it's just you and me and the couch."

I AWOKE shortly after 0200 hours. I'd fallen asleep with my shoes still on. The dog was licking my face and whimpering.

"What is it, Lassie?" I said, rubbing my eyes. "What? Timmy's fallen down the well?"

Cuddles quickly trotted to the front door and looked back at me, then at the door, then at me, wagging his tail.

"You need to use the little boys' room?"

He paced up and down on his front legs like he could barely wait. I may not be able to read horse, but dog and cat, I've got down pat.

I rose and opened the door. Instantly he shot out of the cabin and made a beeline into the wind-blown snow like he was breaking out of jail. I didn't yell at him to get back in the house before he froze to death because I didn't want to wake my hostess. I grabbed my coat instead and went after him.

The raccoon he was chasing clambered up the side of the barn, skittered across the roof, and dropped down through a sizable hole in the shingles. Cuddles seemed equally familiar with the aging barn's structural deficiencies. He dove straight through a section of wall to the right of the barn's double doors, which had been latched closed. The wood, unprimed and unpainted for probably a century, already was falling apart before the dog crashed into it. Three slats flew off like they'd been tacked on. Instantly the barn was filled with a cacophony of barking, neighing, and a raccoon screaming shrilly. A coon can make short work of even a large dog. I didn't want any animals getting injured or worse. I went charging in to break up the melee. What I saw when I stepped inside and clicked on the pull chain of a naked light bulb dangling from a beam overhead made me freeze in my proverbial tracks:

Sam McBride's other "car" was no car. It was a black Chevy Silverado pickup. The right front fender was damaged, like it had rammed another vehicle—say, perhaps, retired CIA analyst Rico Perris's vintage Porsche.

But that wasn't all.

Two large cardboard cartons were stacked under a green canvas tarpaulin against the wall that Cuddles had butted open. A third carton had fallen over and spilled open. Two dozen paperback copies of the same book lay sprawled on the ground. I stooped to pick up one of them. On the cover was a drawing of a man with red eyes contorted in the trunk of a car, lying on his side, and aiming a short-barrel up through the rear seatbacks. The title of the book was *Lancer's Last Day, the CIA and the Murder of John F. Kennedy*, by P.S. Plaissance.

With no warning, a bullet slammed into the wall, inches from my head.

TWENTY-SIX

It's impossible to sleep with a revolver wedged in the small of your back. Which explains why the one I had "borrowed" from my gold mining acquaintances, Zion and Malik, was still sitting on Samantha Bride's coffee table, not in the barn and in my shooting hand, where I could've used it.

McBride was standing five meters away in the doorway, aiming the very same gun at me.

Bang! Bang! Bang!

Her second, third, and fourth rounds whistled just over my head, exploding chunks of barn wood behind me. Only then did I realize she'd been shooting not at me, but at the raccoon, who dove under the truck and scurried to freedom through the hole in the wall Cuddles had broken open. The chase continued out into the snow, the coon running, the dog barking, Frou-Frou the horse neighing in its stall.

McBride was now pointing the revolver at me.

"Well, Doctor," I said, "looks to me like you've got some explaining to do."

"Go to hell."

Bang!

Blood instantly soaked the right leg of my jeans and I fell to the ground. The pain in my upper thigh was blinding. I could smell the cordite from the discharged rounds. I could hear Cuddles barking far off in the pines, still racing after the raccoon.

"You should have never come in here," McBride said.

"I was only trying to save your dog."

"You're lying. You've been after me this whole time."

The next round, I knew, would be fatal. The only viable weapon I had was my mouth.

"I read your book," I said, lying. "It is your book, isn't it, *Lancer's Last Day*? Fascinating premise."

"Another lie. All you do is lie."

"No, seriously, I did, Sam. I read it when it came out." My thigh felt like it was on fire. I struggled to focus. "The second gunman in the trunk of JFK's limo, that's groundbreaking stuff. The autopsy results, the ballistics, it's all there, everything you laid out in that book. I can't believe the Warren Commission never considered the possibility."

Her eyes were narrow, angry slits. "The Warren Commission was bought off by the mob. Warren himself wanted Kennedy dead. Everybody knows that."

"You bet they know it," I said, "they all do. Only even now, the powers that be won't say so publicly. That's why your book is so important. Warren was as dirty as they come."

That I was slandering the memory of a former chief justice of the United States Supreme Court was of zero concern to me. The longer I kept McBride talking, the more I could persuade her that I was on her side, and the less likely she'd be to put another bullet in me. A thin hope, to be sure, but thin was better than none.

"Get on your feet," she said.

"I'm not sure I can."

"Either you get on your feet right now, you son of a bitch, or I will kill you where you sit."

"Well, when you put it that way."

The bullet had exited the back of my thigh. The femur wasn't broken. Had it been, I would've never been able to put weight on it. That I could and somehow fight off the searing, nausea-inducing pain of my wound en route to a standing position was, all modesty aside, miraculous.

McBride gestured with the barrel of her gun. "Walk. Let's go."

"Where to?"

"You'll see."

She kept her distance as she followed me out of the barn and into the swirling snow—close enough behind me that I made for an easy target, but far enough away that I couldn't turn and take her down even if I had wanted to.

"Look, for what it's worth," I said, "I know folks in high places, including a few at the CIA, even the White House. What if I got them to endorse your book? It would be a best seller in no time. What do you think?"

"Those people are liars. Just like the people who work for them. Just like you."

"Rico Perris and Joe Zyra down in Phoenix, they worked for the CIA. But you knew that already, didn't you?"

"Shut up."

Ahead of me was a wooden outhouse that looked like it predated the barn.

"Is that why you ran Perris off the road and ran over Zyra? Because they lied?"

"Hell, yes, they lied," McBride said. "And they were mean about it."

"Mean how?"

"Online. Their reviews. They hated my book. Do you know how *hard* it is to write a book? All the research? All those sleepless nights, writing and rewriting? You put your entire life into it, every fiber of your being. Why? So it can be held up to public ridicule? Made fun of? I don't think so. Not me. Not my book."

People have died for less, certainly. But to kill someone over having expressed an opinion, seemed to me comical. I almost laughed.

"You killed two men because they gave your book bad reviews? What about Cyril Tomasello, Sam? Did he write a bad review too?"

She slammed me face-first against the outhouse and quickly patted me down for weapons.

"His was the worst."

I was too weak from blood loss and too much in pain to resist. Satisfied I was unarmed, she shoved me inside the tiny shed and heaved the door shut. I heard the dull metallic thud of a padlock closing.

"How long are you planning to keep me in here? I could freeze to death."

Bang!

She put a round through the outhouse door that barely missed my right shoulder before slamming into the wall behind me.

"Keep quiet or the next one's gonna be in your face. I need time to think."

I could hear her footfalls on the snow growing fainter as she walked back to the cabin.

Logan, you idiot. Running outside after the dog without that revolver? Not bothering to look inside McBride's garage before the one time I had, when her horse had blocked my view? I shook my head. Had I been paying closer attention, been more on guard, I would not have been in this mess.

The outhouse was as drafty as it was cramped. Wind whistled through pencil-thick gaps in the wooden slats. I was shivering, but I knew that the subfreezing temperature was beneficial, in the short term anyway. Cold meant that the vessels in my leg would constrict. That meant less blood loss. The bracing air also helped clear my mind. I was hardly functioning at 100 percent, but I could still think tactically.

I removed my belt and secured it snugly around my thigh above the wound—not enough to cut off circulation, but enough to slow it. Groping around in the dark, I found a crushed cardboard roll devoid of toilet paper. I tore the roll apart and, gritting my teeth to stop from screaming in pain, stuffed the pieces into the holes in my leg.

Option one would have been to boot the door open, but that was a showstopper when factoring in my wound. Exercising my second option, trying to shoulder the outhouse side to side and off its foundation proved pointless. The structure may have looked dilapidated, but it wasn't going anywhere.

My final option, I knew, was also likely the most precarious.

McBride had discharged four rounds at the raccoon in the barn and missed four times. She'd shot me in the leg and fired another into the wall of the outhouse. I was no math major but that added up to six rounds. The revolver held six rounds. In other words, unless she had a carton of .38-caliber cartridges lying around in her cabin, the gun had been rendered effectively inoperable.

I would lure her outside, get her to unlock the door of my tiny makeshift prison, hope she hadn't remembered to reload, then jump her. True, I had just been shot. With the amount of blood I'd lost, I had to will myself to maintain consciousness. But men had stormed the beaches of Normandy. They'd successfully landed on the moon. How difficult, I told myself, could this be?

That's when I shifted my weight and inadvertently slammed my thigh into something sharp protruding inward from the outhouse wall. The pain was more than I could bear.

I passed out.

Minutes? Hours? I had no notion of how long I'd been out of it, only that it was still night and still snowing. I shook uncontrollably from the cold.

Behind me, a jagged beam of light about as wide as a quarter penetrated the wall of the outhouse where the bullet McBride fired had exited. Contorting myself and bending forward, pressing my eye to the hole, I could see part of her cabin and, more significantly, her silhouette through the curtains. My captor was pacing maniacally back and forth.

"Hey! Hello? I'm still in here!"

She couldn't hear me yelling.

Her dog could though. He was padding around and whining outside the outhouse.

An idea formed. I quickly unstrapped the belt from around my thigh and removed my hiking shoe attached to the leg that wasn't shot.

"Cuddles, hey buddy, what's going on out there? It's me, your best friend, the one with the ice cream, remember?"

He pressed his black wet nose against the bullet hole and sniffed while I frantically knotted the shoe to the belt's brass buckle, then folded and threaded the tip through the hole in the wood.

"Hey, who's up for another exciting game of tug-of-war? Here you go. C'mon, boy. Get it."

Cuddles did the rest. Growling playfully, he grabbed the leather in his teeth and began backing up until my shoe, tied to the belt buckle, was firmly anchored against the inside of the slats.

"That's it, Cuddles. Good boy! Now, pull!"

Pull he did, for all he was worth, while I pushed and shoved at the wood for all I was worth.

Alas, it wasn't enough. The boards held firm. Cuddles eventually lost interest in the game and wandered away.

I was screwed.

Or was I?

Call it wishful thinking, but the slat with the bullet hole now felt a little spongy. When I reached back and palmed the wood where it had been nailed to the outhouse's structural framing, I realized that all of Cuddle's pulling had produced results. A couple of rusty nails were partially pried out, creating a narrow gap between the slat and the frame that hadn't been there before.

I put my shoe back on. Pivoting as best I could and girding myself for the agony I knew was sure to immediately follow, I kicked out with my good leg. Pain shot through my bad leg and the rest of my body like I'd been zapped with an electric cattle prod. I thought for a moment I might pass out again, but didn't. I reached out in the darkness and felt the gap in the wood. The two nails had been pried out a little more. No additional incentive was required.

I kicked and I kicked. The slat fell away. I kicked some more. Another weathered board fell off. The gap that was left was so wide, I didn't have to squeeze through.

My break to freedom lasted all of five seconds.

McBride emerged in search of her wayward dog—"Cuddles, you get in this house right now!"—and was on the front porch, pulling him by his collar, when she saw I had escaped. In a flash, she ducked back into the cabin, grabbed the revolver, and came charging at me through the snow with her teeth bared.

Three things, the Buddha said, cannot be long hidden: the sun, the moon, and the truth. At that moment, I would've added a fourth thing that can't be hidden for very long: whether the six-shot, .38-caliber handgun you foolishly left inside the home of a homicidally deranged individual has been reloaded or not.

No way I could outrun her. Not with the bullet hole passing through my leg. My only choice was to face her and charge. I may have been hobbled, but if Sam McBride had thought to put live rounds in that revolver, I figured she was still going to have to hit a moving target.

An experienced shooter would've stopped when she was within range, formed a two-handed combat crouch, and consciously slowed her breathing to help steady her aim. She would have swiftly and smoothly aligned the fixed blade of the gun's front sight on her intended target to ensure that her first round didn't stray left or right. She would've taken care to ensure the front sight was nestled squarely within the notch of the V-shaped rear sight, so that the round didn't hit below or above where it was intended. Only then would the experienced shooter have gently squeezed the trigger.

McBride didn't do any of that.

She raised the gun as she converged toward me at full speed and opened fire from about five meters away.

Click.

Click.

Click.

The revolver, mercifully, was empty.

Thank you, Buddha.

By the time McBride realized her error, her momentum carried her into me and we fell together like gladiators locked in mortal combat.

Ordinarily, I would've made short work of her, but she was big and strong in that maniacal way all crazed killers who have nothing to lose are strong, and I was wounded.

She grappled and clawed at me, snarling, while Cuddles circled us, barking furiously, unsure whose side to take. He finally took hers. I nearly had her in a carotid restraint when the dog lunged, nipping a healthy chunk out of the back of my good leg. McBride took the opportunity to break free and bolted toward her cabin. I knew she was going to retrieve the rifle I'd seen propped in the corner inside her door.

I also knew I was toast. Nowhere to run. No way to run. I sat there in the snow, bleeding anew.

"Some friend you are, Cuddles. No hard feelings though. You were just doing your job."

You could tell he felt bad about biting me. He came slinking over with his head down and ears back, rolled over on his back and wanted me to scratch his tummy. I did, smiling at the irony of my ultimate fate. All the hardcore, high-value bad guys I'd ever tangled with in the far corners of the rock and now, here I was, about to get smoked by a female cardiologist and third-rate writer. No one could ever accuse me of chauvinism.

Suddenly colored strobes and headlights cut through the trees, accompanied by the throaty roar of approaching cars.

McBride burst out of the cabin with her rifle at the very instant a Denver police car came fishtailing through the snow, followed by an unmarked detective's Crown Vic. Two burly uniformed officers jumped out of the cruiser and took cover behind their open doors with pistols drawn.

"Put the gun down!" one cop yelled.

"Don't make us shoot, Dr. McBride!" the other one shouted.

McBride blinked a couple of times, as if in disbelief.

"It's over, Sam," I said.

She lowered the rifle to the ground and got down on her knees with her fingers interlocked behind her head without being asked. One of the cops handcuffed her while his partner covered him.

Only then did I notice the driver of the unmarked detective unit was Steve Weiss. He holstered his pistol and went to assist in taking McBride into custody as Layne Sterling climbed out of his passenger seat. She came running over as best she could, considering her recent surgery, and knelt beside me in the snow.

"You look like you just went ten rounds with Hulk Hogan."

"Touché."

"You OK?"

"Other than the hole in my leg, couldn't be better. How'd you find me?"

"Buzz called. That photo you analyzed, showing that Zyra owned a copy of *Lancer's Last Day*, just like Perris and Tomasello, that was it. You covered yourself in glory, Logan. Can't believe I missed it. Langley ran P.S. Plaissance through the cyber center in Utah, determined that Plaissance was Samantha McBride's nom de plume. I needed backup ASAP, somebody I could trust, so I called your friend, Detective Weiss. His wife gave birth to a healthy little girl, by the way."

"That's not what I asked. I asked, 'How did you find me?'"

"That tracker I put on your phone. Don't you remember?"

"The battery's dead."

"Logan, I work for the CIA. Let's just say we have our ways."

"CIA. How do you spell that?"

She smiled. Then she kissed me.

TWENTY-SEVEN

Funny thing about a bullet wound. Weeks later, you swear that you can still feel the bullet in your leg, even though you know the slug passed through.

I didn't tell Mrs. Schmulowitz I'd been shot. My limp, I said, was the result of having fallen off a step stool while trying to change a light bulb inside my garage apartment. She said she could relate, having recently taken a minor tumble while skateboarding, an activity Mrs. Schmulowitz had added to her long list of recreational pursuits. Let me just say, you haven't really lived until you've agreed to videotape your octogenarian landlady launching herself down a concrete half-pipe in pink pads and matching helmet at Rancho Bonita's beachside skateboard park, rotating 360 degrees while airborne, then sticking the landing to the cheers of riders young enough to be her great-grandchildren.

"Did you get that?" she asked excitedly.

"I got it, Mrs. Schmulowitz." I showed her the video I'd shot on my phone.

"Gnarly. I'm uploading it on YouTube when we get home. When you get all better, I'm gonna teach you how to shred, bubby. You'll love it, believe me. Way less dangerous than flying that rickety little airplane of yours, or screwing in a light bulb on a ladder. You do know, don't you, how many skateboarders it takes to screw in a light bulb, right?"

"No, Mrs. Schmulowitz, I'm afraid I don't."

"Just one—but it takes twenty tries. Get it? Because you're always falling off the board, so twenty tries to get the trick right is par for the course. Is that funny or what?"

"Hysterical," I said, unable to generate the kind of smile she was looking for.

"OK, forget I said anything. Listen to me, bubeleh, it's just my opinion, OK, but you need to start getting out more. All you do since you got back from Wyoming is work and hang out with that silly orange cat. Sometimes, by the way, I think he must be related to the president. They have the same complexion!"

"I was in Colorado, Mrs. Schmulowitz, not Wyoming."

"Colorado, Wyoming, same deal. My point is, you're not having enough fun in life. Live a little, Cordell. Trust me, you'll be dead soon enough. Then you'll be kicking yourself, wishing you'd listened to Mrs. Schmulowitz."

What woman that old referred to herself in the third person? Mrs. Schmulowitz was one of a kind. She was also right.

Nearly two months had elapsed since that night outside Samantha McBride's cabin. I'd spent two days in the same hospital where she'd worked. The doctor said that I was lucky; the slug had narrowly missed my femoral artery. Two centimeters to the right and I would've bled out. I could expect to eventually make a full recovery, he said, but he was talking about my body, not my head. Call it post-traumatic stress. Call it whatever you want. I only knew that I was deriving little joy from anything. That was unusual for me.

Had I been a psychologist, I would've said that part of what I was going through stemmed from having to sit through multiple interrogation sessions between McBride and ranking CIA officials. With Alpha, the targets of intelligence operations in which I participated usually ended up pushing daisies or whatever euphemism for lifeless you care to use. I'd sit through a relatively cursory debriefing with one or more intelligence-collecting desk jockeys, file my after-action report, and start planning for the next op. I didn't have to sit across the table at a safe house in suburban Denver, staring evil in the face for two solid days, while evil was interrogated by ranking CIA officials. I didn't have to dwell on how closely I had come to death at evil's hands.

At first, McBride maintained her innocence. She didn't need a lawyer, she said, and was happy to "clear up any confusion" regarding her alleged involvement in three murders.

Presented with forensic evidence showing that paint from Rico Perris's Porsche had been found on the damaged front fender of her Chevy Silverado pickup, she laughed. "I bought the truck used," McBride insisted. "That fender was that way when I took possession."

Showing her grainy, time-stamped footage recovered from various security cameras that placed her truck—or a truck identical to it—near the scene of Joe Zyra's murder in Phoenix, and of Cyril Tomasello's in Denver, produced more defiant denials. The images had been doctored, McBride claimed. They were of another Silverado, not hers.

What about the search history on her computer at the hospital? Had she not recently worked up dossiers on all three men, including their home addresses?

"Plenty of people have access to that computer," she said. "I'm a Stanford-educated, board-certified physician, as well as a published author. I really don't think I deserve to be treated in this manner."

Layne Sterling was the one who got her to crack.

Five years earlier, McBride had spent a night in jail after allegedly attacking her soon-to-be ex-husband and fellow physician with a letter opener during a heated argument. While the case eventually was bargained down to a misdemeanor, a psychological evaluation that Layne unearthed, one prepared in conjunction with McBride's probation report, concluded that the doctor was particularly hypersensitive to criticism. She had anger management issues, the report stated, attributable to her childhood spent with her demanding, emotionally distant father.

McBride folded her hands on the table and smiled placidly. "I've undergone extensive therapy sessions," she said. "I am no longer that woman."

Then Layne read aloud the review of *Lancer's Last Day* that Tomasello had written for a website called Bookworm. com a week before he was killed. Tomasello, she said, had belonged to the same book club as Perris and Zyra. All three men had posted similarly snarky reviews of McBride's tome, along with a handful of other readers around the country.

"How this book ever got written," Tomasello's review began, "is beyond me. The second gunman was hiding in the trunk of Kennedy's limo and fired through the back of the seat? A bigger pile of horse dung I have never read. I want my money back *and* punitive damages for cruel and unusual punishment. This writer has no business writing a birthday card, let alone a book about something as important as the Kennedy assassination."

McBride's nostrils flared. Her neck veins bulged. You could see the anger building that she claimed had been counseled away. Layne continued reading:

"If bad writing was a crime, this author should be locked up for twenty years. Seriously, he should stick to writing about subjects that are more his speed, like the Tooth Fairy or how the earth is flat and the moon is made of green cheese. P.S. Plaissance is a moron."

McBride exploded out of her chair and lunged at Layne— or would have, had she not been chained to the floor.

"*I'm* the moron? I've been all over the world," she said, seething. "More places than any of you losers have ever been or ever will be. Not once, not *ever*, have I seen a monument or a statue devoted to a goddamn critic."

Layne's boss, an otherwise implacable South Carolinian with burgundy fingernails, who was standing behind McBride, slammed her back down in her seat. She reminded the accused that two of her victims had been employees of a national intelligence agency. That made the case federal, not state, and that meant she would almost certainly get the needle—unless she was willing to cooperate in exchange for the possibility of spending the rest of her life in a prison cell. McBride looked away, pondering the possibilities.

"Here's one thing to think about while you're thinking about it," I said. "All that uninterrupted time you'll have to write."

The idea of it seemed to resonate with her. "I never much cared for medicine anyway," she said. "Too many sick people."

Professing her pride at having sent a message on behalf of "unfairly ridiculed" authors everywhere, she began talking. She admitted to having created different identities through multiple phantom e-mail accounts. Using one account, she'd sent Perris threatening messages. Using another, after discovering that he lived close by, she had lured him out of his cabin the night of his death with promises of an illicit rendezvous. She insisted she never knew that Perris and Zyra worked for the CIA. She had killed them, she said, because they, like Tomasello, were merely within easy driving distance.

"I would have killed all these other stupid sons of bitches who think they can write a book and have the audacity to insult mine," McBride said matter-of-factly, "only they lived too far away."

None of the CIA officers in the room spoke. They were too stunned.

Layne looked over at me. "Any further questions for Ms. McBride?"

"*Doctor* McBride," she said, correcting her.

"Yeah," I said, "I have a question for the good doctor. I'm curious. Your pen name, P.S. Plaissance, where did that come from?"

"Patricia Sewell Plaissance was my high school English teacher. She passed away eight years ago, bless her soul. She was the first one who ever told me I had the talent and should think about becoming a writer."

"So I suppose we have her to blame for the lunatic you became."

She seethed. "I saved your life, Logan. The least you could do is show me a little respect."

For a millisecond, I actually felt sorry for her. "You won't be punished for your anger, Sam," I said. "You'll be punished by it."

I got up and walked out.

CONDITIONS COULD not have been more perfect. One of those warm but not too warm days in Rancho Bonita, when the winds are light and variable and the sky is so vividly blue, it hurts just to look at.

After being retrieved from Winslow, Arizona, the *Ruptured Duck* was flying like a fine-tuned machine, not like a winged bucket of bolts approaching retirement age. Even my London-born student, Oliver Vickers-Todd, a moppish, thirty-four-year-old professor of biomolecular science from the local university, was in the groove.

"OK, Ollie," I said, "maintain 3,000 feet. Give me two standard-rate turns to the right, roll out smartly on a heading of two-seven-zero—not two-six-five, not two-eight-zero—then two full turns to the left."

"Right-o."

"The correct response is 'roger.' All pilots love to say that word."

"Roger."

Ollie was a deft, natural aviator, what we older aviators call a "good stick." *The Duck* was a compliant dance partner in his hands.

For a few minutes, I stopped playing flight instructor and simply enjoyed the ride. I relaxed enough that I almost forgot Layne Sterling had given me the old brush-off.

It wasn't me, she said, it was her—or, more specifically, her work. Assignments were piling up. A retired case officer from Atlanta who'd gone missing on a canoeing trip in the Great Smoky Mountains. A former administrator from the agency's Office of Terrorism Analysis shot to death, purportedly by accident, while cleaning his gun alone in his car outside a shopping mall in Seattle. Layne's bosses were breathing down her neck, she said. She'd give me a call, she said, as soon as she could. Five weeks had gone by since, and not a word from her. We hadn't gotten to the "I love you" part yet, so it was really no big loss. I told myself that anyway.

Oh, well.

"Outstanding air work, Ollie. Looks like our hour's about up. What do you say you take us back to the barn? You have the airplane."

"Right-o. I mean, roger."

I filled out his logbook on the tarmac after we landed and taxied in. Another couple of hours of instruction, I said, and he'd be ready to solo. I thought he might explode from excitement, but he caught himself in that refined, stiff upper lip British way.

"Excellent. Then we shall see each other next week. Same time, same day, I presume, if that works with your schedule?"

I dug the classy way he pronounced it—"shed-yule." He made it sound like I actually had one to keep, with a surplus of paying students.

"I'll be here, buddy," I said.

I chocked the *Duck's* nose wheel, tied down the wings, and headed for my office inside Larry Kropf's hangar where I planned to finish a crossword puzzle and maybe peruse the job listings on craigslist.

Larry was plopped in a lawn chair with a sixty-four-ounce Big Gulp, next to a Grumman Cheetah with a bad alternator that he'd been working on since morning. Face tilted up to the sun, shades on, shirt off, catching a few rays. His belly looked like he'd swallowed a beach ball.

"You're late on your office rent, Logan. Again. And I'm having to remind you. Again."

"I'm aware, Larry. I'm still waiting on the check for that charter I flew back in Colorado."

"A 'charter,' huh?"

"Yep."

"Logan, what is it exactly you do? I mean, when you're not doing this—whatever *this* is? Why can't you just be honest with me for once?"

"You'll get you the money, Larry. It should be here any day."

"One can only hope," he said, shaking his head and slurping his soda.

I patted him on the shoulder as I limped past him, into the hangar.

"By the way," Larry said, "you've got somebody in your office. I don't know how you do it, Logan, a dude with your marginal looks. I told her to come see me if she wanted a real man."

"Student?"

"Yeah, right. I don't think so."

Layne Sterling was kicked back with her suede boots on my desk. Her smile filled the room. My breath came shallower. I resisted the urge to start singing like we were both in a Broadway musical.

"Good flight?" she asked.

"Great flight. Slipped the surly bonds and all that poetic good stuff. I thought you were in Atlanta. Or was it Seattle?"

"Nuckled both files, no problem," she said.

". . . Nuckled?"

"No Unusual Circumstances Known, Legal Expiration. That's what we call it—Nuckled." She started to get up. "I'm sorry. Would you like your desk back?"

"Relax. You're good. I've been sitting all day." I pretended to stretch, flexing my biceps over my head à la the Hulkster to remind her what a hunk I was.

"Gosh," she said with her tongue planted firmly in cheek, "look at all those big strong muscles. You must work out. I'm so impressed. Will you make sweet love to me?"

"That obvious, huh?"

She grinned. "Pretty obvious, yeah."

Whatever word transcended beautiful, that was Layne Sterling. But it was *who* she was, not what—her smarts, her quick wit, her convincing self-confidence—that made me realize in that instant how much I needed her in my life.

She said she thought I'd be interested to know what was happening with our case. I said I was, even if I was having trouble concentrating on anything other than her face.

Samantha McBride had been arraigned on three homicide charges and two counts of attempted vehicular homicide, the latter stemming from her having read-ended Layne and me in her truck on the highway that night. She remained in jail on a no-bond hold, awaiting a preliminary court date. Her horse and dog had been adopted out by animal rescue organizations.

Spruce County Sheriff Harlan Weber had been indicted on charges of embezzlement. Florida authorities had reopened investigations into the two mob killings in which he was rumored to have participated in the 1960s. He denied knowing anything about any murdered drug dealers in Spruce County.

Back at the National Archives, meanwhile, administrators were still searching for the missing Kennedy documents. The official explanation was that they had been inadvertently misfiled and stored in some obscure location on campus. Unofficially, the fear was that they'd been stolen. By whom or for what reason, no one was willing to speculate.

"Intriguing," I said. "Thanks for reading me in. Is that why you're here?"

"Two reasons," she said, digging through her shoulder bag. She pulled out an envelope and laid it on my desk. "Reason number one was to get you paid. My sincere apologies for the delay. I would've put the check in the mail, but you know how the post office can be these days."

I smiled. "And reason number two?"

"I quit."

"Say again?"

"I said I quit. Hit my twenty and punched out."

"Well, as mayor of Pensionland, I'd like to officially welcome you to retirement."

"Thank you."

"I suppose you'll be playing a lot of shuffleboard now and learning how to watercolor, right?"

She came around the desk. "Actually I had this crazy idea. What if I became a private investigator?"

"Not so crazy. You definitely have the résumé."

"As do you. So here's an even crazier idea: What if *we* opened an agency?"

"We, meaning, like, *together,* a partnership?"

"That's exactly what I meant. Maybe even right here, in Rancho Bonita."

"There are certainly worse places to live," I said.

"Indeed."

This time, she didn't kiss me. I kissed her.

Five minutes later, we were still kissing, and five hours after that. We didn't really stop kissing for the rest of the day or, for that matter, the rest of the night.

True happiness, the Buddha observed, is where you find it. Sometimes, if you're lucky, it finds you.

In that moment, I was as happy as I'd ever been.

ACKNOWLEDGMENTS

The anthropology of any career is traceable; every opportunity is twined to the next. The writer of mystery novels navigates them as he would stones across a river, striving to tell a compelling story while balancing other no less slippery concerns, like paying the bills. Perseverance is integral to the process. So is chance.

This series of novels never would have come to pass had I not had the good fortune to cross paths from the outset with many supportive individuals who took their own chances on me. From Aurelia Valley, my high school English teacher, to publishers Martin and Judith Shepard of The Permanent Press, each has helped shape my work as well as the very course of my life. The culmination of their influences is embedded in these pages, and I am indebted to them all.

I would like to thank John Windhauser, Ed Will, Ben Burns, Michael Howard, John Swagerty, Charles Carter, Dale Fetherling, Dick Barnes, David Rosenzweig, Noel Greenwood, Shelby Coffee III, and Jenifer Siebens for helping further my reporting career. Thanks also to Scott Stossel, Pat Trenner, Diane Tedeschi, Linda Shiner, and Maria Streshinksy for the magazine work they've thrown my way over the years.

My gratitude to Maggie Field, Maggie Roiphe, and Dean Schramm for helping me earn my keep in Hollywood; to Chuck Pfarrer, John Jarrett, and Ed Heinbockel for ushering me inside the federal intelligence community; and to Ann Gill and Greg Luft for showing me what fun teaching college kids can be.

A shout-out to graphics designer Lon Kirschner for his always splendid covers, to copy editor Barbara Anderson for helping keep me honest in print, and to Jill Marr, my indefatigable, ever-charming book agent. Cordell Logan would be but a figment of my imagination had she not believed in both him and me.

Finally, to my brilliant and beautiful partner, Dr. Betsy Bates Freed, who took the greatest chance on me anyone ever could and who each day helps me strive to reach the far bank of that river, I owe you everything.